THE MARSHAL MAKES HIS REPORT

THE MARSHAL MAKES HIS REPORT

MAGDALEN NABB

HarperCollins*Publishers*

This book was first published in 1991 in Great Britain by
The Crime Club, an imprint of HarperCollins Publishers.

FIRST U.S. EDITION

Library of Congress Cataloging-in-Publication Data

Nabb, Magdalen, 1947–
The marshal makes his report / Magdalen Nabb.
— 1st U.S. ed.
p.   cm.
"Originally published in Great Britain in 1991"
—T.p. verso.
ISBN 0-06-016914-1 (cloth)
I. Title.
PR6064.A18M33   1992
823′.914—dc20   92-52560

92   93   94   95   96   HC   10   9   8   7   6   5   4   3   2   1

1

The Marshal's memory of the scene that night remained vivid in every detail. And yet, there was something about it that made it seem more like the memory of a spectacular film or the climax of a stage play, so that it crossed his mind even at the time that it didn't look real. Maybe distance had something to do with it, because the tower, when he at last reached the top of it, gasping for breath, was so very high and the figures acting out the drama below in the courtyard looked so tiny.

The Florentine night was hot and the sky velvety with a big bright moon. It was just possible to make out that there was a light on down there in the huge iron lantern that marked the entrance to the courtyard, but the bulb was so weak that if it hadn't been for the moonlight he would hardly have been able to distinguish the colonnade and the well in the centre. The body was lying face down near the well and he could see the dark shape of the woman kneeling over it. Everything was silent. Other dark figures were closing in, emerging from the deeper gloom of the colonnade and moving hesitantly towards the central tableau, but before any of them reached it they paused and settled more or less in a circle. A torch was switched on but went off almost at once. No one disturbed the kneeling woman who was as still as the body. She might have been a mother watching over a child's sleep, afraid that any movement might wake it. No voices reached the Marshal at that height. The tableau held its stillness for what seemed like an unnatural length of time until the ambulance men attempted to get to the centre, with a white rectangle between them. The circle of heads widened and separated.

The Marshal's big hands clutched the warm stone para-pet and he leaned further over. His body was tense, waiting for the woman to break down. She surely must, now, and it would bring a sort of relief to him, too. He saw the white rectangle placed on the ground and one of the black figures bend over her. He saw her head go back, the face turned up towards him as though to accuse him, though she couldn't have seen him. He felt the wail of pent-up grief leave her body but he never heard it, because right then the first of the fireworks went off, drawing a glittering red fountain on the black sky and exploding in soft hissing blobs that fell down towards the rooftops in slow motion. For a few seconds all the roofs and towers of Florence appeared in a warm glow, a flash of pink river snaking between them, and the crowd along the embankment roared and clapped its approval. Then it was dark again and a cloud of rosy smoke obscured the moon. The Marshal was dazzled and distracted, hearing only his own heavy breathing, and feel-ing the smooth warm stone beneath his hands.

His memory of getting his great bulk down all those hundreds of stairs was vaguer. He remembered only that the staircase was so narrow that he frequently bumped his right shoulder against the rough wall and that the worn steps were treacherous in the gloom. He went slowly, not wanting to catch up with the uneven thump and shuffle of the small figure struggling down below him. That, at any rate, was his reasoning then. Now it was over he could admit, at least to himself, that he'd been in no great hurry to face the scene in the courtyard. In the event, hardly anyone had noticed him. The chief public prosecutor had caught his eye for a second but he was fully occupied with the Marchesa, so he waited until she had been calmed and led away and then went quietly across the dim, hushed courtyard and out into the noisy street. There he paused to wait for a gap in the traffic and drew in a deep breath of relief as the bright lights of Gino's and a waft of hot pizza dough welcomed him back to life and blessed normality.

So now he sat in his office in the carabinieri station at the Palazzo Pitti, two fat fingers poised over the typewriter keys, examining his conscience. What really bothered him was that when he'd come to his own conclusions about what to put in his final report his conscience hadn't made any objections at all. That came later when the chief public prosecutor asked him to do what he intended to do anyway. A man like that . . . well, not to put too fine a point on it, if you agreed with a man like that, you must be as bad as he was. The Marshal didn't like the chief public prosecutor. A non-commissioned officer like himself could reasonably expect to pass his whole existence without ever so much as setting eyes on the chief public prosecutor. Even the substitute prosecutors who directed the cases he might be involved in would normally communicate directly with the Marshal's superior officers. He typed 'On the evening of June 24th' and stopped. To agree with a man like that . . .

The idea that two very different men might reach the same conclusion for two very different reasons was beyond the Marshal's powers of reasoning. He wasn't very good at reasoning. He wasn't very good at writing reports either, even simple HSA reports, and this one was far from simple. What was it his wife had once said to him when they'd quarrelled over something or other and he'd said that whatever it was wasn't right. 'It may not be right,' she'd said, 'but what's right isn't always what's good.' He'd been too furious at the time to think of asking her what the devil that was supposed to mean, but he wished he had because it described the way he was feeling now.

'On the evening of June 24th . . .'

'Oof!' He yanked the page out of the typewriter and crumpled it with one big hand. His large, slightly bulging eyes stared at the map of his Quarter pinned on the opposite wall. The sun was shining in on it. He was hot. He was hungry, too. A phrase came into his head: '*Whoso foregathers with great people is the last at table and the first at the gallows.*' That young Englishman had said it, or read it. True enough, too. He felt again the Marchesa Ulderighi's beautiful eyes turned on him that first time, making him feel like some sub-human creature who was soiling the air she breathed. The memory made him squirm and he got up, irritated with himself for such weakness, and began plodding about the room. As he plodded he periodically bumped into the rubber plant his wife had bought him and placed right in front of the window just where he liked to stand and stare out. Grunting a little, because the pot was heavy and he was more than a bit overweight himself, he pushed the thing to one side and opened the window. The warm air came in from the Boboli Gardens, carrying with it a strong savour of tomato sauce with garlic and basil, the clink of cutlery and the signature tune of the lunch-time news. The lads were up in the barracks kitchen eating and he hadn't noticed the time! With a sigh of relief he shut the window and abandoned his office. A good lunch, a rest, and a chat with Teresa and the boys in his own quarters and then he'd start all over again, right from the beginning.

It began, at least for the Marshal, on the second Sunday in June and with the first round of the football tournament. That wretched football business could be said to be at the root of the whole affair, that and the Marchesa Ulderighi's bright freezing eyes. Not that the Marshal had anything against football, real football that is, in which he took a vaguely benevolent interest and in front of which he dozed and woke alternately in his armchair in front of the television on Wednesday nights. But this Florentine version was something else. He'd never forget the first time he saw it, more than fifteen years ago, it must have been. He'd enjoyed the procession through the city. Halberdiers and guildsmen and so on in their mediæval costumes under the brilliant sunshine, the drummers and the flag-throwers and the restive horses constrained by the narrow streets and the crowds. Picturesque, he thought, a nice show for the tourists who sat peaceably licking melting ice-creams on the stands around the sand-covered city square. They and the Marshal too were diverted by the prize, a white cow with gilded horns, looking a bit dazed as it was led into the arena among the flying silk flags and rattling drums.

It was only when the fancy dress brigade had cleared off and left the field to the players that the Marshal began to have vague doubts. They were in fancy dress too, but the slashed sleeves and knee-breeches and long, coloured socks did nothing to soften the impression made by their bull necks and murderous expressions. The Marshal, being on duty that first time, was right on the edge of the pitch and the tension, the threatening language and certain gestures were not lost on him. The tourists, placed at a safe distance in the expensive seating behind the city nobility and the mayor, were still licking their ice-creams and chatting. But in the other stands where the local supporters were sitting, waves of unrest were building up. The Marshal looked about him uneasily as some announcements were read over a loudspeaker in various languages. Nobody else seemed to look worried. The supporters, after all, were throwing nothing more lethal than dyed carnations, flying dark silhouettes criss-crossing against the blue midsummer sky and settling in a pattern of the teams' colours on the sandy pitch.

Near the Marshal stood the Master of the Games, decoratively dressed in a cloak and hat of black velvet and wearing a sword which he clutched with his right hand, to the Marshal's amusement, as though about to draw it for a fight. That was his last thought before a cannon shot boomed and echoed round the square. He just had time to notice the ball fly upwards in one direction when the bulk of the players rolled itself into one struggling mass moving the opposite way and a desperate fight broke out. The local crowd stood up, roaring. The Marshal's mouth fell open and he gazed about him. Shouldn't he intervene? Good God! Somebody should intervene. Hadn't he seen a referee? There was a referee. After a while he emerged from between the legs of the fighting mass, got to his feet and started yanking at the shirt of one of the more vicious fighters. At first he was ignored but then the huge player noticed this irritating attack from behind, turned round, picked up the referee and tossed him over the paling that bounded the pitch. The roaring increased. The Marshal heard a metallic swish beside him. The Master of the Games strode forward, almost at a run, his black cloak flying and his drawn sword raised. The sword was not decorative. Within seconds order was restored. When the tangled mass of men was separated and the point was argued out it appeared that one particular player had been the designated victim, the biggest and most ferocious man on his team. The idea had been to eliminate him as early on as possible. Now he stood, red-jowled, sweated, and howling in fury. The remains of his T-shirt hung in ribbons around this slashed breeches. His nose and the side of his head were bleeding. Somebody had bitten his ear off but the real cause of his fury was that he was being sent off as injured. He disdained the stretcher that was brought and managed to get in a good right hook at one of the enemy before being dragged away. A search was instituted for the ear but the Marshal never knew whether it was successful because the cannon boomed and play was resumed; the Marshal lifted his sunglasses and mopped his sweating face. For the rest of the match he contented himself with occasionally murmuring 'Good

God . . .' and keeping an eye on the reassuring figure of the swordsman beside him.

After so many years, of course, he'd got used to it all and had learned to distinguish the four teams sent by the four Quarters of the city, only two of which were really dangerous on the field. One of those, unfortunately, was the white team of his own Quarter. Unfortunately, because his own two little boys, when they and his wife at last moved up from Sicily to join him in Florence, became instant supporters of the Whites along with their schoolmates from the Quarter and expected that in his position he should produce tickets for the match. His feeble attempts to claim that the only tickets he could get were for the play-off between the Greens and the Reds met with disgusted howls of 'Oh, Dad!' He had allowed himself to be bullied into producing tickets for the match between the Whites and the Greens which should turn out to prove fairly innocuous. Anything to avoid the inevitable final battle between Whites and Blues, a floodlit and terrifying spectacle on the night of San Giovanni, the patron saint of the city. The night of June 24th.

So it was that on the second Sunday in June as he pushed his bulky dark-uniformed figure through the crowds on the narrow pavement of Via Ulderighi, the only thing really worrying him was the fact that the boys would be at the match with their mates, that and the burning afternoon sun which was making his sensitive eyes stream a bit despite his dark glasses. Every now and then he was obliged to fish for his handkerchief and pause, jostled on all sides, to try and dab them dry without actually removing his sunglasses. He could hear drums behind him thundering out a tattoo that echoed between the high eaves of the buildings. The procession was on its way. He'd had to spare quite a few lads from his station for duty at the match but he had no reason for going there himself other than wanting to keep an eye out for the boys. Even so, he had to admit, as the grey horse leading the cortège came level with him, that despite his disapproval of the violence of the tournament he did rather enjoy the pageantry. The drums and trumpets and the shining silk flags spinning upwards in the narrow streets towards a strip of blue sky made Florence look as it ought to look, and the people leaning out to watch from high windows between the bunting made a cheerful atmosphere that was infectious.

His cheerfulness was short-lived. He had paused for a moment, distracted by the antics of the grey horse which was getting too excited for comfort. It was snorting and trying to throw up its head and a lather of sweat was forming on its neck and shoulders. The cloaked nobleman in the saddle maintained a stern and competent expression but, in the Marshal's opinion, his stern rigidity was impressing the crowd but not the horse which was trying to break into a trot and sidled towards the crowd when prevented. People were pressing back on the Marshal. He felt someone tug sharply at his sleeve.

'Here! Marshal!'

He turned. A very tall man was standing directly behind him, intent on photographing the antics of the grey horse.

'This way. Quick!'

'Who the devil . . . ?'

A woman tapped his arm and pointed to a pair of gigantic studded doors surrounded by scaffolding, one of which was open just a crack.

'He went in there.'

An odd little face peered out and a hand beckoned impatiently, then vanished.

Puzzled, the Marshal went nearer to the great doors and peered into the gloom beyond. He could see nothing. He took off his sunglasses, pushed on the door and went in. He had hardly stepped inside when the door boomed shut and a small figure dodged out from behind him.

'This way.' He unlocked high wrought-iron gates. They were in a large colonnaded courtyard in the centre of which was a stone well. It was cold and dark after the brightness and heat of the street and the noise of the procession barely penetrated. Instead, he could hear faint music coming from somewhere above. The Marshal followed the agitated little figure that ran before him and came back to urge him on, the way dogs sometimes do. Now he was waiting by a door under the colonnade on the right. The Marshal reached him and said, 'Well?'

The man was a dwarf and barely reached the Marshal's waist, but to judge by his face he was well past forty. He was fishing for a key now in the pocket of his black overall.

'I locked the door. Well, you never know. Not that *he'll* be going anywhere!'

The Marshal waited in silence. He could already sense that something very serious was afoot and he couldn't reconcile this feeling with the dwarf's attitude. So he just waited.

The dwarf unlocked the door and went in with the Marshal following him. It was a gun room, quite small and windowless. A light was burning. Apart from the rifle rack and a cupboard, there was nothing but a table and a leather chair in the room. Nothing, except the man lying dead on the floor.

'Who is he?' The Marshal's big eyes were taking in every detail of the room and the body.

'Gaffer. The boss, or so he liked to think. Now he knows better. More of what they call a Prince Consort. Know what I mean?'

'No.' The Marshal bent to look at the dead man more closely. He had been shot at point blank range close to his throat. Or more likely he'd shot himself. He was lying on his back and a rifle lay across his chest. He wore a silk dressing-gown over evening clothes and there was a dark patch on one side of his face.

'Who is he?' repeated the Marshal, adding, as the dwarf opened his mouth to answer, 'His name.'

'Corsi. Buongianni. You must have heard of his famous apéritif. "Perks you up when you're feeling down"—you'll have seen the ad on the telly. Mind you, it'd take more than one at this point—'

'And what's your name?' said the Marshal, glowering.

'Me? I'm usually known as Grillo.'

The Marshal could well believe it. It was the common name for a cricket, which was just what this rattling little creature looked and sounded like.

'Well,' said Grillo, rubbing his hands together with relish, 'she'll have to be told so you're the man to do it. I was just wondering what to do when I saw you out there through the window. Not in here—' he was quick to catch the Marshal's glance at the blank walls—'from next door. *I'm* not going up there. Not my job, is it? I don't operate "up there". The porter ought to deal with it but him and his wife are "up there" already, tarted up as butler and maid for the do. I wonder what she'll say to this?'

'Sit down.' The Marshal was beginning to look dangerous. Grillo sat down. There was only the one chair and the Marshal stood over him glaring down with his huge bulging eyes. Grillo folded his arms and stared back brightly.

'At your service, provided you don't expect me—'

'Shut up.' But having shut him up, the Marshal wasn't at all sure where to begin. Buongianni Corsi . . . The apéritif business rang a bell, though he never touched the stuff himself. The faint sound of a fanfare of trumpets came from outside. It seemed to come from another world. The Marshal began to feel suffocated in the small room. It was a feeling that was to stay with him for a long time. With a sigh he looked from the dwarf to the dead man and back again.

'What time did you find him?'

'I haven't a watch!'

'What time approximately?'

'Might have been half an hour ago. I came in—'

'Why?'

'Why? To clean the guns, of course. It's my job, always has been.'

'And did you?'

'Clean them? No point, was there? He'll not be needing them. I didn't get that stuff out if that's what you're thinking.'

He didn't miss a trick. The Marshal had deliberately not looked at the rags and gun grease on the table.

'Cleaning it himself, wasn't he? I mean, he must have been. Shot himself, I suppose, wouldn't you say so?'

The Marshal expressed no opinion.

'You said it was your job.'

The only answer was a long-drawn-out cackle.

'What's so funny?'

'Nothing. He spent a lot of time in here, playing with his guns. Many an evening. Playing with his little pistol.' He grinned lewdly at the corpse. 'Preferred that to his wife and her friends. Now why do you think that would be, eh? Ha ha!'

The Marshal glowered. He was beginning to feel like the straight man in a comic act. He decided to try a policy of threatening silence. It worked. At first the dwarf, too, maintained a defiant silence but he soon began to look uncomfortable.

'Well, anyway . . . she'll have to be told. I expect . . . I expect you need to know who and where to find . . .'

The Marshal shifted his feet slightly and settled into still-ness again. The room was so bare, windowless and severe.

You'd have to be in a bad way to want to spend long silent evenings in it.

'It's the Marchesa you want. The Marchesa Ulderighi. His wife. You'll find her on the first floor. There's a concert going on, there always is on Sunday afternoons.'

The Marshal turned to go out the door.

'I'll lock it again, shall I? I'd better, don't you think?' Grillo came chattering after him. The Marshal waited as he turned the key, then took it from him and slipped it into the top pocket of his uniform. He looked up to where the music was still playing.

'Where's the lift?'

'You'll have to use the stairs. Only the family have keys to the lift.'

'Where can I phone?'

'Phone . . . there's one in the porter's lodge but you can't use that, can you? Locked. They're "up there" like I said, in fancy dress—'

'All right.'

The Marshal started plodding up the broad stone staircase. Perhaps, after all, it wouldn't be politic to fill this Marchesa whatshername's house with carabinieri and ambulance men before she even knew her husband was dead, though he'd rather have got the business off his hands and left an officer or a magistrate to tell her . . . tell her what? If he had to do it himself he'd better be careful how he phrased it. An accident . . . probably that's what it was anyway if the fellow was cleaning his gun, happens all the time. For a number of reasons already firmly lodged in his mind, he didn't believe what he was thinking. What he did believe, wrongly, as it turned out, was that anything involving high and mighty people like this would instantly be taken out of his hands.

'Oof!' He paused for breath and mopped his brow. At the first turning in the great staircase a carved wooden shield painted with the family coat of arms hung on the wall. The Marshal came upon it on turning the corner and it stopped him in his tracks. It was at least twice his own height and there was something about the way it leaned forward from the wall at the top that gave it a threatening air. The muffled, gentle music continued playing somewhere above. He continued his climb, slightly out of breath, and on the first-floor landing he stopped. There were high double doors to his right and left. The music was coming from the right. A concert, Grillo had said. He looked at the bell on the wall, imagining the interruption its pealing would cause. A brass plate above it was engraved in copperplate: *Bianca Maria Corsi Ulderighi Della Loggia*. That must be her—but why only her name? What about the husband? He hadn't been dead when that plate was put up. Prince Consort, the Grillo had said . . . What a creature!

The Marshal didn't ring the bell. When it came to people who had that many names on their doorbell you did well to tread softly or you might wake up one morning and find you'd been transferred to some godforsaken spot at the other end of the peninsula. He raised his big fist and tapped gently. The music continued. It was a sad but pleasing tune, the melody picked out by what he thought was probably a flute. He knocked discreetly three more times and then tried the door. It opened. After all, it was a concert and presumably open to the public, so he stepped gingerly in. He was in a broad corridor with a terracotta floor of tiles so old and darkened with polishing that they seemed almost black. There were no windows, but light came from small silk-shaded lamps on four half-moon tables flanking more double doors to the right and left. The flute continued its soft lament and the Marshal tried to tread the polished floor in his big black shoes without making too much noise, his fists clenched with the effort. He reached the door on the left, took off his hat and pressed the brass handle.

As the volume of the music increased he got a brief impression of a high-ceilinged yellow and white salon with the same darkly polished floor and an enormous central chandelier. There were perhaps sixty or eighty sleekly dressed people in there sitting on tiny gilded chairs. He drew the door shut quietly and stood thinking what to do for the best. Wait for an interruption in the music and slide in under cover of the applause? This was ridiculous. The woman's husband was lying dead down there. Why the devil hadn't she even missed him if they had all these guests? Perhaps the best thing to do, after all, would be to go out and phone for help from a bar now that the racket caused by the procession would likely be over. The only thing that made him hesitate to do just that was the thought of that chattering Grillo who was undoubtedly waiting below to see how he'd got on. By this time he could well understand why the dwarf had balked at coming up and barging in on that lot himself and could just imagine his grinning triumph at the Marshal's own lack of courage and aplomb.

'Blast,' he said to himself, and thought again about waiting for an interruption in the music. Then he heard the door behind him open. He turned round to see a plump woman of middle age dressed in a maid's uniform. She was still holding the doors open wide and was staring at him in apprehension. With a little wail of fear she turned and vanished. He could hear her calling for someone urgently.

'Mauro! Mauro!'

'What's up with you now, woman?'

'*Mauro!*'

The Marshal had followed in her wake. The room to his right was almost identical to the other but a bit smaller and it contained two very long tables covered in white damask and set with glasses and bottles of the famous apéritif. A small service door had been left open at the other end of the room and now a man appeared there. He had a wizened, monkeylike face and was dressed in black trousers, a short striped cotton jacket and white gloves. His wife—for this was surely the porter, reappeared behind him to peer anxiously over his shoulder. Her white face was now blotched with red. It was plain that they felt as incongruous as they looked in their 'fancy dress' and that this exacerbated their distress at the sight of the Marshal. The porter looked not so much at the Marshal himself as at his uniform and let out a single word under his breath.

'Shit . . .'

'What did I tell you?' wailed his wife. 'Time and time again I've said it and nobody takes a blind bit of notice. Well, I'm glad, do you know that! I'm *glad*. Because even she'll think twice before helping him again if you ask me, and so that'll be the end of it. Even if they put him away, at least it'll be the end! You'll not listen to me but you'll learn—'

'Keep quiet, you stupid cow!'

The Marshal, understanding nothing, stood where he was and remained silent. The woman shuffled back through the service door and continued her sobs and imprecations out of sight.

'Well?' The porter pushed his hands into his pockets in an attempt to look nonchalant but at once pulled them out again because of the white gloves. 'Is he hurt himself or has he damaged somebody else, or what?'

The Marshal, nonplussed, only stared back at him with large bulging eyes.

As if remembering something, the porter said, 'What time is it, anyway?'

'The time . . . ?' The Marshal glanced at his watch. 'A quarter to six.'

'But they only kicked off at half past five, so how could you have got here—or did it happen before?'

'Before . . .' Did he mean the concert?

'Well, whatever happened, he's not to blame, you can take that from me. What can you expect? They go for him, they always have done. You can stand so much but then sooner or later something has to give, am I right? You haven't said whether he's hurt?'

'He's dead.' The words were no sooner out when the expression on the porter's wizened face told him that they couldn't be talking about the same person. He'd taken it like a blow in the stomach and was swaying on his feet now as though he might fall.

'Easy,' the Marshal said going closer and getting hold of the smaller man's arm. Nobody was that fond of their employer. 'Buongianni Corsi. I'm talking about Buongianni Corsi. There's been an accident. He's dead. You'd better sit down a minute.' The porter let himself be led to a chair and sank down in it with a white-gloved hand against his chest.

'Nearly did for me . . . heart's not so good. Nearly did for me.'

'I'm sorry. Shouldn't you take something?'

'Ada! Ada!' Loud sobs were still issuing from the room beyond and his wife didn't hear him.

'I'll get her,' the Marshal said. He went through the service door into a small kitchen-cum-storeroom. She was sitting on a cardboard box with 'Bottles. With Care' printed on it, her feet planted wide apart, her fists descending limply on her knees in time with her sobs.

'Your husband needs some medicine,' he interrupted her a bit brusquely. There would be time enough later to find out what all this was about and he didn't want another dead man on his hands.

She got to her feet and pushed her hair back, forgetting about the little lace cap, which went askew.

'Yes! Medicine! It's me that'll end up in hospital between

the two of them but they'll not listen. I can talk till I'm blue in the face . . .' Nevertheless she went off through a further door, presumably in search of whatever her husband required.

The Marshal filled one of the wineglasses from the table with water and went back to the porter. He was still sitting down and there was a bluish tinge about his lips but he seemed calmer.

'Your wife's bringing you something.' He gave him the water.

'Thanks.' He sipped at it, keeping his eyes fixed on the double doors which stood open. The music was still playing.

'They'll be coming through before long. I'll have to—'

'Sit where you are,' the Marshal said, 'or maybe we should go back there.' He indicated the kitchen.

'If we're not ready for them there'll be hell to pay. The Marchesa—'

'The Marchesa will have other things to think about. Her husband's dead.'

'That's true . . . You said, didn't you, an accident. In his car?'

'No. Why wasn't he up here at the concert, do you know?'

'Him? He never comes. Not his style. Leaves all that stuff to her.'

'Will there be any other members of the family in there with her? Someone who'd know how to break the news to her?'

'Well . . . the aunt'll be there, I suppose. Even so, I wouldn't worry so much on that score if I were you.'

'Are there any children?'

'Neri . . .' The porter grimaced. 'You'll not see him, nobody ever does. He'll be above.' He took another sip of water and put his head down near his knees. 'Feel a bit dizzy . . .'

The Marshal took the glass from him. 'Your wife's a long time coming back.'

'It's all those stairs . . .' He fell silent as though it fatigued him to talk. The wife did come back at last, out of breath and with her cap still askew. She gave him two tablets which he gulped down greedily. She turned to the Marshal. She had stopped crying and her look was defiant.

'Well? What's he done?'

'You have a son, is that it? Is that who you're worrying about?' By this time the Marshal had put two and two together.

'Who should I be worrying about? If he went for somebody he had good reason! They all pick on him—I've warned him to give it up, I've warned him—'

'Hold your noise!' shouted her husband, and then clutched at his chest again. He shut his eyes at the pain and said, 'He's come about Corsi. There's been an accident. He's dead.'

The woman was silenced. She gaped about her at the serried ranks of bottles as though their presence must indicate that their producer was still alive.

'What happens next?' the Marshal asked, nodding his head towards the other room where the music had ended and there came the sound of applause.

'They'll all be coming in here.' She straightened her apron. 'Just look at the state I'm in . . .' She didn't think of the cap and the Marshal didn't like to say anything.

'And who's going to tell her?'

'I am.'

'Rather you than me. Not that there was any love lost . . . Even so . . .'

'Can you two carry on as normal here?' the Marshal interrupted. 'I'll keep her in the other room, if possible—'

But the two of them got to their feet, not listening to him. With a smartness that surprised him they had taken their places, one behind each of the long tables, and were pouring very modest amounts of the famous apéritif into the rows of shining glasses when the doors of the salon opposite burst open.

2

The crowd that poured into the room caused the Marshal to back up slightly but then he stopped, his face set and expressionless, standing his ground. He was well aware of how out of place he looked in his dark uniform among the pale silk and linen, in his silent immobility against the swirl of chattering movement. One or two women gave him a questioning glance before turning away to continue their conversation or reach for their glasses. No one spoke to him. They were almost all women and none of them young. One, very formally dressed and heavily made up, walked with the aid of two sticks. The room filled up with an oppressive mixture of strong perfumes. A woman backed into him as she withdrew from the long table, glass in hand, and turned as if to apologize but her expression froze as she saw him. With a swift icy glance that took him in from head to foot and dismissed him from her world, she turned and went on talking.

'*So* talented, I think, and rather good-looking, but of course you saw "the friend" . . . My dear, Bianca for once was rather at a loss but what could she do . . .'

'She should have refused. Of course, I agree we wouldn't want to lose dear, dear Emilio. Nevertheless—'

'Oh, Bianca gets away with anything, even this!'

The Marshal, watching and listening, wondered what 'this' referred to and thought perhaps she didn't care for what was in her glass. There was nothing else on offer, he noticed.

'Do you think,' a voice whispered, so close to his ear that he thought he was being spoken to, 'that Emilio is actually homosexual?' It was the heavily painted old lady with the two sticks speaking not to him but to a much younger woman who looked amused.

'Of course. You can't imagine he's ever tried to hide it.' She noticed the Marshal's turning to stare which seemed to amuse her even more. The other woman, noticing nothing, insisted: 'But you're young and know about these things— is it a genetic defect of some sort or, as they say, psychosomatic? I don't understand . . .'

The porter appeared at the Marshal's elbow with a tray of full glasses.

'You might as well . . .'

'No, thanks.'

'Well go through, then. She'll be in there.' He nodded towards the opposite salon.

The Marshal pushed his way through to the door. The bigger room was now almost empty. Three men, all impeccably dressed in silk suits and with sleek grey hair, stood talking seriously near the rows of empty gilded chairs. One very young man sat alone on a plain wooden stool almost behind the door, where the Marshal had been unable to see him when he had first glanced in so briefly. At the front of the room stood a grand piano. To the Marshal's surprise there were no other instruments, only a stereo set on an antique table. In front of this stood a good-looking young man, 'dear Emilio', perhaps? He was talking animatedly to a tall, elegant woman in white who had her back to the Marshal. Avoiding the tiny chairs that would surely collapse if his great weight so much as brushed against them, he trod the polished floor almost on tiptoe and, hat in hand, approached them.

As he came near, the young man stopped in mid-sentence to stare at him. The woman turned.

'Signora Marchesa . . .'

'Yes?' Her eyes took him in from head to foot just as the other woman's had done but with a good deal more effect.

They were very large black eyes but her hair was blonde and her skin white. She wasn't young, certainly over forty, but she was an extremely beautiful woman indeed and there was an aura surrounding her that deterred the Marshal from going too close. The expression in her bright disdainful eyes so unnerved him that he could hardly have felt more humiliated if he had skidded on the shining floor and smashed a dozen of those frivolous little chairs. He swallowed and looked at the young man as he spoke so as to avoid her eyes.

'I have some bad news, I'm afraid. If I could speak to you alone . . .'

'Bad news . . . ?' She inclined her head slightly as if making an effort to believe him, then she turned to the young man and smiled. He was dismissed. The Marshal watched him go. Near the door he spoke to the man seated on the stool, who got up hastily and with a backward scowl at the room in general went out with him.

'Rather a fortunate interruption . . .' the Marchesa murmured with a faint smile. 'Artists are a race apart, don't you feel? So that whatever their origins . . . but one must draw the line . . . Dear Emilio. Well, I'm quite sure he won't make that mistake again—What exactly can I do for you?'

The sudden change of tone took him aback.

'I . . . It's bad news, I'm afraid—'

'Ah yes, so you said. Shouldn't you tell me who you are, exactly?'

'Guarnaccia. Marshal of carabinieri, Palazzo Pitti station.'

'Palazzo Pitti? There's a carabinieri station there? What an extraordinary thing, but how nice for you. Would you care to sit down?'

'No! I . . . no, thank you.' Nothing would have induced

him to risk planting his weight on one of those tiny chairs. He was beginning to sweat with embarrassment and didn't really take in a word of what the Marchesa was saying. He could only stare at her with his big eyes. He felt he was looking at someone wearing a mask, trying to fathom her real expression behind it. The mask was one of faint surprise touched with disdain. The eyes looked out through it as hard and bright as ice.

'I was passing here,' he began after a slight cough, 'when I was called in by a man . . . a dwarf—'

'Grillo?'

'Grillo, yes—I presume he works for you?'

'Works? Well, yes, he does odd jobs about the place. He's been with us since he was a child. Part of the family in a way.'

The Marshal took this to mean that they didn't pay him and that his position was uninsured and illegal, but he had no intention of going into that. He had enough on his plate already without stirring anything up in that direction. Noticing that he was turning his hat slowly round and round between his large hands, he stopped himself doing it and, holding the brim tightly, said his piece.

'This Grillo took me to a room off the courtyard, a gun room. He told me he'd gone in there himself to clean the guns. Your husband was there. Possibly he'd been cleaning one of the guns himself and there was an accident. He's dead, Signora Marchesa.'

'Buongianni? Dead . . . ?' The mask was recomposed into one of distressed astonishment. The eyes didn't falter for a second. She didn't even find it necessary to look away from him and he knew as surely as if she'd confessed it that she'd been ready for him, or for whoever else might have brought her this news. The Marshal himself, however, was far from ready for her next move. There was no pretence of grief or anything approaching it. The hard icy glance held his for long enough to establish her hold on the situation and his own irrelevance. Then she turned her head very slightly and raised her voice.

'Gianpiero.'

One of the silk-suited men at the back of the room detached himself from the other two and approached.

'What's going on here?' He took in the Marshal's uniform and then turned to the Marchesa and took her arm. 'Has there been an accident of some sort? You look distressed.'

'It's Buongianni. An accident, yes. This is Marshal . . .'

'Guarnaccia.'

'I do beg your pardon. Dear Gianpiero, thank goodness you're here, I suppose we must go down and look. Do you think . . . ?' She glanced down the room to the remaining two grey-haired men.

'They should certainly be with us.' He addressed the Marshal then in brusque authoritative tones. 'What sort of accident, and where?'

The Marshal was nettled. For the moment, at least, he was supposed to be in charge of the situation but he might have been one of the servants.

'It may or may not have been an accident. That's something we must look into. He's in the gun room on the ground floor.'

'Dead? Speak up, man, dead or injured? We could be losing precious time.'

'Dead.' Who the devil did this chap think he was?

'Right. You've told them?' This was addressed to the Marchesa who was coming back followed by the two men. 'Then we'll go down.'

They went down in the lift but not before the Marchesa remembered to complete the introductions. 'Dear Gianpiero' turned out to be the chief public prosecutor of Florence. The other two were 'family lawyers' who remained nameless. The descent was made in silence. The Marshal, still clutching the brim of his hat, could hear his own heart-beat and his ill-judged words re-echoing in his head. 'It may or may not have been an accident. That's something we must look into.' How could he have been such a damn fool? His only hope was in his not being important enough to matter. All he had to do was keep his mouth shut until he could escape from this house never to return. They'd find some tactful, respectful, high-ranking officer . . . They could hardly get him transferred just for that one remark . . . He wasn't important, that was the main thing he could count on . . .

And yet, all the way down in the lift, all the time they were in the room with the body, around which two or three flies were now buzzing, beneath the tension and distress caused by the fear of his own position there was another thought which persisted. 'Dear Gianpiero' was a close friend, that was obvious, but even so, as the lady said, how very *fortunate* that he happened to be here.

'HSA job, is it?' asked Lorenzini, munching. The usual Homicide, Suicide or Accident report in case of sudden death didn't seem to him much of a reason to call in for assistance but he was glad enough to find himself eating an excellent pizza.

'This is great.'

'Mm.' It wasn't clear whether the Marshal was agreeing about the 'HSA job' or the pizza. He didn't seem to have his usual good appetite, though. Every so often he would cease chewing and stare into space as though his mind were on other things. He had sent for his young brigadier from the station at Pitti partly because he would need his help but more because he found his presence reassuring. At this early hour in the evening very few people in Gino's, the pizzeria opposite the Palazzo Ulderighi, were eating. Most of them seemed to be friends and relations of the owners and were smoking and drinking coffee around the television set on which a local channel was showing a recording of the mediæval football tournament.

'After all,' Lorenzini went on, raising his voice as the crowd round the television set up a roar of protest over yet another bout of violence on the field, 'if he did kill himself they won't pay up, will they?'

'No.' He popped a slice of the crackling pizza into his mouth and when he'd dealt with it said, 'His wife's from Naples, that's why.'

'What? This Marchesa what's she called . . . Ulderighi?'

'Eh? No, no. The woman who makes this pizza. So her husband was telling me while I was waiting for you. That's why it's so good. The stuff they make in Florence as a rule, all that thick rubbery dough with tinned stuff slopped on it and what tastes like motor oil . . .' He continued munching in silence, frowning a little as the television caught his eye. 'I hope there wasn't any trouble. My boys were there. Perhaps I should call home.'

Lorenzini turned his head to look. Three Green players had fallen in a heap on top of one of the Whites. Their long slashed breeches were covered in sand and not one of them still had a T-shirt on his back. The group round the set stood up shouting and blocked their view. The Marshal got up from his chair.

'I'll just telephone . . .' He went off to the back room, fishing for a token in his pocket. He wasn't gone long. As he sat down again he sighed and said, 'What a business . . .'

Again Lorenzini wasn't sure whether he meant the football or the dead man across the road, but he knew the Marshal well enough to be sure that this grumpy vagueness meant he'd got his teeth into something. He had the look of a bulldog about him and, like a bulldog, he was unlikely to let go. Young as he was, Lorenzini ventured on a word of warning.

'With people like that, of course, it doesn't do to stick your neck out, especially—'

'Especially with the chief public prosecutor taking a personal interest?'

'That, too. Even so, he's given you a free hand, hasn't he? I mean, checking on the tenants and what they might have heard. Establishing the time of death. From what you've said he's not blocking you.'

'No. And why? Why me?'

Lorenzini was silenced. The Marshal wiped his mouth and took a sip of wine.

'I'll tell you why. Because I'm nobody. Anything I say, anything I find out, can be ignored. And if I don't like it I can be transferred from Florence—' he snapped his thick fingers—'like that!'

'Well, yes, that's what I meant, but I'm sure if you tread carefully, stay clear of the press and so on—'

'I don't like being made a fool of,' the Marshal said quietly. 'And if I were to tell the truth I don't like this being made a fool of much either.' As he said it he placed his large hand on the hat with its gold flame above the peak which lay on the empty chair beside him. After which he finished his meal in silence, gazing in bleak disapproval at the television screen.

They were half way through their coffee when he suddenly took up where he left off: 'And bear in mind, when you say he's not blocking me, that we're to question the tenants but we're not to disturb the Signora Marchesa—that wouldn't do at all—and not her son either, who's too delicate, they say, so nobody ever sees him.' He unbuttoned his top pocket and fished a black notebook out from behind his sunglasses.

'This lot,' he said, flipping the book open beside his coffee cup, 'are the ones we're allowed to waste our time on, starting with this Filippo Brunetti—that's the one they call Grillo, I told you about him.'

'The dwarf?'

'That's right. I suppose I ought to feel sorry for him but he's a nasty little beggar, sharp as needles, too, and if anybody knows everything that goes on over there, he does. But . . .'

'You don't think he'll talk?'

'He'll talk all right. I've never met anybody who talked so fast. But he knows which side his bread's buttered on and if he had to leave the Ulderighi place where would he go? Didn't seem to care much for Corsi, but then . . .'

'But what?' Lorenzini had a great respect for the Marshal, but he was young and active and couldn't always conceal his impatience with the older man's slowness and the half-formed irrelevant observations he left hanging in the air. 'But what, Marshal?' he said again, his bright grey eyes glancing through the window at the great house. Left to himself he'd have been over there an hour ago taking accurate, methodical motes, but here they were taking time over the coffee as they'd taken time over their pizza and still the Marshal didn't answer. Lorenzini turned from the window to look at him and found him once again staring over at the television screen in silence. When he did speak he had drifted from the subject.

'Florentines are a funny lot. After all these years I haven't got used—no offence meant, you understand.'

Lorenzini, a died in the wool Florentine, pointed out that we all have our funny ways, but the point didn't get home.

'If you'd seen him, standing there with a dead man at his feet and cracking jokes.'

'Better a corpse in the house than a Pisan at the door?'

'Eh?'

'It's an old Florentine saying from the days of the wars with Pisa.'

'Mph.' The Marshal thought this over and then said, 'So I'm the Pisan, is that it?'

'You or anybody else threatening the set-up.'

'Well . . . Maybe you're right. Perhaps you should talk to him, you might understand each other better—just look at that! He's trying to strangle the referee! I remember that face, too. Isn't he the one who got his ear bitten off one time?'

'Might be. It was years ago. I think I was still at school.'

'Well, I don't like it. At least half of that lot should be behind bars, if you ask me. Anyway, you talk to him. Then there's the porter and his wife. Mori, the name is, and there's a son, too, and if I've got my facts right he's among that lot.' Another black look at the screen and then he prodded the notebook with a huge forefinger. 'This is the old "tata". Nursed all the Ulderighi children since the year dot. Her name's Marilena Binazzi. Ninety-one and stone deaf. All these family retainers live in rooms off the court-yard. The other rooms there are rented out as studios. The musician, Emilio Emiliani, who has a flat up on the third floor uses one for practising. One's a doctor's surgery . . . here she is, Flavia Martelli, likewise has a flat upstairs. The last one, near the entrance on the right, is rented to an English girl called Catherine Yorke who does some sort of restoration work. She left last week on a trip to England so we won't see her anyway. Now: there's another flat on the third floor . . . wait a minute . . . Martelli, Emiliano . . . This one—Fido.'

'Sounds like a dog.'

'Well, he's a painter. English again, but you're right, it's a funny sort of name. Oh, and there's a ballet school on the first floor but that doesn't concern us since it's closed between Saturday and Monday. Well, that's the lot. Now

we go and ask them if they heard anything and they'll all
say no.'

'But, Marshal, surely, these people who are tenants and
not family retainers—I mean, a shot like that echoing
round a courtyard would wake the dead.'

'Yes.' The Marshal slipped the notebook back in his
pocket. 'It would. If that's where it happened. But I don't
think he died there, not like that. He was lying on his back
but the blood had settled along one side of his face. There'll
be a post-mortem, of course, there'll have to be, but I'll
never get to see the results of it.'

'Do you think he shot himself, then?'

'How should I know whether he shot himself? My point
is that I'll never get to know—but I'll tell you one thing I
do know, you don't wear evening dress to clean a gun. And
another thing I know is that there wasn't enough mess in
there, not by a long chalk. Not a spatter. We'd better pay
and get going.'

Paying and getting going wasn't so easy. Their waiter
was too involved with the noisy crowd around the television
to notice their attempts to attract his attention. In the end,
Lorenzini got up and went to fetch the proprietor, who then
delayed them further by wanting compliments for his wife's
pizza. Lorenzini was happy enough to oblige but all he got
out of the Marshal, scowling out of the door from behind
his sunglasses, was a mumbled repetition of 'Not enough.
No, no, not by a long chalk . . .'

As the two uniformed men crossed the street and rang
the bell at the Palazzo Ulderighi, Gino, the proprietor
stared after them. He reckoned their pizzas were the biggest
ones in Florence. And the Marshal had eaten two!

'I hope you're feeling better.'

The porter peered out suspiciously at the Marshal. He
had only opened the lodge door a crack.

'I'm all right.'

'Then if you don't mind we'll step inside with you for a minute. Is your wife at home?'

'She's having a lie-down. It's been an upset for her. She's bad with her nerves.'

He let them in but didn't offer them a chair or sit down himself. The room was small and stuffy and overcrammed with a mixture of old and new furniture. It evidently served as both kitchen and living-room. The air was thick with the smell of fried onions and meat and a large pan of water was coming to the boil on a gas ring. A washing-machine which looked new stood in one corner with a bit of fringed cloth over its surface and a vase filled with plastic flowers on top. The Marshal's big eyes took in each detail and his sharp ear caught a faint rustle in the next room.

'Your wife seems to be awake.'

The porter hesitated, his glance shifting to the inner door.

'We'll have to talk to her at some point. Best get it over with and we'll try not to have to disturb you again.'

The porter went through to the inner room and shut the door behind him. A murmured argument went on and it was some time before the two of them appeared.

'Good evening, Signora. I'm sorry we're obliged to disturb you but we won't keep you long.'

The woman's face was still blotchy and a rolled-up handkerchief was clenched in her fist. She didn't so much as look at the Marshal, let alone answer his greeting. She sat herself down at a formica table and stared reproachfully at her husband.

The Marshall persisted. 'Very fond of your employer, were you?' But she didn't answer.

'She's bad with her nerves,' the porter repeated.

He still didn't offer them a chair. It was all wrong. In the Marshal's experience a couple like this one, shut in all day, bored and probably underpaid, would be only too glad to settle down at the table there, perhaps with four glasses and a bottle of vin santo between them, and spill the dirt on their employers. It was the chance of a lifetime to be the centre of attention and get all their accumulated grudges off their chests. Instead of which they wanted the Marshal and Lorenzini out, and quick. Yet it could hardly matter to them whether Corsi had died by accident or by his own hand.

The Marshal's face was bland, expressionless, his voice reassuring as he addressed the woman.

'There's not much we need to ask you.'

He asked little and learned less. They had last seen Corsi when he left with the Marchesa the evening before to go to a dinner. They had opened up for them on their return but without looking out. They had heard the lift go up. They hadn't heard any shot.

'What time was it when they came in?'

They looked at each other and hesitated. The woman opened her mouth but her husband put in quickly: 'Lateish. I went to bed at one more or less and I'd been asleep, I don't know how long but the lad wasn't back, so it wasn't four in the morning, I can say that.'

'The lad?'

'Our boy, Leo. He's a bouncer in one of the clubs. They shut about four and he has breakfast before he comes home so it's half past four or quarter to five when he gets in.'

'And that wakes you, I suppose?' He didn't add 'though a shot, of course, wouldn't' but he might as well have done because the porter was immediately on the defensive.

'Well, it's bound to, isn't it? He has to come through. We sleep in here, on that.' He indicated a divan. 'It makes a double bed.'

'And your son has the bedroom?'

'He has to sleep all day. How else could we manage?'

'He's a good lad. He's always been good to his mother *and* to him.' The woman had dissolved into copious tears again and was plying her handkerchief.

'Pack it in, will you?'

But there was no stopping her.

'That's right! Never a good word for him but you've no objection to the money he brings in.'

'I've never taken a penny of his money. It's you—'

'Yes! Me! It's me he gives it to and where would we be if he didn't? It's all very well shutting your eyes to it!' She dabbed at her own eyes but the tears continued to flow. She blew her nose and said to the Marshal, 'He bought me that.' She stabbed the air with her handkerchief in the direction of the draped washing-machine. 'Only the other day he bought me that washer.'

'He doesn't want to know that!' The porter made to raise his fist but thought better of it and pushed both hands into his pockets.

The Marshal felt the closeness of the four walls, imagined this quarrelling going on day after day, year after year. Three of them in this tiny place, with its accumulated smells of cooking, the son in bed most of the day.

Then the dressing up to serve the Marchesa's friends. They hadn't much to lose but he knew they weren't going to risk losing it any more than the dwarf was. It was a roof, a living, both of which were hard, almost impossible, to come by in Florence. He felt pretty sure the Marchesa had paid them to say nothing, or promised to.

'I don't think we need you any longer,' he said. What was the point? He was wasting his time. He knew it and so did they. When they were outside the door they heard the quarrel continuing and the supper plates being slammed on to the table. This noise was drowned almost at once by an echoing series of piano chords.

*

'Oh! Oh, that's right. I'd heard you might be on your rounds. Sorry if I didn't hear you right away.' The musician, dressed in white linen trousers and a crisp striped shirt, looked cheerful, even amused, as he let the Marshal in.

'That's all right.'

Two grand pianos faced each other in a carpeted room lined from floor to ceiling with shelves filled with volumes of sheet music. A lamp was lit on one of the pianos, for this room, too, was devoid of windows.

'Do sit down.'

They sat on a white divan that stood against the wall, the only seating there was. It was so very low and squashy that the Marshal wondered as he sank into it whether he would ever manage to get up from it. The young musician leaned back happily, propping one leather-slippered foot on to his knee to exhibit an expanse of smooth leg, and fixed the Marshal with a bright and wicked eye.

'So! Family dirt is what you're after, isn't it?'

'Well . . .' It was true that that's what he'd been hoping for from the porter, but when it was put to him so bluntly he felt a bit embarrassed.

'No?'

'I . . . in a way, I suppose . . .'

'Well, there's oodles of it and I'm in rather a wicked mood today!'

The Marshal, red and uncomfortable, wished he'd sent Lorenzini here instead of to the dwarf. He'd never be able to deal with this. As it turned out, he didn't really have to since 'Dear Emilio', once launched, hardly paused to draw breath.

'I suppose you want to know whether the Prince Consort shot himself so that it can be proved that he didn't for the insurance—well, of course he shot himself, who wouldn't in his place? Needs courage, naturally, and I wouldn't have said he had much of that myself, but then *she* had it to spare and probably gave him a helping hand. Oh dear, now you look shocked. But you don't know the people you're dealing with!'

'I—'

'But you were there at this afternoon's débâcle, I saw you. That, just that alone, should give you an idea!'

'You mean the concert?'

'Concert? Those aren't concerts that she has every Sunday, my God, no. Now, how shall I put it? You must imagine La Bianca—the Marchesa Ulderighi to the uninitiated—as a sort of high priestess of musical appreciation and yours truly as the acolyte brought in—for a small consideration—to distinguish between one note and another on her behalf. A lady with so many heavy social responsibilities can't be expected to concern herself with the trivial or artisan aspects of the art of music. So: I play them a gramophone record—avoiding anything they might recognize and be able to hum—and I then seat myself at the pianoforte and analyse it. I explain it to them while they fix me with expressions of well-bred attention and think to themselves, "Isn't Bianca *musical*!"'

'And is she?'

'Well, you know, it's my opinion that she might be if she gave any time to it—I'm being desperately generous, considering what happened this afternoon—but the son's got a talent, squashed to death but it's there, and if he gets it from anywhere it's from her. However, be that as it may, the amount of time she does give to it is about equal to the amount of time she would spend choosing a lipstick, that is, sufficient to establish that it's of acceptably good quality, the right brand and becoming to her. She's sufficiently well informed to be able to make an intelligent remark at a first night and to know when to keep quiet and avoid a gaffe in the Nini style. You must have heard Nini's famous one about Chopin, it was all over Florence!'

'No—if you don't mind my asking—'

'You *must* have heard it. Just after Christmas when I gave my Chopin recital and of course all the dear old bags from Bianca's Sunday afternoons wanted tickets, but Ninì, the contessa—absolutely my favourite of them all—came up to whisper in my ear, 'It won't all be lieder, will it?''

He shut his eyes and was shaken by a gale of merriment so heartfelt and infectious that the Marshal couldn't help his own expression lightening a touch though he hadn't understood the joke. He waited, hat planted on his knees, until the laughter subsided and he had the young man's attention, to say: 'You mentioned something that happened this afternoon. If you mean my arrival on the scene—'

'No! You mean you didn't notice? But you'd have died! I don't know how I kept a straight face through that lecture, I really don't, and I didn't dare catch Simone's eye. He was livid, but I'm used to these people and I couldn't help—even if I think about it now—' Thinking about it now he was again shaken by laughter that left his face pink and his eyes watering.

'Simone's my friend, you understand. Well, needless to say Bianca's Sunday afternoons are desperately exclusive but Simone particularly wanted to come today, so yesterday I asked her—note that I didn't just bring him along, I *asked* her. So, you can imagine the position she was in. She didn't want him but, since she had to have me or there'd be no Sunday afternoon, through gritted teeth she said yes. And then she found a solution to mollify her exclusive friends. I can't believe it yet though I saw it with my own eyes. Simone was allowed in, *but*—he wasn't allowed to sit on a gold chair! Can you believe it? He was given a nasty little stool right by the door so that he looked as though he were there to sell tickets!'

Though he had seen the young man on the stool by the

door with his own eyes, the Marshal did find it rather difficult to believe.

'Perhaps the other chairs were all full . . .' he murmured.

'Fifteen of them were empty. Fifteen! Poor Simone, but how can you not laugh at the mentality of these people? Well, *I* can't help but laugh but I must say I wouldn't care to be in your shoes. I'd help you if I could, but I imagine you're only meant to help cover up whatever happened.'

'You could help me find out what it is wants covering up.' Almost despite himself, the Marshal was beginning to like Emilio. He was intelligent, something he always admired, and a musician, too, and he seemed to know the Ulderighi people without being prejudiced against them or even frightened of them. 'Do you seriously think he killed himself?'

'I do. He wasn't like her, you know.'

'He wasn't?'

'No, no. Different sort altogether. He came of an old family himself, of course, or she wouldn't have married him, but unlike the Ulderighi, the Corsi accepted the new world and got on with surviving in it. An old family that made new money. Follow me?'

'The apéritif business?'

'Exactly. Well, somebody had to pay for the upkeep of all this.' He shot a bright ironic glance at the ceiling above his head. 'So he coughed up the ready while Bianca pretended, at least on the surface, that nothing had changed since the days of Cosimo De' Medici.'

'Well, if he was happy doing it . . .'

'He was miserable doing it, take my word.' He threw open his long white hands. 'The outdated pride of the Ulderighi sucking the enterprise of the Corsi dry. And for what? If the son had been anything decent—No, he was miserable. They led completely separate lives, probably both had lovers but very discreet. There's still a country house, you know, though the Ulderighi have lost just about everything else they owned, including the land which now belongs to the next estate. He used to go there a lot to shoot—'

'Why did he keep his guns in town, then?'

'Oh, the place is shut up except during August. You can hardly keep a gamekeeper on when all you've got left is your back garden. He goes out there a lot but he's usually a guest in somebody else's house. *She* only goes in August because it's not socially acceptable to be in Florence in August, but they never went there together. I'd swear he shot himself and I don't blame him.'

'But did you hear him?'

'Hear? Oh, I see what you mean but I can't help you there. I spent the night at Simone's flat and we came round here together in time for this afternoon's lecture, so that's no help to you, is it?'

'No. No . . . Well, I'll leave you to your practising.'

'Will you be going to see the other tenants?'

'I'll see them, yes . . .'

'For all the good it will do, is what you're not saying. Well, you never know. I've been here less than a year. If you find somebody who's been here longer—or at least someone who was in all night . . . But as you say, or don't say, for all the good it will do . . .'

Out in the courtyard the daylight had faded. The square of sky far above still glowed with the dusky greenish light of a summer evening and one star glimmered there. But the spent light didn't penetrate to the centre of the great building and the colonnade was already in deep shadow as the Marshal began to walk slowly round it, his step falling in automatically with the rhythm of the music which had begun again almost as soon as the door had closed on him.

He passed a door with no sign on it and no bell. By his

reckoning that ought to have been the room of the old nurse, the 'tata', who was reputed to be stone deaf. Would she even hear him if he knocked? In any case, he didn't pause there but continued round the corner and stopped before the doctor's surgery to read the hours engraved on a brass plaque. She wouldn't be there at this hour on a Sunday. He could of course go up to the third floor and try her flat. But he walked slowly on past the broad staircase and the porter's lodge to come out of the colonnade at the gates. As he did so, the light in the huge iron lantern over the entrance came on. A light-bulb so weak that it only seemed to accentuate the gloom. If there was one thing that annoyed him about the Florentines almost as much as their hard cynicism it was their obsession with economizing. He walked on past the English girl's empty studio and the unmarked door of the gun room. Hearing muffled voices as he reached the dwarf's tiny door in the far right corner, he remembered Lorenzini's response to his grumbles on the subject. One of his jokes about the three Florentines sharing a boiled egg and quarrelling about what to do with the leftovers. Well, with any luck Lorenzini would get more sense out of Grillo than he'd been able to do.

Having completed his round and reached the music studio again, he stepped out from the colonnade and approached the stone well in the centre of the courtyard. It was covered by a heavy wooden lid with an iron ring in the middle. Very heavy. He couldn't shift it an inch, never mind lift it. How many hours did that fellow practise? The music, which had been pleasant company at first, was now getting on his nerves. He also felt a prickling at his back as though someone were watching him. He turned to look but all the doors were shut. Even so, he could have sworn . . . Perhaps the old 'tata' wasn't as deaf as she was made out to be and had taken a peep at him. Natural enough, and if it hadn't been for that blasted everlasting piano music he'd have heard the door. He kept an eye on it for a while but it didn't open. He ought to go in and see her. After all, it had to be done sooner or later, might as well get it over with.

This piece of advice to himself went unheeded. He was feeling uncomfortable. He stood for a moment staring round him at all those closed, dark-varnished doors, with a peculiar feeling of being at once inside the building and yet shut out. Still, he might as well be, for all his presence mattered to the place. Or surely, he should rightly say, to the family. It wasn't what he'd thought, though. It was the place, this great house, that gave a sense of malevolence and he wished he were out of it, out of it for good and away from that music. With a sense of relief he at least managed to pinpoint the problem. It was certainly the music he'd heard this afternoon when he'd gone up there. That was all it was, an unpleasant association with the dead body, the icy face of the Ulderighi woman and his own anxiety at having made a fool of himself in front of the chief public prosecutor. Yes, it was the same music, he remembered it perfectly now. Thinking he'd heard instruments and it turned out that there'd been a gramophone . . . a flute, he thought he'd heard—but surely, that was a flute? Emilio, alone, behind his closed door was still playing, but from some other direction, from somewhere above, the melody was being tentatively picked out by a flute.

The Marshal remained by the well, looking up. The first and second floors were a blank, the tall brown shutters were all closed. On the third floor one rectangle of yellow light shone out. That could only be the doctor or the artist chap with the funny name. Not that there was any law against their playing the flute but he could swear it wasn't coming from there. Somewhere higher up, if anything, it was so faint. He backed round the well and craned his neck. Above the corner where the dwarf's door was, the building was much higher. There was some sort of tower at that corner silhouetted against the blue-green darkness of the summer night where more and more stars were appearing. Well, if the flute was being played up there, where he could make out two windows without shutters, it was being played in the dark.

'Enough's enough,' muttered the Marshal. Enough of the whole lot for one day, the Marchesa Ulderighi and the chief public prosecutor included. And especially enough of this great prison of a house with its grim lines of columns, its closed gates and shutters and that single dismal light. Let it keep its secrets to itself if that's what it wanted. With loud decisive steps that rang out on the flagstones the Marshal approached the dwarf's door and hammered on it with his big fist.

3

'Salva! What are you thinking of? You've got every light in the house on!'

The Marshal only grunted something incomprehensible from the bathroom. His wife, Teresa, waited a moment and when he didn't emerge she slid the shirts she was holding into a drawer and went out of the bedroom, turning off the central light and one of the bedside lamps as she went.

When he joined her in the living-room she was watching television by the light of a small lamp with her knitting in her lap. He switched on the chandelier.

'What's the matter? Are you looking for something?'

'No.'

'Well, turn that off. There's a lamp on already and we can't see the television properly like that—why are you in your dressing-gown? Are you tired?'

'A bit.'

'Switch that light off, Salva, will you?'

'You're knitting. You'll ruin your eyes.'

'I don't need to look at my knitting and I don't need six bulbs burning all night for no reason. You'll be the one to complain when the bill comes.'

'Me?' He was disconcerted. He switched off the light and sat down beside her, staring glumly at the screen.

'What's the matter? Have you had a bad day?'

'A bit . . .' He knew well enough that she could read him like a book. It was his habit when he came in to have a shower and exchange his uniform for something comfortable, but if he did it without pausing for a chat first, or if he stayed overlong under the shower washing away the day, then she knew something was up. Getting straight into pyjamas and dressing-gown was an obvious sign that he was putting a stop to a day that had been a disaster. He wished he'd thought of that before and not done it, but it was too late now.

She looked at him sideways, still knitting.

'If you haven't had enough to eat I can make you something.'

'No . . . no.'

'The boys wanted to wait up for you to tell you about the match but they've got school tomorrow.'

'Mph.' He stared at the news for a bit without taking a word of it in and then said, 'Isn't there a film or anything on?'

'I don't know. Look in the paper.'

But he sat where he was. If the worst came to the worst and he did get transferred, how would she take it? She'd spent years stuck down at home in Sicily looking after his sick mother while he was here in Florence. And when at last his mother had died and she'd come up here with the boys it had taken her a long time to settle in a strange city. She was settled enough by now, but when he tried to imagine telling her that they had to uproot again—and what about schools? The boys would have to change school and what if it were some way-out godforsaken place . . .

'Salva!'

'Eh?'

'I'm asking you if you want a hot drink!'

'No. Yes—I don't know . . .'

She rolled up her knitting and went off to the kitchen, her felt slippers flapping softly on the marble tiles. 'I'm making some camomile tea,' she called back.

He got up and trailed after her, hovering.

'Don't plant yourself right there, I want a pan.'

He shifted, watching her.

'Or there, I want to put the water on—Here, you do it.'

He lit the gas under the pan of water and stood watching it while Teresa got mugs and teabags.

'I was wondering,' he said to the pan.

'Wandering, more like. What about?'

'Well, if you feel really settled here now . . .'

'Of course I am. What brought this on? I haven't complained.'

'No . . . no. Only at first you—'

'These things take time, Salva. More for me than for you. You've got your work and your colleagues wherever you go. And even though it's so bad for the boys to change school, they soon make friends. If it's taken me longer it's because I'm on my own—is it boiling?'

'Yes.'

'Mind out of the way. You can't be going out making new friends at my age. I haven't the time. Salva, will you *move*, I want to get to the rubbish bin. Anyway—' she put the mug of tea in his hand—'I don't know what you're worrying about. I'm used to Florence now and I like it. And thank goodness we won't have to move again.'

They watched a film, or at least Teresa did. The Marshal tried his best to follow it in the hope of distracting himself, but for all his efforts at following the story he would continually find his thoughts back with the Ulderighi house, its inhabitants, the gloomy courtyard filled with piano music. Lorenzini, he'd noticed, had been quite unperturbed by it all, even by Grillo, who had evidently been less on the defensive with a fellow Florentine. A rum sort of character, Lorenzini had admitted.

'Even so, you can be sure he knows everything that's going on in that house.'

'That's what I thought.'

'You know what his real job is?'

'Some sort of odd job man, isn't he?'

'Nothing of the sort—oh, he probably does do odd jobs, but his business is looking after the young master.'

'Ah, the son . . .'

'Neri Ulderighi, who apparently hardly ever leaves his apartments which are at the top of the tower above where Grillo has his lair. It seems that was the original Ulderighi house, thirteenth-century. The rest, with the courtyard, was added three centuries later when they were in their heyday.'

'How old is the boy?'

'Early twenties, I gather.'

'Mph. Not quite right in the head, is that it?'

'Difficult to tell. Delicate is the word used. In and out of clinics all his life, never went to school. There even seems to have been some doubt about his surviving at all when he was a child. Mother smothers him, father never went near him. Mother's latest plan is to marry him off to some suitable girl who'll produce the next heir before it's too late.'

'And he's not willing, I suppose.'

'Oh, he willing all right. According to our friend Grillo, he can't wait, though he's never been near a girl in his life. Wants to escape from his ivory tower, perhaps, and Grillo's all for it. "He needs to get married," were his words. You know, he's a pretty poisonous little creature but I'm convinced he's really attached to the boy.'

'And the others?'

'Difficult to say. I reckon he's a bit frightened of the Lady of the Manor, for all his cockiness. Corsi I'd say he never gave much thought to, dead or alive. The ones he really loathes are the tenants.'

'Why?'

'No reason I could pin down. Just for being there, I think. Breaking up the great family residence, not belonging. It may be they torment him, of course, but I wouldn't have thought it. They're all respectable people by the sound of them.'

The Marshal, who had long since had his faith in 'respectable people' thoroughly shaken, made no comment, and they parted in Piazza Pitti, Lorenzini to go cheerfully off to his young wife and baby in their little flat down Via Romana, the Marshal to climb the sloping forecourt in front of the Pitti Palace towards his station under the arch on the left. He wanted his own home, a shower, normality. He wanted, at least for tonight, to forget it all. So why was he thinking about it yet again? A better film might have helped. This one seemed to be nothing but one long quarrel between a husband and wife. What they were quarrelling about was beyond him.

'What did I tell you!' announced Teresa, pointing an accusatory knitting needle at the screen.

'Eh . . . ?'

'He knew all along. I told you she was being followed when she supposedly went to the hairdresser's.'

'Oh.'

'By that man in the red sports car. I think he's in league with the husband as well as blackmailing her.'

'Ah.'

'Salva, I've never known anybody as slow to catch on as you—see, he's phoning him, so I'm right.'

She was right, thought the Marshal, about his being slow to catch on. Anybody with their wits about them would have kept quiet in front of any friend of the Marchesa Ulderighi's until he'd found out who it was. He suffered his way through the rest of the film, the knot of anxiety in his chest growing tighter every time he tried to reason it away. He wanted to go to bed, though he was convinced that he'd never sleep. Oddly enough, he did fall asleep, and almost at once, but he woke much earlier than usual with the same thoughts running through his head as when he'd closed his eyes.

'It's a beautiful day,' Teresa said, opening the window and pushing back the shutters. A shaft of fresh morning sunlight lit the room, carrying with it the scent of bay leaves from the Boboli Gardens. The knot of anxiety in the Marshal's chest tightened.

'Where was it stolen from? Where did you leave it?'

'Right under my house in Via del Leone. The chain was on the wheel but it wasn't chained to a pole or anything. I could kick myself. Ever since I got it I've hoiked it up three flights of stairs to my flat every night but last night after I'd been out to the cinema I was just so exhausted and I thought, well, who'd want to steal a bike like mine? It's one of those mini things and I got it second-hand so it can't be worth more than the price of a meal.'

'The price of a fix, perhaps.'

'I suppose so. I shouldn't be wasting your time on it, I know.' She was young, probably a student. Pretty, too, but that wasn't why the Marshal was letting her waste his time, as she put it. He had a whole queue in his waiting-room of typical Monday-morning complainants with stolen bikes, mopeds and cars and minor break-ins after a weekend's absence. On top of that were the season's tourists glumly reporting snatched bags and cameras and lost passports. And he was going to give them all the time they wanted.

'Have you checked with the *vigili*?' The municipal police sometimes removed bicycles as well as towing away cars if they were left in a street due to be cleaned that night.

'I did check. Tuesday's our night for street cleaning but I called them anyway. They said they didn't take anything from Via del Leone last night.'

Lorenzini tapped on the door and came in.

'Excuse me, Marshal, but do you think I'd better deal

with the German couple? Their flight's at three this afternoon and they'll have to go back to the consulate from here and get themselves temporary passports . . .'

'All right.'

'I can deal with all of them if you have to—'

'No. No . . . just the Germans. I'll see to the rest. Now then, Signorina, I suppose you don't happen to know the frame number of your bicycle?'

Lorenzini shot an astonished glance over his shoulder as he went out but the Marshal didn't care. He was doing his job, wasn't he? His job was here, doing what he was doing now, not playing a part in the farce going on at the Palazzo Ulderighi. He had about as much chance of making a serious inquiry there as he had of finding this girl's bicycle.

'Do you know what I mean by the frame number?'

'Yes, but I don't know it. To tell you the truth—I know I can't expect you to go looking for it but I was so blazing mad when I saw it had gone and that I'd miss my lecture that I started marching around the streets in a fury looking for it. Well, somebody's got it, haven't they? And I thought: Just let me see anybody riding past on my bike and they're for it. I even thought I might see it parked somewhere and get it back for myself, you never know. Then I remembered a friend of mine doing that when his moped was stolen, only it turned out that the one he found wasn't his, just looked like it. Needless to say the owner caught him apparently stealing it and he was arrested. He hadn't reported his own being stolen, thinking it was a waste of time, and he spent two nights in jail before it got sorted out. So, anyway, now I've told you, if you hear I've been arrested for stealing a small orange bicycle you can help to get me out of prison.' She stood up, smiling, and tucked her bag of books under her arm. 'It was kind of you to let me get it off my chest. I can't tell you how angry I was, especially because it's worth so little. I mean, aren't the poor supposed

to steal from the rich or something? Oh well, I suppose I'll
have to find myself another one second-hand.'

The Marshal stood up and saw her to the door. As she
went she laughed and said, 'You can get them quite cheaply
but of course they're probably stolen.'

'Very probably.'

As the girl crossed the waiting-room an elderly woman
got up with difficulty from her chair and approached the
Marshal with an anxious face.

'Marshal, you have to help me. I can't go on like this.
I'm frightened to go in and out of my own house. Right on
my doorstep they're doing it, injecting themselves! Why
can't you do something?'

'Come in, Signora,' the Marshal said. 'Come in and tell
me all about it.'

And so he passed the morning, patient, dogged, doing
his job. But for all he tried to give a hundred per cent of
his attention to the small problems of the people in his
Quarter, he was aware all the time of that knot of anxiety
which never loosened and which tired him more than any
amount of work could tire him. Every so often, as he listened
to a tale of woe or reduced its human content to a series of
dates, times and places on his typewriter, his large eyes
would stray to the silent telephone beside him. For most of
the morning his glance was one of apprehension as he half
expected a furious call from the public prosecutor. Later,
when it was obvious that no such call would arrive, his
expression changed. Nobody cared, it seemed, whether he
went round there or not, whether he went through the
motions of an HSA inquiry or not, provided that he turned
in a report to their liking.

When the last of his visitors had gone, he sat for a while
considering the idea of a telephone call to his commanding
officer at Borgo Ognissanti Headquarters across the river.
Captain Maestrangelo was a good man, a serious man. But

he was also an ambitious man, the sort who would one day
be a general and one of the better sorts of general. With a
sigh, the Marshal gave up the idea of turning to him for
help. Go through the motions, that was all that was
required of him, so go through the motions he would. And
if he was being made a fool of, it wasn't the first time and
wouldn't be the last. Lunch, then a rest, and the Palazzo
Ulderighi.

He ate but he couldn't rest. Making some excuse to
Teresa about having a lot to do and not being tired, he
buttoned up his jacket and left the building, slipping his
sunglasses on as he came out under the stone archway into
the dazzling brightness of the forecourt. Heat shimmered
in the air above the parked cars and the piazza smelled of
fresh pizza and coffee. The coffee attracted him, though
he shouldn't really have another. He resisted for a while,
pressing his way as best he could along the narrow pavement thronged with tourists who paused in front of every
shop and monument, consulting their maps, arguing, translating prices into marks or dollars. He wished for once that
he were one of them, that he could stare up at the shrouded
façade of the Palazzo Ulderighi like that couple were doing,
consult the guidebook and then wander on to look at at a
leather shop further on, heedless of what was behind those
great doors where he now paused, hesitating to ring the
bell. For a moment he stood there, his bulky uniformed
figure blocking the way so that the passing tourists had to
step off the pavement to get by. Then he turned away and
crossed the road to Gino's.

'Ah, it's you . . .' Gino looked surprised, given the Marshal's parting remarks the night before. 'I was afraid you
didn't enjoy your pizza last night.'

'What? No, no . . . it was very good. You couldn't give
me just a cup of coffee, could you?'

'Well, we don't usually, but seeing as it's you . . .'

He served the Marshal himself. 'You can sit down over there if you want to. We're not so full by this time.'

'No, no.' The Marshal stood where he was at the cash desk, staring out across the street.

'Something going on over there, is there? I heard her husband was dead?'

'Yes, he's dead.' Her husband, the Prince Consort. Was that how everybody thought of him? Yet he had his own business, he must have been a person in his own right, at least for those who worked for him.

'No offence meant.' The unfortunate Gino, feeling himself repulsed yet again by the Marshal's lack of response, made himself scarce.

'Doctor Martelli? I've disturbed you, I see. I'm sorry.'

'That's all right. You must be the Marshal who . . .'

'Guarnaccia. That's right. I won't keep you a moment.'

He had woken her from her siesta, that was obvious. Her face was flushed with sleep, her cheek creased, and she was still buttoning her cotton shirt with one hand as she held the door with the other. She was fortyish and still pretty, with a mop of brown curls.

'Do come in.'

Still pretty but a spinster, the Marshal thought, looking round, hat in hand, as he entered a dainty and immaculate drawing-room. Sunlight from the tall window filtered softly through a pale silk blind.

'I'll have to ask you to excuse me while I make myself a coffee or you won't get a sensible word out of me. Will you have a cup, too?'

'No. No, thank you. I just had one over the road.'

'Do sit down.'

He sat himself gingerly on the edge of a silky light green sofa, laid his hat down beside him and then took it up again and kept it on his knees. While she was in the kitchen he took the opportunity to have a good look around him. It was all very nice, he thought. Some antique stuff, some very modern, a lot of books. Too many ornaments, though . . . those enormous vases and brass stuff and fancy boxes . . . you'd knock something over if you so much as moved . . .

The Marshal sat very still, his big eyes roving. He heard her light the gas and then she looked round the door.

'Are you quite sure you won't join me?'

'No, no . . .'

She brought in a little tray with a silver sugar bowl on it and a prettily decorated coffee cup. 'I see you're fascinated by my father's collection. You're fond of chinoiserie? I must confess I'm not passionate about it myself but having inherited it I'd feel rather guilty about selling. People are always nagging me to get it all properly valued and insured, but you know the way it is with these things . . .'

'Of course.' He wasn't at all sure what she was talking about but he noticed that though her voice was still a little hoarse with sleep the flush had faded from her face and she looked paler and older than she had seemed at first.

'That's the coffee coming up. I'll be right back.'

She moved briskly, efficiently. He could imagine her going along a hospital ward, white coat flapping, though he knew she was a GP.

'Monday's such a heavy day for me.' She sat down opposite him in a large white linen chair and poured the coffee. 'A thing I never noticed when I worked in a hospital, but then every day was a panic. Being a GP is neither ambitious nor exciting but at least I get time to shop! That's better, I think I'm awake now—though I don't know how I can be much help to you. It was suicide, I imagine?'

'That or an accident.'

'Hm. Well, people do strange things, of course, and nothing's impossible but surely it all happened in the middle of the night?'

'That's one of the things I need to find out. That and whether it was suicide. The insurance, you understand . . .'

'Of course. Well, I heard a commotion but it's all a bit vague, so not much help really.

'At what time?' The Marshal slid his black notebook from the top pocket of his jacket. Go through the motions. Don't let it matter. Those were the rules of the game. 'If you can remember . . .'

'Oh yes, I think so. It was around half past two.'

'You're so sure?'

'Nothing strange about that. I'm not a very good sleeper, so I'm often forced to take a tranquillizer. I try to stick to half a tablet, though I'm often obliged to take the other half during the night. I have to be careful about that because if that happens too late in the night I feel groggy when I get up—not the sort of thing to do in a job like mine.'

'No, no . . . I understand. So you woke up and looked at the time so you could decide whether or not . . .'

'Oh no, you see it was Saturday night. If you've ever suffered from insomnia you'll know that half the problem is caused by worrying about not getting to sleep because you've got to get up and work next day.'

'I don't think I ever . . .'

'Well, think yourself lucky. Of course, different people have different ways of reacting to anxiety. Some people can't eat.'

'I don't think . . .'

'No . . .' her glance at his portly figure was involuntary and withdrawn at once, but even so she couldn't help adding, 'And others eat too much to comfort themselves.'

The Marshal was silenced.

'Anyway, where was I? Oh, Saturday night. Well, since I don't absolutely have to get up early on Sunday I try not to take anything. I do hate to think of being a slave to any drug, so Saturday night I make my bid for freedom.

Sometimes it works and sometimes it doesn't. That night
it didn't—at least, I did fall asleep reading, but then, as
often happens I woke up with a start about two hours later.
It's not just a question of waking up, you understand. More
of a leaping from the pillow like a gaffed salmon, heart
beating fit to burst.'

'Had you heard a shot?' asked the perplexed Marshal,
his pen poised hopefully.

'A shot . . . ? No, no, I'm just explaining the way I wake
up in the night when I'm anxious. When that happens I
have to give in and take the tranquillizer. Do you follow
me?'

'I think so . . . and you looked at the time so that—'

'Exactly. It was half past two, near enough. I took a
whole tablet. I was annoyed about it because even though
it was Sunday the next day I'd wanted to get up at a decent
hour because there were various things I wanted to do, but
since I wouldn't have got them done after a totally sleepless
night . . .'

'But the noise you heard?'

'I'm coming to that. That was after I'd taken the pill.'

'You didn't fall asleep at once, then?'

'Good heavens, no! It takes me half an hour or so to calm
down. I read for a bit. Then I heard the row. I think their
bedroom must be directly below mine.'

'The Ulderighi?'

'Yes. I hear all their quarrels. Heard I should say—
though mostly I heard her. Hysterical woman. He always
tried to keep his voice down and I often wondered whether
it occurred to him that I could hear it all. He was always
very civil to me.'

'And the Marchesa isn't?'

'No. I don't know if you've any idea what she charges
for these flats, but I can tell you that it's plenty. All of us
are good tenants who look after the property and pay regu-

larly and we're treated like we were squatters or something. She loathes us. She can just about force herself to say good morning if you meet her in the courtyard but her face is saying "how dare you set foot in this building". You know we're not allowed to use the lift?'

'I heard not.'

'But the rent is based on precisely that sort of thing, you know, whether there's a lift and so on. She charges us for it but we don't get keys to use it. She wouldn't let us use the main entrance if there were another, you can be sure of that! They're all alike, these people, keeping their old life-style going at the expense of the middle classes and looking down their noses at us at the same time. That's the reason, of course. They're dependent on us and that's why they hate us, whereas creatures like that poisonous little gnome and their mad old nurse are dependent on them and so get treated well.'

'You must be very unhappy living here,' observed the Marshal.

'Well, I'm looking for something else, yes.' Dr Martelli's face which had become flushed during her short diatribe paled again. Even so, her fingers which had been tapping on the polished arm of her chair continued their rhythmic movement. Her small hands were strong-looking, the nails short and neatly trimmed. For some reason he couldn't explain, the Marshal felt convinced that as a child she had bitten them. She had, of course, made it clear that she was an anxious person. As gently as he could he persisted.

'Can you tell me anything more about this commotion, this row? Can you actually hear what's said from here?'

'No, not at all. You can imagine how thick these walls and floors are. No, just that they were quarrelling—and when they stopped someone, I suppose it was him, went down in the lift. The lift's the last thing I can remember hearing, so at that point I must have fallen asleep. It's awful when you think about it, isn't it? I heard someone in the last stages of desperation going down there to shoot himself and I turned over and fell asleep.'

'But you didn't know,' the Marshal pointed out.

'I know I didn't know. It's just ironic, that's all. The way we can all live in such proximity but we might just as well be miles apart for all the help we are to each other. I didn't know him very well but what bit I did know of him I liked. His eyes were sad . . . He looked as though he had a heart, do you know what I mean? And for a man with a heart to live with a woman like that . . .'

'He married her,' the Marshal said.

'Well, people do marry people, don't they? She's a very beautiful woman, even now. Think what she must have been like twenty years ago. She's also sexy, which is something else again. Men do like her. You must have met her.'

'I . . . yes.' All he could remember feeling was fear. He could hardly admit to that.

'Then you know what I mean. Hugh fancies her, I'm convinced. Hugh Fido, the painter next door. She's commissioned a portrait from him. Of course, being a man he doesn't get treated as badly as I do, and the same probably goes for Emilio. Have you met Emilio? The pianist?'

'Yesterday.'

'And of course they're artists, which might have something to do with her accepting . . . Anyway, Catherine and I probably get the worst treatment, though even Catherine's been invited to tea once—I've just thought of something!'

'Yes?' The Marshal prepared to make a note.

'No, no, sorry, nothing to do with all that. It's amazing. I'd never have got it if it hadn't been for talking to you. Do you know what it is? Hugh is her court painter, Emilio is her court musician, and Catherine—that's Catherine Yorke who has a little studio flat on the courtyard—is a restorer and the Ulderighi woman has got her to work on the books that were damaged in the flood, books and documents, plans of the house and so on. Don't you see?'

'No . . . No, not really.'

'You must see! She can ignore the fact that they pay rent and mentally fit them into her feudal system. I'm the odd one out! There's no excuse for my presence here except that I pay her rent. I don't fit in at all.'

'I think I understand. Even so, you're a doctor so if she wanted . . .'

'Good Lord, you must be joking. I'm not a grand enough doctor to attend the Ulderighi. Still, you've got the idea. If I *were* grand enough that would solve her problem. Anyway, she wouldn't call someone like me in if her cleaner had a cold, so that's that. You should see the fleet of specialists who descend on her son every six months. Only one is Italian. Two are from London and the rest from Switzerland.'

'What's wrong with him exactly?'

'I couldn't say. I've never seen him. Certainly, I've never heard anyone mention any specific illness, so it may well be that it's just a question of nine hundred years of in-breeding.'

'You mean he might be a bit mental?'

She smiled at him, her face relaxed and pretty again once they had abandoned the personal for the medical. 'That's not a term a doctor would use.'

'I beg your pardon. I just thought . . .' He wasn't really thinking but remembering an image. A gloomy courtyard and the sound of a flute high up in a darkened tower. You couldn't call that normal. 'I mean . . . he could be strange.' That was just as bad. She was still smiling, perhaps even laughing at him.

'It's quite probable that his health is poor and that he could be, as you put it, a bit strange. As I say, I've never seen him. As far as I know, he doesn't go out. Emilio's seen him, though, because when he's feeling well enough he does appear at the Sunday afternoon music lectures—and Catherine's seen him a few times. He collects coins and medals or something of that sort and she took him some things she found among the flood-damaged stuff down there. She didn't seem to think he was all that strange. He spent all his time at his desk by the window messing with his coin collection and watching the world go by in the courtyard below. I know she felt sorry for him, but she also said he was highly intelligent. Oh . . . ! You surely don't think—'

'No, no. I don't think anything of the sort.'

She looked disappointed. It was evident that a Crazed Son Shoots Father story would vindicate her feelings about these people. The Marshal had enough trouble on his plate without starting rumours of that sort within the Palazzo Ulderighi.

'The official feeling is,' he lied rather pompously, 'that the victim died by accident while cleaning a rifle. Naturally, I have to make these inquiries so as to be sure there was no possibility of his having taken his own life.'

'Well,' said Dr Martelli, unabashed, 'I suppose you know your own business best, but even so—' she leaned back in the big white chair and pushed back a bunch of crisp brown curls—'nobody will ever convince me that it was anything other than suicide. Quite ridiculous. Going down to clean a gun at two-thirty in the morning.'

'We don't know that he did.'

'I've just told you that I heard him!'

'You heard the lift.'

'What? Ah . . . You're right. Well, as I said, you know your own business best. What time did he actually die?'

'I don't have an autopsy report yet.' He didn't add that he'd never have it. He was feeling very uncomfortable with himself. This woman was far from stupid and he didn't much care for reciting official lies to her while she observed him with lively and intelligent eyes. But it wasn't just that. It was—

'I can't make you out,' she said, interrupting his thoughts as she observed him. 'This accident story—it's exactly what a family like the Ulderighi would claim, as much to avoid a scandal as to collect the insurance, and of course if it's the official line you have to give it out in just the way you did and in just the tone you did. That far I can follow you. And yet you really seemed to mean it when you rejected my suicide theory and even more the suggestion that the son or somebody might have been responsible.' She was almost but not quite laughing at him. 'So! What in the world *do* you believe happened?'

It was fortunate that the doorbell saved him from having to reply because he didn't know the answer to that himself.

He looked at his watch as she was answering the door. He should get on. There was no point in spending more than the minimum time necessary on these visits since he wasn't meant to be finding out anything. The Martelli woman was talking rapidly to whoever had called on her. Talking rather under her breath, it seemed to him. Was she talking about him, sending someone away because of his presence? 'Come back later when he's gone and I'll tell you all. He seems to be a bit stupid and contradicts himself all the time.'

That wasn't what he was hearing. He couldn't make out a word. He was getting paranoid, that's what. This house did something to his nerves, made him uncomfortable in his skin, unsure of himself.

'It's Hugh!' Dr Martelli re-entered the drawing-room, followed by a very tall man with limp brown hair and a crumpled linen suit. 'Hugh Fido. I mentioned him before, didn't I? The painter from the flat next door.'

'Oh . . . yes. Yes.' The Marshal got up stiffly, clutching his hat.

'Please don't get up for me. Hugh Fido. Pleased to meet you. Flavia says you're coming to talk to all of us about Corsi's death. Are you coming to me now?'

'If it's inconvenient . . .'

'Not at all. Flavia, is that all right for Friday?'

'Of course. I said so. I can't believe you really need me, but I'll be there with pleasure.'

'Fine. Great. Er . . . Marshal, is it? If you've finished here I'll take you next door to the studio.'

'If you need me again, do come back.' Dr Martelli touched the Marshal's arm lightly as he left. 'It was interesting talking to you—Hugh, I must tell you afterwards about a theory we worked out about the way things function in this house. It's absolutely fascinating. I'll invite you for a drink after evening surgery and tell you all about it.'

The Marshal, following the Englishman, was amazed at his lankiness. He really was extraordinarily tall. Nor was he the very young man he had seemed at first sight. The hair that fell forward over his eyes as he fitted the key into the lock was greying at the temples. He was probably as old as the Marshal himself, but looked twenty years younger.

'Do come in. Where would you like to sit? Let me move this stuff and we'll sit on the sofa, it's the most comfortable spot.' He lifted a pile of art magazines, foreign newspapers and catalogues and, finding no uncluttered surface to place them on, dropped them on to the floor. The Marshal was staring about him in amazement. He had never seen so much colour, so much elegant clutter, so many paintings, drawings, sculptures. Mountains of discarded sketches were piled on pieces of antique furniture, one whole wall was painted with a mural of prancing naked figures in a garden vivid with huge flowers, and everywhere in the long, light room grew plants that trailed and twisted and climbed and intertwined and cascaded.

'It's a bit untidy, I'm afraid,' the painter said, watching the Marshal's face.

'Oh no . . . Well, yes, but it's very interesting . . .' His voice tailed off as his glance came round again to the mural and took it in better than the first time. Most of the figures in it were involved in or observing with glee an explicitly depicted orgy.

'It's . . .' What on earth had he intended saying? Why hadn't he kept his mouth shut? He could feel himself blushing and wished to God he'd noticed that thing better before accepting a seat on this sofa where they would have to face it for their entire conversation.

'Allegorical.'

'Eh?'

'The mural. That's perhaps the word you were looking for.'

'Ah. Yes. I expect . . .'

'Actually it's not a mural. It's detachable, since of course this is not my own flat. Still, I'm very dissatisfied with the figure of Spring. I wanted her to be spread out in a sort of limp—limp's not the right word—*abandoned*, yes. Abandoned, giving attitude on this great soft heap of flowers. But I think—possibly because of the problem of the pose and wanting to keep the pudenda fully visible—I've made her right leg look too stiff. It really should be open and relaxed, not in tension like that. I don't know if you understand what I mean.'

This was terrible. Pornography, when he came across it in the course of duty as he sometimes did, left the Marshal feeling cold and disgusted. But this was something quite different and he was feeling anything but cold. He was hot and distressed and sweat was starting to trickle down the inside of his collar.

'Would you mind showing me your passport?'

'My passport?' Fido looked puzzled. 'Well, of course, if you need to see it. I've got a five-year police permit if you—'

'No, no. Just your passport will do. A formality, that's all.'

And the minute he was out of the room the Marshal got up and looked for somewhere else to sit. It wasn't easy. There were a good many attractive-looking armchairs but they were all occupied by papers and books. In the end he removed an ashtray and a glass from a bamboo stool and sat himself gingerly on that to wait.

Fido came back with his passport, giving the Marshal an odd look as he handed it over.

'I'm afraid you can't be very, very comfortable there.'

'That's all right.' He opened the passport. 'British nationality.'

'Yes. Ahem . . . I don't want to appear fussy but I do think you'd be more comfortable on a chair.'

'A stool's fine.'

'Yes, of course, but it isn't. Isn't a stool. I mean, it's more of an occasional table, if you follow my meaning.'

The unhappy Marshal got to his feet. He wasn't going back to that sofa, though, not at any price. The effects were only just wearing off. Frames were removed. He was given a chair near a tall window.

'If you don't mind my saying so, it's a funny sort of name, yours. Not English-sounding.'

'Not as common as Smith, I agree. Actually it's a corruption of Fitzdieu.'

And he was forty-eight! Who would have thought it?

'Thank you.' He handed the passport back and got his notebook out. 'I believe you're painting a portrait of the Marchesa Ulderighi.'

'Yes. Would you like to see it?' He hurried from the room, cleary delighted to show off his work. There was something childlike about his anxious expression as he carried the canvas in and set it up on an easel for the Marshal to see.

'It's nowhere near finished, you understand, and with her being in mourning now . . .'

'It's very like her,' the Marshal felt safe in saying.

'Hm. I'm not satisfied. It's the length and curve of her neck and the soft fall of hair that interest me—you know the Winterhalter portrait of Elisabeth of Austria? The pose is taken from that because there is a resemblance, but only a physical one. Bianca has a much stronger character.'

The Marshal got up and came closer. The woman in the painting was looking back at the viewer as though inviting a glance at two heavily framed paintings hanging on the wall in the background.

'Lucrezia Della Loggia and Francesco Ulderighi,' Hugh Fido informed him. 'Painted to celebrate their betrothal but they never married and the paintings are still hanging in Bianca's drawing-room.'

'If it weren't for the clothes . . .' the Marshal said, amazed.

'They could be the same woman? Well, there's nothing so surprising about that. That's where Bianca inherited her looks from.'

'And do you work on the painting in the Marchesa's drawing-room . . . I mean, with these two other pictures behind her and so on?'

Hugh Fido laughed. 'No, no. I made sketches of the portraits, but I work on the painting here. I don't think Bianca would appreciate smears of oil paint on her furniture—and be careful yourself, incidentally.'

The Marshal looked down at his uniform but it seemed unspotted.

'You get on very well with your landlady.' The word, applied to the Marchesa Ulderighi, sounded ridiculous as

soon as he'd said it and he felt rather foolish, but persisted.
'Better than some of her other tenants.'

'Oh, you mean Flavia. Well, she gives Flavia a gigantic
inferiority complex. Bianca, you see, is that very rare
phenomenon, a real lady and a real woman.'

'That's as may be,' said the Marshal, whose inferiority
complex in the face of the Marchesa was much worse than
Dr Martelli's, 'but some of her points are valid. Doesn't it
bother you that you pay such a high rent and that you're
not allowed to use the lift, and that the porter—'

'Oh God, Flavia *has* been spitting fire. Just try to imagine,
Marshal, what it means, after nine hundred years of glory
to have to break up your house and let it as flats.'

'Why did she?'

'Money, of course. Marshal, strictly between the two of
us—and I really mean that—I rather think Corsi had
started keeping a tighter hold on the purse strings of late
on the grounds that this place should start paying for itself.
The biggest thorn in Bianca's side is the dancing school, of
course, not only because of the constant comings and goings
but because they've got the best reception rooms in the
house because of their size. They've also got the most
beautiful ceilings, as you may have noticed.'

'I haven't been in there. It's my business to talk to people
who were in the building between Saturday night and Sunday afternoon when the body was found.'

'That's right, yes. Including me, of course. Well, I was
here.'

'Did you hear any noise or disturbance?'

'A shot, I suppose you mean. But no, I'm a heavy
sleeper.'

'Sleeping pills?'

'Oh no. Just that.' Hugh Fido pointed to the whisky
bottle standing among a clutter of books and magazines on
the low table between them.

'Ah. You don't like Italian wine?'

'I love it. Wine with dinner. A glass of whisky at bedtime.
Helps one to sleep through people's shooting themselves—
I suppose that's what he did?'

'So does everyone. It may have been an accident. Have
you lived here long?'

'In this house? About a year.'

'No. I meant in Florence. In Italy.'

'Oh.' Fido relaxed in the deep armchair and crossed one
gangly leg over the other. 'From the minute I could get
away. Practically from the day I left Eton. I decided at the
age of fourteen that I wasn't having anything to do with all
those appalling English girls whose idea of conversation is
a sort of donkey-like braying interspersed with hysterical
giggles and who lose their virginity in the saddle—I can
see that none of this means anything to you, but then you've
probably never been to England.'

'No, no . . . I haven't.'

'You wouldn't like it. There's far too much sexual
ambiguity—I'm not referring to homosexuality, nothing
ambiguous about that—no . . .'

The Marshal, barely listening to all this stuff he couldn't
understand anyway, was gazing down from the tall window
into the courtyard. The porter was opening the inner gates
for someone. Nobody entered. A box was handed in, groceries it looked like. The porter went and rang the bell on
the dwarf's door and Grillo appeared to take it from him.
As far as the Marshal could tell, not a word was exchanged
so probably there was no love lost between the two of them.
Grillo looked after the young master, they said, probably
even cooked for him, all those groceries were never for one
person. Why didn't he eat with the rest of the family? The
Marshal's gaze travelled up from the base of the tower
where Grillo had his lair to the first window of Neri's rooms
at the level of the roof of the renaissance building. The

brown shutters were open and behind the glass a white face was looking back at him. The distance was such that it was impossible to swear to it, but the Marshal was convinced that the eyes in that white face were staring straight into this room. Almost as if this must prove him right, he shifted in his chair, leaning forward to make it obvious that he was looking up. The face vanished.

'You know what I mean?'

With a start, the Marshal tried to pick up Hugh Fido's incomprehensible discourse.

'It's a very particular sort of ambiguity. Plump, rather limp men with high peevish voices married to jolly, straight-legged women with masculine jaws and voices like referees. I don't know what causes it but I know I don't want any part of it. I like women who are women!'

The back of the Marshal's neck began to prickle hotly at the thought of the mural behind him. It wasn't enough to face the other way. The whole of this great room with its hot colours and over-luxurious plants was alive with sexuality.

'You're looking restless,' the painter said, smiling. 'I'm afraid I'm wasting your time, but as there's nothing useful I can tell you . . . I suppose if I'd heard the shot you could have established the time of death and so on. It's really a great pity that Catherine's away. She actually lives down there and right next door to the gun room, so that would have solved your problem for you—without, of course, resolving whether it was an accident or not. The family's hoping for a verdict of accidental death, naturally?'

'This girl Catherine, how long ago did she leave?'

'Mm. I can't tell you to the day, Thursday or Friday, perhaps. She was going to a course or convention or some such thing on restoration.'

'Well, thank you for your time. I'd better get on.'

The painter got up to show him out and the Marshal kept his eyes firmly fixed on his back as he followed.

'Thank you again.'

'It was a pleasure.' Fido held out his long thin hand. 'And don't take me too seriously about England. If you go for a holiday you'll enjoy it. You'll like the parks, there's so little green in Italian cities, and your wife will enjoy the shops.'

Well, he was a nice man, very nice really, and then he was an artist so you had to make allowances. He'd said some funny things, especially about the English—but then he was English himself and they were a bit peculiar, all of them.

The Marshal plodded on down the great cool staircase, puffing unhappily as he went as though he were climbing rather than descending. There was a distressing feeling in the pit of his stomach, a mixture of excitement and dismay. It could be that it was still the effect of Fido's painting, since the images were still strongly imprinted on his brain. Yet it couldn't be only that because there was some other feeling mixed in and it felt very much like fear. Fear of what?

The last turn on his descent brought him to the broad landing where the gigantic family shield hung. He paused and stared up at it. Orange, red, gold and green. Burning hot colours like those in the artist's studio. These had a film of age and dust on them but they were just as powerful, and the menacing effect of the shield's looming forward as though about to crush him was just as strong as it had been the day he came across it by surprise. Was that the source of his fear? The Ulderighi could certainly crush him and his family with a fleeting blow, the way you might swat a fly that irritated you. But he was doing his best not to irritate, wasn't he? Going through the motions, not finding out anything. In the absence of strong proof to the contrary a verdict of accidental death was inevitable. And why not? Why should he feel angry about it? Why be in revolt about it? Even if the poor man did shoot himself, what was the good of a scandal? What was so very awful about covering it up, if cover it up was what they were doing? There was no sense in the way he felt.

He stood there, feet planted wide apart, his hat turning and turning in his big hands, staring up at the shield, his breath still short and distressed.

'There's something not right,' he murmured to himself. 'Not right at all . . .'

A splutter of laughter exploded behind him and he turned just in time to spot two very tiny girls dash past him and round the staircase out of sight, where they let their suppressed giggles loose in a gale of merriment at the memory of the fat uniformed man talking to the wall.

4

'Marshal Guarnaccia from the carabinieri!' He raised his voice even more but the old nurse peered out from her lair with narrowed, crafty eyes.

'You can't come in.' She was almost bald and her few remaining white hairs were scraped back and skewered with a multitude of thick black hairpins. Her lower lip hung loose, dropping a thin trickle of saliva on one side.

'It's all right,' he shouted, 'I just have to talk to you. It won't take a minute.'

'This is the Palazzo Ulderighi!' she shouted up into his face. 'What are you doing in here? I don't know who you are. Be off!'

What was he supposed to do? Put his foot in the door like a salesman? He tried again.

'The Marchesa sent me. She wants me to talk to you.'

'The Marchesa lives here with me. This is the Palazzo Ulderighi. I don't know you. I don't know who you are.'

He shouted his name again, peering into the small room over her head. One entire wall was a mass of tiny red icon lights illuminating small pictures. Apart from the infirmity of her great age, she was evidently something of a religious maniac. Oh Lord . . .

'Be off! Be off!' He stepped back a pace as she raised her stick to him while supporting herself against the door jamb.

'Do you hear me? Be off or I'll call the police!'

The door slammed in his face.

The Marshal mopped his brow, replaced his hat and turned away. He didn't lose his temper. He had endless patience with the old and knew that the harridan who threatened him with her stick one day would quite likely

invite him in for a coffee the next as if nothing had happened. Even so, his distress and apprehension still lay
heavily inside him as he crossed the courtyard and made
for the gates. He was anxious to get out of the building
which so oppressed him. The gloom and the interminable
piano music—and surely today it was coming from somewhere new? He paused as he passed the foot of the
staircase. It was coming from up there and a loud
woman's voice was calling out instructions over it. The
dancing school, that would be. That must have been
where those two little girls were going, running up the
stairs late for their lesson.

As he went on to the gate another bunch of girls came in
at the great doors. Older girls, long-legged, wearing baggy
T-shirts and carrying large bags slung over their shoulders.
The Marshal opened the gate and stood back to let them
in. They all seemed to have very long hair. All of them were
chattering loudly and he remembered the Englishman's
remarks, imagining the Marchesa's icy face if she should
encounter them. He went through the gate, hearing their
voices echoing loudly on the staircase, then fading as they
turned the first corner. As he reached the great doors he
found that the girls had left them ajar, surely another bone
of contention with the Marchesa. As he reached for the
handle the door began to open of itself. Expecting another
group of girls, he stood back, but it was a young man who
entered, wished him a pleasant good-evening and stepped
smartly through the gates using a key. The Marshal stared
after him. He had met all the tenants and that, if he was
any judge, was never the Ulderighi son and certainly not
the porter's son, either. He looked too . . .

'What the devil!'

The young man, whoever he was, had let himself into
Catherine Yorke's supposedly empty studio with a key.

'Blast!' The gate slammed closed a second before he got

to it. Why was he so slow? He was forced to ring for the porter to readmit him. The porter looked none too pleased and not a little surprised.

'I thought you'd already—'

'Open up.'

Once inside he drew close to the porter and glowered at him. 'You told me the English girl's flat was empty, the studio there.'

'It is empty.'

'I've just seen someone go in with a key. Who was it?'

'I didn't see anyone.'

The Marshal turned away from him with an impatient grunt and crossed the courtyard. Whoever was in there wasn't alone. He was talking to someone, his voice raised in anger. As he reached the door the voice dropped suddenly. He paused on the step.

'Yet she must die . . . No . . . Yet she must *die* . . .' An inaudible mumble and then: 'Put out the light!'

The Marshal rang the bell.

The door opened and he was confronted by the young man who had passed him at the gate. He held a glass in one hand and a book in the other and was staring at the Marshal with a look of faintly surprised inquiry.

'Could I have a word with you?' the Marshal said, frowning.

'Of course. Nothing wrong, is there?' When the Marshal didn't answer, he added, 'You'd better come in.'

The Marshal stepped inside without a word. The room was as small as the gun room next door and was just able to contain a single bed, bookshelves, a worktable, a shower alcove and one armchair.

'Have the chair,' offered the young man.

'No . . . No, thanks. I understood from the porter that this room is rented by a young lady, English. Catherine . . .' He felt for his notebook.

'Yorke,' said the young man. 'Catherine Yorke. I'm her brother, William.'

'Ah . . .'

The other was evidently waiting for some sort of explanation. When it wasn't forthcoming he pointed out: 'If you saw me coming in, then you saw me use the key. You couldn't have thought I was breaking in. Besides—excuse me for asking—why are you here at all? I mean, has something happened? I've just arrived from Venice, so . . .'

'Yes, I see. Well, I beg your pardon. Nothing for you to worry about. There's been a . . . an accident. Buongianni Corsi died in the room next to this between Saturday and Sunday. He may have been cleaning the rifle that killed him. At any rate it's my duty to establish whether his death was accidental and so I've been making a few inquiries of the tenants. I was given to understand that this studio was empty . . .'

'I see. That's a turn-up. A nice man, too, I thought, and I know Catherine liked him a lot.'

'She knew him well?'

'Fairly well, I should think. She was doing some work for the family. Various documents and stuff that were damaged in the flood—Good Lord! You mean when you saw me come in here you registered me as a suspicious character?'

'No, no, I—' Then he remembered the raised, angry voice he'd heard. 'You were talking to somebody when I rang the bell.'

'Talking? But there's nobody . . . Oh! Oh, do sit down—I'm sorry, I can see you're a carabinieri but the ranks are beyond me . . . ?'

'Marshal Guarnaccia. It's quite all right, I—'

'No, please! Please sit down, Marshal. You have to give me time to undo this terrible impression I've made, walking into a flat not my own and starting an argument with the empty air—threatening murder, like as not, wasn't I?'

'I don't know if—'

'Oh yes I was! Listen!' He put his wineglass on the work-table and raised his free hand to declaim:

> *'Yet I'll not shed her blood,*
> *Nor scar that whiter skin of hers than snow*
> *And smooth as monumental alabaster—*
> *Yet she must die, else she'll betray more men.*
> *Put out the light, and then put out the light.'*

The Marshal, seated now in the only armchair, stared with bulging eyes at the young man who now dropped his arm and laughed.

'*Othello!* You must know *Othello!*'

'Ah. Verdi's opera . . .'

'Well, as you like. There's an English version, you know. Anyway, we're giving a performance here next week. I belong to an English theatre company in Venice. Mostly we do things designed to help Italian students studying English literature at the Liceo and the university, so we choose the plays we know they have to study. So! I was rehearsing, that's all.'

'And you have your sister's keys?'

'Ah! Not to be deflected from your original point, eh? Yes, I have my sister's keys. I always have my sister's keys and when we play in Florence I sleep here.' He caught the Marshal's glance at the one narrow bed. 'Underneath there's another that slides out.' He waved his glass. 'Can I offer you something to drink? This is only water but there'll be wine somewhere.'

'No, thank you. You didn't bring any luggage?'

The young man laughed. Though his face was pock-marked and his figure slight, his deep grey sparkling eyes and his readiness to break into laughter made him attractive. 'You don't miss anything, do you?'

'You did say you'd just arrived . . .' The Marshal felt a little embarrassed. He liked the look of the youngster and didn't suspect him of anything at all. It was just a question of a lifetime habit of noticing. Still, the boy wasn't at all offended.

'I've arrived,' he said, 'but my luggage, such as it is, hasn't. I came by train from Venice as I always do. Some members of the troupe drive down in the van with all our luggage, props and costumes. I'll be going to the theatre in an hour or so to collect my stuff. I keep a clean shirt and the odd pair of socks here anyway. I like to come and see Catherine for a day or two when I can, even when I'm not here for work.'

'You're very close?'

'I suppose we are, in a way. We're orphans and have no family except each other. I suppose that does make a difference. She lived in Venice with me for a time but I think she found it too decadent. Now I love decadence—theatrical decadence such as you only find in Venice. Catherine's better off here really, given her job. What happened to Corsi exactly? Or aren't you allowed to say?'

'We don't know a great deal as yet.' Was he being over-cautious? It was only by talking more openly that he would encourage people to talk openly to him. That was the way it always worked. That was the way to find out things. Again he had to remind himself that this time nobody wanted to find out anything—or if he did no one would want to be told about it. But mightn't he feel better, relieve himself of the feeling of stress and fear that persisted inside him? He might. But in that case he'd better keep what he found out to himself or he'd really have something to be frightened about.

As these thoughts wandered through his mind, his eyes drifted over the shelving above the worktable which held labelled jars, brushes and sponges, like a painter's studio except there were no colours. William Yorke followed his gaze and tried to interpret his silence.

'I understand. You can't say anything. Still, a rifle . . . everybody in the place must have heard.'

'No!' said the Marshal abruptly. 'Nobody.'

'Well, of course, it's none of my business. I'm just interested in the family—decadence again, you see. You can follow the whole history of Florence through the history of this house.'

The Marshal didn't like to say that the house gave him the creeps, so he said nothing.

'From a purely personal point of view the place gives me the creeps,' continued William. The Marshal's heart warmed to him. 'Give me the faded colour and elegance of Venice any time. These Florentine palaces are fortresses, built to keep people out, not to receive them, don't you find?'

'I hadn't thought of it but I don't like this place.'

'Exactly! Of course you don't. You were never meant to. It was built to keep you out, like the whole of this city. Whoever heard of a city where all the great houses turn their backs on the street and have their gardens and façades on the inside? Do you realize what that implies about the character of the Florentines? You're not a Florentine yourself, I can tell from your accent. Sicilian?'

'That's right.'

'Then I wouldn't like to be in your shoes. I suppose La Ulderighi won't receive you?'

'I've seen her once but—'

'You must have seen her by accident—and I suppose, whatever did happen to Corsi, she'll want an accident verdict. She needs the money.'

'You seem to know a lot about her . . .'

'I do rather. Catherine tells me things, of course, and then, when I'm here, La Ulderighi invites me to tea.'

'She invites you?'

'Certainly. You look surprised.'

'Well, I . . . I understood—particularly from Dr Martelli—that the Marchesa took a rather snobbish attitude to her tenants. Of course, you're not a tenant.'

William's dark grey eyes twinkled with merriment. 'No, no. You're not there. Dr Martelli—she's a nice woman—comes from Milan, in case you hadn't noticed. You come from Sicily, which is worse, altogether unforgivable, but I come from England, which makes me an honorary Florentine with no other credentials required. Now do you understand?'

'I've been here over fifteen years—' the Marshal rubbed his face glumly with a huge hand—'and I decided long ago I'd never understand the Florentines. You must have been in Italy a good while yourself?'

'Donkey's years. My mother came over after the flood doing volunteer restoration work—nothing fancy like Catherine does, just shifting mud and that sort of thing. Then she and my father bought a part share in a country cottage in Chianti, so we all used to come over for the holidays. We were still at school when my parents were killed in a road accident. We'd have liked to keep the Chianti cottage on but we weren't old enough to decide for ourselves . . . Anyway we both drifted back here, as you see. After death duties and our school fees and so on we were left without a bean. When I think what that cottage would have been worth today . . . Well, that's us. The proud poor. Still, we are both doing what we like to do and that's important.'

'Oh yes,' agreed the Marshal, who thought it all very precarious, imagining his own little boys adrift in a foreign country with no family and no money.

'You said', did you,' he went on, picking up on an earlier remark, 'that the Marchesa was in need of money. Why was that?'

'She'll want to collect on the insurance, won't she? I
mean, surely it has to have been an accident. If it
wasn't . . .'

'You have reason to think he might have wanted to kill
himself?'

'Mm. Lots of people have good reason to kill themselves
but they don't, do they? I mean, think of people dragging
round with incurable diseases, no money, no friends, no
family. There are people like that and they struggle on. You
have to be the suicidal type and I wouldn't have thought
it of him particularly. Not that you can always tell. You
ought to talk to Catherine when she gets back. She may
know things I don't know. They won't thank you round
here for suggesting suicide, though, will they?'

'No,' the Marshal said glumly. 'No, they won't.'

The Marshal liked William Yorke. He was intelligent,
sympathetic. He wished . . . Well, it was no use wishing.
But as though reading his thoughts, William made a tentative suggestion.

'Perhaps . . . If you think it might be any use to you, I
could listen around, chat to people while I'm here. I'm
afraid there'll be no invitations to tea if she's in mourning,
but I'm on good gossiping terms with everybody in here,
just about.'

'Well . . .'

'If I'm talking out of turn just say so.'

'No . . . No. I was wondering, do you ever talk to the old
nurse?'

'The tata? Always. I always go in and take her a few
sweets. She reminds me of the witches in the Scottish play
except that she tends to tell you about the past rather than
the future. She's pretty batty though, you know.'

'But you like going in to see her?'

'I've already told you about my taste for the decadent
and the theatrical! She's both in a big way.'

'I ought to talk to her myself . . .'

'But she waved her stick at you and warned you off the Ulderighi territory.'

'That's about the size of it.'

They smiled at each other like good friends.

'She's done that to me before now,' William admitted. 'There are days when she doesn't recognize me. I go back five minutes later and she welcomes me with open arms. Half the time she thinks I was one of her Ulderighi babies.'

'But why . . . I mean, why do you . . . ?'

'Why do I bother? I collect eccentrics. One day I'm going to write a play of my own. In the meantime I keep a notebook—no doubt you keep one yourself?'

'I—yes, but for information—'

'So is mine for information.' He whipped out a notebook very like the Marshal's own. 'Listen to this: *Two large and wealthy ladies are floating down the Grand Canal and one says to the other as she stares at the crumbling grandeur drifting by, "I thought these places were supposed to be beautiful." And the other one says, "They* are.*" Then she looks at them for a bit and adds uncertainly, "On the inside . . ."*'

'I don't—'

'Wait—wait! A Florentine one: *Tourist couple standing looking at the Baptistry. Wife reads from guidebook: "Probably built between 1059 and 1150. Nine hundred years that's been standing right there!" And her husband says, "Well, it'd probably cost too much to pull it down."* You see? I collect treasure everywhere and one day I'll write a comedy. While collecting for me I can be collecting for you. I often think I could have been a policeman. What do you think?'

'I'm sure you'd be a great detective with your brains.'

'Another Sherlock Holmes? Is that how you think of your job?'

'My job? Good Lord, no. My job's just routine stuff. We don't often get anything more exciting than handbag-snatching at my little station, and just as well since I haven't your brains.'

'But you notice things.'

'What?'

'You notice things. My lack of luggage, the invisible spare bed, that sort of thing.'

Once again that lurch of anxiety. He'd pushed it to the back of his mind, but he had noticed—how could he not have noticed?—a dark patch on the side of Corsi's face and him lying on his back and nobody had touched him, they said.

'I hope I haven't offended you? You did notice those things. It's to your credit, after all, isn't it?'

'I'd better go.' He'd hardly heard what the lad said. 'I really must . . . I'll come back, though—when will I be able to talk to your sister?'

'Sunday. She'll be back Sunday afternoon—I'm hoping she'll be in time to come to the theatre. Sunday's our last night. I'll tell her you were here—and, as I said—I'll be chatting to people. You never know, I might just hear something useful.'

As he opened the door, the Marshal saw between the columns a short black figure approach the lift and stand waiting. The lift door opened at once and the man stepped inside. When he turned the Marshal saw his dog-collar and also that he was carrying a small black case. The lift doors closed on him but the Marshal had got a glimpse of the person who had brought the lift down for him. It was the Marchesa Ulderighi. Her face was very white. She appeared not to have noticed the Marshal.

Under the brilliant June sunshine the cathedral square was swarming with people. It always was, of course, and the traffic swirling round it made matters worse. But now there was this demonstration as well, so that the cars and buses were blocked and exuding useless exhaust fumes into the shimmering air. As usually happened in these cases, the Marshal had 'lent' two of his men but where the use of it was he couldn't see. They had called in a half-hour ago saying that although there was no danger it was quite impossible to get the traffic through and that it looked as if there was little to be done until the demonstration broke up. The Marshal himself, on his way to the Palazzo Ulderighi, had missed lunch to stop and check on his boys and for the moment at least he was thoroughly stuck. He had got into a sort of backwater between the cathedral and the bell tower and was trying to dry his streaming eyes, but even there he was getting crushed. He had been glad enough to delay another attack on the Ulderighi house because of the claustrophobia that overwhelmed him there, but the crush of people, the burning heat and the stench of exhaust fumes had pretty much the same effect here.

He had managed to get over to the other side of the square to where his boys were but hadn't succeeded in getting back as yet. He finished drying his eyes and now mopped his brow. His hat felt too tight. A voice was exhorting the crowd through a megaphone and leaflets were being passed over people's heads, many of them taken and then dropped on the ground by tourists who couldn't read them. The Marshal caught one as it fell and folded it up and put it in his pocket without looking at it. He couldn't read properly with his sunglasses on and he had no intention of taking them off. Besides, he had already signed the double petition, a copy of which had come to his office.

'The administrative factions in the Palazzo Vecchio are struggling for power, for political power. But political power is not what the administration of Florence is about. The administration of Florence is the administration of an inheritance. A priceless inheritance which belongs not only to Florentines but to the whole of the civilized world . . .'

A gang of youngsters roared by on mopeds, drowning the voice for a moment.

'They'll surely never get away with it,' commented one of the bystanders squashed up against the Marshal.

'That other lot got away with it near the Ponte Vecchio.'

'Yes, but not *on* the Ponte Vecchio, for God's sake . . .'

Perhaps they would get away with it, but the Marshal hoped not. A hamburger joint practically within the precincts of the cathedral was going too far and he'd been more than willing to object to it along with the traffic business, though where the cars would go if they didn't flow round the cathedral neither he nor anyone else could say. He tried to remember when he last went inside the cathedral. Had he taken Teresa and the boys when they first moved up from Sicily? He wasn't all that sure. They'd gone up to the top of the bell tower, he remembered that. The boys had insisted. And they'd looked at the doors of paradise, one panel of which had been missing, being restored after the ravages of exhaust fumes. It was a bad business.

And now hamburgers. Exhaust fumes mixed with the greasy fumes of fried meat and onions. There'd always been a little trattoria in that sheltered corner. He'd never eaten there but remembered three or four tables with snowy cloths set out under the green shade of a vine. Presumably their lease had run out and they couldn't compete with the world-famous hamburger chain. Still, they were fighting back. You had to hand it to the Florentines, they didn't take that sort of thing lying down. Reluctant though he was to move out of the shade, he had to do it. He shouldn't hang about here. He must really be on his way. There were enough police there, as well as carabinieri, to sort this mess out. Besides, his boys were quite right, there was no danger and it would soon be over.

As he began to push his way forward a delicious smell floated to his nostrils, sharp, aromatic, cutting through the smell of car fumes. A pity, he thought, that he was in uniform, otherwise . . . The enticing smells got stronger as he made his way through the crowd. He couldn't see the long table from which the demonstrators were being served but he knew what was on it. He could smell the hot toast with garlic, oil and salt, the crisp, wafer-thin pizza with rosemary scattered on it—and surely that was Tuscan sausage? Well, there was nothing to be done, so it would do him no good to think about it. Some good at least came from the fact that the crowd was shifting in the direction of the food, which meant he could get along better. And get along he did until a voice shouted, 'Marshal!'

He paused. Of course, whoever it was need not be calling him. The square was full of uniformed men.

'Marshal!' He recognized the voice though, he thought.

'Over here!' Foreign. That was it. Yorke, the English boy. An umbrella was being waved furiously above the heads of the crowd. The Marshal stood still and waited, letting the people flow round his great black bulk as though he were a rock in a choppy sea. The umbrella disappeared, reappeared, then its owner came into view. 'Ah!' The umbrella was lowered. In his other hand he cradled a miniature pizza, still sizzling on a small paper napkin, as carefully as though it were a baby bird. A swift mouthful disposed of it.

'Excuse me.' He waggled his umbrella in the direction of the source. 'But it's in a good cause.' And to the Marshal's mild astonishment he folded the little paper napkin as though it were of silk and slid it into the top pocket of his blue linen jacket, adjusting the protruding folds with a little flourish.

'Never drop litter,' he said. 'I saw you from a distance,' he went on. 'Well, you're very visible for one reason and another. You, of course, didn't see me.'

'No, no, I . . .'

'An umbrella is a useful object. Look!' He pointed to where a tour guide held a large red umbrella aloft and strode off with a crocodile of weary-looking people straggling after him, their arms burnt to the colour of the umbrella. 'Very useful—really I've always regretted not joining the Guards. Too small, you see, though nicely made. There are things I want to tell you. Which way are you going?'

'Me? I—to the Palazzo Ulderighi . . .' He almost added, 'Unfortunately.' He felt at ease with this young man, strange though he was with his quick way of talking and the odd things he said that you couldn't at all follow. And though he was so young he had a way about him that was old, a sort of mock-gravity which, combined with the umbrella, made the Marshal think of Charlie Chaplin.

'In that case,' William Yorke said, looking about him solemnly, 'we shall leave this merry scene and hope that all this effort, including my heroic champing of all that good food, will prevent the barbarians from opening their hamburger joint in the precincts of the cathedral. We'd better not talk Ulderighi talk here. Follow me!' He raised his umbrella, pressed the spring and snapped it open. The Marshal, the ghost of a smile flitting across his face behind the dark glasses, followed him.

For the Marshal, it was a relief not to have to ring the bell and affront the sullen face of the porter who always made him feel like an unwelcome guest rather than an official caller. William let them in with his keys. In the courtyard the piano music filtering down from the dancing school was almost entirely drowned by that of Emilio who

was practising something very loud and, the Marshal
thought, modern.

'I like a nice tune, myself,' William said as he opened up
the studio. But he said it in such an odd voice, despite a
serious face, that the Marshal, who had been on the point
of agreeing with him, hesitated and said nothing.

'Tea!' William announced, parking his umbrella and
whipping off his jacket. 'That's the first thing. Why don't
you take off your jacket, too?'

'Shouldn't do that on duty.' He would have liked to,
though.

'Well, sit down, at least.' William put an electric kettle
on to boil in a corner of the worktable. 'My throat's so
dry from rehearsing and in a few hours it will be time
for the matinée—you do drink tea, don't you? I know
Florentines do but you're not from here. Sicily, you said,
didn't you? I guessed from your accent if I remember
rightly.'

'That's very clever of you. I mean . . .'

'You mean considering I'm a foreigner. But speech,
accents, that's my business as an actor. What's your
decision about the tea?' He held the spoon poised over the
teapot, waiting for an answer. The Marshal, more kindly
than truthfully, said he would be glad of it.

'Very wise. I see there's only instant coffee, anyway, and
you wouldn't like that. We don't have fancy teacups, only
mugs. Very English. It's good tea, though, not teabags. I
fired a shot last night.'

'You . . . you *fired* a—' The Marshal's already protruding
eyes almost popped out of his head. He gaped around the
studio as if in search of the offending weapon.

William laughed at him. 'Only in a manner of speaking.
Don't worry, it wasn't a gun but a firework. A very small
banger. But if you'd heard the racket it made! Well, I was
in here, of course, but it made enough noise echoing round

out there in the courtyard to waken everybody up and bring them to their windows shouting "What the hell".'

'And what sort of explanation did you give?'

'Me? I was What the helling with the best of them. Now then, I woke: the porter, the porter's wife, Grillo, but not the tata who's genuinely as deaf as a post. I woke Hugh Fido but not La Martelli, Emilio Emiliani, and all the Ulderighi gang except Auntie.'

'Aunty?'

'Fiorenza Ulderighi, Bianca Ulderighi's auntie.'

'What time did all this happen?'

'In the middle of the night—or the early hours of the morning, I should say. About two. We eat after the performance and so I get in very late. It seemed like a good idea to me at the time but I thought I should tell you at once for two reasons; firstly, somebody will tell you—at least, I imagine so—so you'd have been What the helling yourself, which would have been a waste of your time. Secondly, I'm afraid I've set more off than just a firework.'

For once the boy looked deadly serious. The Marshal waited, observing him. It was a moment before the continued and then he was hesitant, which, from what little the Marshal had seen of him, seemed unlike him.

'I said I woke all the Ulderighi except the aunt. Well, among them was Neri. Of course when I put my head out pretending to wonder what the noise was I had a good look about. Naturally, most people switched their lights on. Neri didn't. I went out and looked up at the tower and no light came on. Even so, I know I woke him.'

'How can you be sure?'

'Oh, I'm sure all right. There was no light but I heard him. He was screaming. Really screaming. Up there in the dark. I frightened the life out of him.'

The Marshal, stunned, sat immobile for a while without speaking.

'I'm sorry,' William said, handing him a mug of tea, 'it seemed a good idea at the time—well, to tell you the truth we had a fair bit of wine with our supper—oh, don't worry, I didn't mention it to the rest of the cast.'

When the Marshal still didn't speak he went on, 'Well, you know how it is? What seems a good idea after a glass or two, in the light of day—'

'You didn't—' the Marshal interrupted, and stopped. He liked the boy but liking people never prevented him from seeing things as they were. Many a time he'd wished that wasn't the case but there was nothing much he could do about it, so . . .

'You didn't buy your firework in the middle of the night after your few glasses of wine. You must have bought it when the shops were open.'

William smiled, his face a little red.

'Yes, of course. You're right. I should have remembered how you notice things and not have tried to get that one past you. The truth is that it seemed like an amusing trick to pull on them all after you'd told me nobody had heard anything. So, yes, I did buy the banger after you'd gone yesterday, on my way to the theatre. Then, after seeing what I'd done—or rather hearing what I'd done to Neri— I confess I was rather ashamed. It was childish of me and out of place and I like to think that, even though I had bought the thing earlier, I wouldn't have let it off if I hadn't had a bit to drink. Anyway, I'm sorry.'

'Well,' the Marshal said, relieved by the boy's frankness, 'I doubt if there's any harm done.'

'I'm not so sure.' The boy took a gulp of tea and frowned. 'This morning when I was leaving for rehearsals I saw two men arrive. They were doctors, I'm sure of it. Both of them were speaking English, though one was certainly Italian. So you see there may be quite a lot of harm done.'

The Marshal observed him. Only now did he really

notice that when the boy's face wasn't lit with mischievous laughter, it was a sad and thin face. One moment you saw the dapper, fast-talking comic, the next a schoolboy orphan adrift in the world. More than that, his remorse was genuine. If he had done harm, he cared. It was more in the hope of its being comforting than of its being true that he said, 'You can't consider yourself responsible in any real way. They say the Ulderighi boy is weak and nervous, not a normal person at all.'

'He'd just lost his father. He may or may not have heard the shot. I of all people ought to have known better.'

'They weren't close, from what I've heard,' the Marshal pointed out. He was dismayed to see the dark grey eyes glittering as though with tears and felt the sadness communicate to himself. 'You can't always judge people's reactions by your own.'

'No.' This seemed to do the trick and the Marshal was relieved to see the glitter fade from his eyes. 'No, of course. I was very close to my father. He was a teacher, you know, but his great passion was the theatre. He taught me so much, even when I was very small—what he would have given to leave his boring job and do what I'm doing now . . . The same is true of Catherine in a way. Our parents left us without a bean, as I think I told you, but we inherited their dreams. That's not nothing, is it?'

'No, no . . .' agreed the Marshal, but he rather thought that a roof over their heads and a bit of money in the bank wouldn't have done any harm. His own wife would have an army pension, of course . . . But what if something should happen to both of them, as it had to this boy's parents? How would the boys be fixed exactly? He ought to look into it. These things want thinking about . . . for instance, surely it was better never to travel together without the children? Of course, once you start thinking on those lines you can't live your life at all . . .

'You must be thinking what a childish idiot I am,' William Yorke broke in, 'judging by your face.'

'No, no . . . I wasn't thinking anything, except . . .'

With a sigh, he put down the mug of tea he had hardly tasted. He was here to pretend to do a job so he'd better get on with pretending to do it.

'I wonder . . . the old nurse—'

'Of course! I'll take you to see her, shall I? She's bound to let you in with me if she's letting anybody in at all. There's never any telling how *compos mentis* she'll be, but let's try.'

He was glad to have something useful to do, to make up for having done something stupid, the Marshal could see that. But what about his own motives for involving the boy? Lorenzini could have been with him, *should* have been with him if any second person were really necessary, which he doubted. But since that first evening he hadn't said a word to Lorenzini about this business and he was wondering now if that was to avoid having the young NCO present when he was being used, made a fool of, or whether he was afraid . . .

Afraid of what? As the two of them came out of the studio under the music-filled gloom of the colonnade he knew that he was afraid all right. It wasn't something he could explain because there was no explanation for it. He was afraid of this house.

5

'And there was blood, *blood* . . . all over the place. She never saw it. She never saw it, but her face . . .' The old tata's finger, shiny and crippled with rheumatism, stroked the pale cheek in the picture. 'She was beautiful. There was never anyone like her as a girl. Look at her. They say she was responsible for what happened, but people will say anything. Besides, what else could she do?' She flashed a look at the Marshal which seemed to him to be both lucid and vicious. In his experience you could never be sure with the very aged and the mentally infirm how much they hid behind their weakness, looking out at you. The woman was rambling, that much was certain, and young William was egging her on. It was obvious that he'd already heard this story, perhaps more than once. If only there were a window in the room. There was barely room for their three chairs because of the size of the double bed. The Marshal tried to close his nostrils against the faint, sickly smell of very old age. His hat was on his knees and his dark glasses in his hand. The only light came from the hundreds of icon lamps with their dim red glow.

'They caught the men who did it, though, didn't they?' William shouted close to her ear.

'Caught them. They caught them, all four of them. As for the girl, it was no more than she deserved, an adulteress and a nobody. But *he* was the villain of the piece and he got his come-uppance and no mistake.'

'And he stank! Tell us, Tata, how he stank!'

'Stank? When he walked through the streets he'd leave a stench behind him that didn't clear for days. He never changed his clothes from one year's end to the next. He was no better than a pig. He was never anything to look at, of course, even as a lad, not like Francesco. Now if she'd married Francesco as she should have done by rights— He was a victim if ever there was one, and oh, he was a good-looking lad. Bonny, he was. And they dressed him all in white with a garland of flowers, a garland of spring flowers . . . I can see him now. His head was crushed in at one side—'

The old woman's voice stopped quite suddenly and she looked at William with narrowed eyes.

'Have you brought me something?'

'Sweets, like you asked for,' William said.

'And are they soft? I've no teeth.'

'They're what you asked for. They're soft. Here.'

She snatched them from him but didn't eat any. Instead she reached out from her armchair to a bedside cupboard with a small square of marble on top. On the marble was a cream lace cover with a bottle of medicine, a glass and a black rosary on it. Her crippled hand struggled with the drawer. The Marshal half rose from his chair to help her but she waved him away, irritated. 'He'll do it.'

William tucked the sweets into the drawer.

'Now what was I telling you? Well, Francesco died, of course, and they say as it wasn't an accident though it was given out that his horse was to blame, and she married his brother. They made her have him, you know. She cried all the night before. Ugly! An ugly man and a soul as ugly as his face. Of course, once she'd had a child he left her alone, you have to give him that, but I never had any time for that branch of the family myself—you know he was cousin to that fellow . . . Wait a minute and I'll tell you his name. The miser, you know who I'm talking about, now what *was* his name—and don't you look at me like that, you young bugger, I'm not too old to know what I'm talking about.'

'Tell us about the murder,' shouted William. 'Tell us where the men came from.'

'Campi.' Her face darkened as though she'd named the Inferno rather than a Florentine suburb. 'They were tanners, you see, great brutes. They got in by the small door, that's how it was done. They got in the day before while *he* was away and not a soul saw them.'

'But somebody sent for them, Tata! Come on, admit it! They were sent for!' William was grinning as he provoked her.

'A wife has her rights. A chit of a girl like that Ginetta and a servant at that, flaunting herself. Flaunting jewellery as he'd given her—well, it was the last time she'd go up that staircase alive. She hadn't a stitch on when the four of them broke in. *That* came out in court. Not a stitch . . .'

She lowered her voice and for some reason, perhaps enjoying a new audience, she addressed herself now to the Marshal.

'It took two of them to hold him down . . .'

The Marshal instinctively drew his face back a little from hers, not sure he wanted to hear what she was going to tell him, but the rheumatic fingers clutched the sleeve of his uniform jacket.

'There wasn't a mark on him but it took two of them to hold him while they did what they did to *her*. They took her body away with them and pitched it in the Arno, but it came up at the bridge . . . two bridges down from this one, what's it called—'

'Ponte alla Carraia!' prompted William in her ear. 'But the head, Tata! What about the head?'

She still had hold of the Marshal's sleeve. A fine string of saliva hung from the left side of her mouth.

'They hung that on his bedpost, hung it there on one of the wooden spikes, the eyes staring out of it, staring at *him* and him staring back. And that's how they found him in the morning. And there was blood, *blood* all over the place. It had soaked right through the bedclothes and through two mattresses and through the wooden base of the bed, and *he* was covered in it but he hadn't moved an inch. Where they'd left him, there he was found, staring at that head with its bloody hanks of hair.' Her grip tightened on the Marshal's arm. 'And he never spoke another word as long as he lived. Now then!'

The Marshal, who felt as though he had been holding his breath for the last half-hour, let it out now with a sigh and shifted his bulk on the hard chair, but she was still holding on to him so that he was prevented from getting up.

'There's nothing goes on round here,' she said, 'that I don't know about. Nothing.'

If only that were true! The Marshal had tried more than once to ask her about the night Corsi died but each time she had raised a crippled hand and stopped him.

'Wait a bit. I'm telling you something . . .'

And she would be off on another of her rambling tales of vicious murder. There was a copy of the local paper tucked behind her in the armchair and the Marshal had no doubt that she collected her gruesome tales from that. More interesting, perhaps, than reading the obituaries to see how many of her friends she had survived. In fact, by this time she had probably outlived them all. Still, it was disconcerting, hearing all those gory details from such a frail and white-haired creature. And the way she told them, you'd think she'd been there at the time. That one about the body in the cellar was enough to give you nightmares, but that sounded more like she'd got it from a book than from a newspaper because that quote about 'Here is an end of all my troubles' and so on sounded a bit old-fashioned. They didn't put stuff like that on tombstones these days. Well, wherever she got it from, it wasn't here that the Marshal would find an end to all *his* troubles, that was certain. The only good thing was that the visit had been paid, his duty done. He had seen everyone he had to see and had collected no evidence for suicide except the story of a late night quarrel. And if every late night quarrel were to be supposed to lead to suicide . . . He must somehow detach the old woman's hand from his arm. Inspired, he asked, 'Will you let me look at your icons before we go? You have so many.' Not that she heard a word he said. William had to repeat the request, bellowing in her ear, before they were allowed to stand up. One wall was entirely covered with red plastic icon lamps.

'But . . .' The Marshal thought better of it and shut his mouth.

'Mm. I thought you'd be surprised. Shall we go?'

Leaving wasn't easy. The old tata clung to William and in the end he had to promise to return the next day.

Out in the courtyard he admitted, 'It's a rotten trick, but you see she doesn't really distinguish the days and if I call in for a minute on Saturday or Sunday it will be just the same. The surprising thing is that she doesn't forget who I am altogether when she doesn't see me more than about twice a year.'

'The surprising thing,' the Marshal contradicted him with considerable vehemence, 'is that those pictures—'

'Ah yes. I thought you'd like those. Did you understand who they all were?'

'I recognized the Marchesa . . .'

'Ah, the photograph. Well, all the photographs on that part of the wall were of her. At various ages. Her wedding picture too, did you see? Not saints, as you thought, but Ulderighi. The photographs go back as far as photographs can go back and then the rest are prints of oil paintings and so on. When she really gets going she's convinced that she's nursed every man Jack of them for the last nine hundred years. Once, on one of her more lucid days, she did tell me that her own mother was wet-nurse to an Ulderighi—I forget for the minute which—so that she grew up in this house herself and was working as a nursery maid by the age of eight. She's ninety-one and has never known anything outside the walls of this place, but she certainly knows about everything inside. It's a great pity that she's so gaga, because she's a mine of information if only you can get at it. She's been a help to Catherine once or twice because, you see, she knew just how many boxes and trunks of papers and books there should have been in the cellar and what was in most of them better than La Ulderighi or anyone else. After the flood damage, I mean.'

They had paused by the well, deep in conversation, not noticing that under the shadow of the colonnade Grillo the dwarf was watching them.

'But surely,' the Marshal said, 'that was twenty-odd years ago?'

'It was, but Catherine's still finding stuff and she reckons it will take years of work yet to restore all the papers. Nobody's a hundred per cent sure how much stuff was lost and those cellars are a labyrinth. You wouldn't believe it.'

'I wouldn't have believed that business of the family icons, either, if it comes to not believing things, not to mention the bloodthirsty tales, but I gather she gets her stories from the papers.'

'Those and books, and hearsay, of course.'

'I thought as much when I saw the *Nazione*.'

'The *Nazione*?'

'I saw it sticking out from under the cushion of her chair.'

William's eyes were bright with merriment. 'All she reads in that rag are the births, deaths and marriages! Listen, you don't have to go yet, do you? Can you spare a quarter of an hour? Let me fascinate you! You've got a lot to learn about this place. Come on.'

The Marshal knew he ought to get back to his office, write that wretched HSA report and get this business off his hands. Had he only known it, this was his last chance of doing just that. He hesitated. He hated this house but it did have a sort of chilly fascination, and besides, he liked the company of this young man so different from himself. He did go as far as to look at his watch. Was it chance that made him decide to stay? That was the way it seemed, and yet, when he looked back afterwards it seemed as though he'd been treading a well-defined and determined path right from the very beginning, right from the moment when he'd stood looking down at Corsi's dark-stained face. So perhaps it hadn't been so important after all that he had thought to say, 'I ought to get back', and instead had said nothing but followed William's smart Chaplin-like step back towards the studio.

''Evening, Marshal.'

That was when he noticed that the dwarf was there. But he thought nothing of it. He followed William into the studio and closed the door.

An hour later he was still reading, or rather, deciphering.

'No . . . I can't make it out.'

'It doesn't matter. Try this. It's not complete but it will give you the gist. Catherine had it photocopied from the Maruccelliana Library. It doesn't always help, but it can sometimes indicate that there's a whole chunk of information missing which means a missing or misplaced page. Here . . . Skip all that stuff about Cosimo the Elder—1490 . . . Neri Ulderighi, there he is: let me . . .

' "*In 1490, Neri Ulderighi decided to enlarge his Florentine house. He purchased the houses adjoining his mediæval tower in the city centre and sent to Rome for a design of the façade and courtyard. The drawing he received, supposed to be by Raphael, was given to the master builder, Lapo Cinelli, for his estimate of the work. The*

drawing was never returned, Cinelli claiming that he had lost it.
Neri applied to Lorenzo de' Medici for help—"'

'Here, you see? This is from the letter you were trying to decipher:

'*"Since the drawing is a very splendid thing and the artist has no time to make another and Your Highness knows that were I to apply to the courts they would only inflict a fine for the loss of a manuscript which avails but little against scoundrels."'*

The Marshal sat bemused as William perched on the edge of the worktable and read to him. 'But did he—'

'Wait . . . Lorenzo's answer is lost but there's a quote from it which proves that he did answer . . . Here it is:

'*"Let the court send for him and the drawing be found."'*

'There may not actually have been a complete letter to Neri, of course, just a note in the margin of some other orders or a mention of the business in a letter to someone else.'

'And was the drawing found, then?'

'Wait! The plot thickens. Listen to this:

'*"Lorenzo's intervention was to no avail. Cinelli insisted that the drawing was lost but that he remembered it well enough to proceed with the work, which he would do at a reduced cost in apology for the drawing's being lost. Not long after work had begun, a rumour reached Neri that Cinelli was boasting of having tricked him and that a drawing by Raphael was worth much more than the reduction in his fee. Within three days of Neri's hearing this, Cinelli was dead, murdered in the cellars where he had begun building and entombed within its walls. Cinelli's son carried out the contract and the Palazzo Ulderighi was completed, but it is said that the son knew who had murdered his father and that it was he who carved the inscription on the cellar wall behind which Cinelli was buried:*

HERE IS AN END TO ALL MY WOES
AND A BEGINNING OF YOUR OWN.

'So it was true . . . The Marshal, who had sat as still and attentive as a well-behaved schoolboy during the reading, shifted in his chair and looked about him, bothered again by the lack of windows in these rooms. He liked to stare out of a window while he was thinking, though he stared without seeing what he was looking at. Here he felt constrained.

William was still leafing through the photocopies.

'It was true all right. The Ulderighi had more bad luck after that—oh, they always managed to stay in power by a system of alliance with the strong, that is, no real alliance to anyone or anything except themselves. They were at court when the Austrian Grand Dukes ruled Florence and even though they thoroughly disapproved of Cavour's machinations for the unification of Italy, there they were at court again when Florence became the first capital of the kingdom of Italy. They've survived two world wars and the rise and fall of Fascism and here they still are. They've lost money, of course, what with taxation and having their neglected country estates confiscated by the new Rupublic. Even so, in that way they haven't been bad survivors. The curse—and everybody regarded the Cinelli inscription as a curse—had to do with the succession.'

'I only meant,' the Marshal said, 'that it was true what the old woman told us. The murder in the cellars. I didn't think . . .'

'You thought she was rambling, I imagine, but all of it was true and all of it attributed by chroniclers of the time to the Cinelli curse. They kept on losing their heirs. Francesco was the first of them.'

'Francesco . . .' The Marshal cast his mind back over the tata's ramblings. 'Ah, the one with the garland of spring flowers on his grave who had an accident of some sort, that one?'

'That's the one. He was the eldest son. There were two

sons and Neri tried to marry Francesco to one of the Della Loggia family, a girl called Lucrezia. Francesco, if you remember, was the good-looking one, and the garland of flowers was what he wore for the wedding. It's a good story . . . Wait, it must be here because it happened almost immediately after the building was finished. I remember seeing it. It begins "*A marriage was arranged*" . . . A marriage . . . Ah: "*Neri Ulderighi had two sons* . . ." this is it:

'"*A marriage was arranged between Francesco and Lucrezia Della Loggia. On June 24th, the feast of St John, the patron saint of Florence, the handsome Francesco, dressed in white with a garland of flowers on his head, rode out of the Palazzo Ulderighi to his wedding. Outside the doors, drums were being beaten and silk flags tossed in his honour. As he rode out from the dark courtyard into the brilliant June sunshine, a flag spun out right in front of his white stallion's head. The horse shied and reared and Francesco was thrown. His garlanded head hit the great stone portal and the Palazzo Ulderighi claimed its second victim. Many blamed the Cinelli curse but some thought that the flag-thrower was in the pay of certain families who were jealous of the combined influence of the Ulderighi and Della Loggia families at Lorenzo's court."*'

'There you are, then.' William shuffled the papers into a semblance of order and dropped them on the table. 'The Cinelli curse in action. That's why they married the poor girl off to the ugly, smelly brother who turned out a bad 'un so that, according to the dear old tata, she couldn't help but have his little girlfriend decapitated. Though I have my theory about why she defends the murderous Lucrezia. She looks so much like the present Marchesa that Tata gets them confused. I just wish Catherine were here because she's got the keys. Anyway, when she gets back she'll take you down to see the Cinelli inscription.'

'I'm not sure,' the Marshal said, getting to his feet, 'that I'll need to—'

He was interrupted by a very sharp knock at the door.

'William! William, are you there?'

It was Dr Martelli, surprised to find the door opened to her by the Marshal who was on his way out.

'Oh. Have I interrupted . . .'

'No, no . . . I was just going.' He reached in his top pocket for his dark glasses.

'What's the matter?' asked William, looking round the Marshal's big shoulder.

'That bloody woman!' hissed the doctor.

'Oops!' William hurried her in and shut the door. 'That courtyard has ears.'

'This whole building has ears,' said Dr Martelli, 'and I suspect that awful Grillo but you can never catch him at it. He knows everything that's going on on every floor but he can't use the lift and I've never once seen him on the stairs—I must get back, I've a queue of patients, but as I had a message for you I came in now to give myself a minute to cool off. I cannot stand that Ulderighi woman any longer. She just tore a strip off one of my patients for leaving the big doors ajar. Would you believe it? A tiny little frail thing of eighty who couldn't hope to shut those great doors without five people to help her. I can't stand it! The cheek of her when there's a porter there, paid for by us, who instead of looking after the doors is forever in fancy dress up there buttling!'

She clenched her small fists and clapped them to her temples with a mock scream of genuine fury.

William looked puzzled. 'She's surely not entertaining, not already.'

'I wouldn't say so, not entertaining. But I've seen a fleet of lawyers go up there while I've been letting my patients in and out. At least they looked like lawyers to me but some of them may have been bankers *and* did you see who was here early this morning?'

'I was out at rehearsals.'

She was telling it all to William but the Marshal could feel that it was directed at him. She wasn't, he thought, a wicked woman, by any means. He rather liked her. But he was quite sure that she had an understandable desire to see the Marchesa get some sort of come-uppance.

'Builders! Oh, not the actual workmen but there was an architect, the one who I used to see when I first moved in, and somebody from the Ministry of Fine Arts taking photographs and measuring. They're obviously going to restart the work on the façade. So!' She turned directly to the Marshal now. 'I hope that report of yours turns out the way she wants it, because it looks as if she's already spending the insurance money.'

'No,' William said, 'there'd be no need of that. The Corsi inheritance is something enormous. She can restore the whole place now if she wants to. Hugh was telling me that yesterday. The insurance money can't matter to her but the scandal would.'

'Do you think they can have read the Corsi will so soon?' the doctor asked.

'Not without my report,' the Marshal said. And they hadn't, now he thought about it, given him a deadline. Not that they should, but in a case like this it was surprising they hadn't tried.

'She'll have no trouble borrowing on an inheritance like that. Flavia, I gave the Marshal some tea, though he didn't like it. Can I give you a cup?'

'God, no! My patients! I'm going—oh, I came to ask you to tell Catherine if she does get back this weekend to come round to me on Monday evening about six, not in the morning. I've cancelled everything in the morning so I can have a long weekend away. You won't forget?'

'I'll write it down—are you going too?' This to the Marshal, who was adjusting his hat as Flavia Martelli hurried back to her patients.

'I must get back.' There were a lot of things in his head, images rather than ideas, that he wanted to sort out by himself.

'But you will come back and meet Catherine? And I wanted you to come to the theatre—wait.' He fished in his pockets until he found what he wanted. 'There you are. Two free tickets so your wife could come.'

'That's very nice of you but . . .' He stared at the tickets before putting them inside his black notebook. 'Didn't you say . . . Well, won't it be in English?'

William's face fell. 'You don't understand any English?'

The Marshal's face fell too and he reddened a little.

'Well, a word or two, you know. Good-morning and that sort of thing . . .' But he recognized the expression on William's face. He'd seen it before on his own little boy Totò's face when the Marshal hadn't been free to go and watch some little effort they'd put on at school. So he said, 'My wife does a bit better than me . . . and then there'll be the costumes and so on. I'm sure we'll enjoy it.'

He'd done the right thing. William produced a programme with a synopsis of the action in Italian. It was, he explained, all geared to people learning English.

'I meant to give a ticket to Flavia—Dr Martelli—but she was so steamed up about the porter I forgot. Still, if she's going away for the weekend . . .'

'She certainly gets steamed up,' the Marshal commented, dabbing at the bridge of his nose with a big white handkerchief ready to put on his glasses.

'Well, you can't blame her. I think she gets a lot of stick one way and another. Anyway, she's right about the porter, he should see to the door instead of playing the butler.'

'I'm surprised he doesn't mind himself. He didn't look too comfortable when I met him up there, yet he hadn't a wrong word to say about the Marchesa.'

'Ha! I bet he hadn't—have you seen their son?' William

had been holding the door ajar but he shut it again as he said this.

'Well, I haven't met him . . .'

'Looks like the side of the cathedral only bigger.'

'He plays in the football tournament, I gather.'

'And could do as the prize if they painted his toenails gold and put a garland of flowers round that great neck. The best thing to do when you see him approach,' said William, lowering his voice, 'is . . . Run away! That's what I do. However, I'm small and sensitive with it. Now the point about the porter's buttling is this: their bonny bouncing baby—his name is Leo but his nickname, if you'll believe it, is Baby—has had a spot of bother now and then with the forces of law and order. I don't know all the details but there was one incident that got into the papers. He was peaceably slicing people up with a broken bottle in some club or other and when the police arrived and interfered with his game he must have lost his temper. Anyway, whether in temper or just playfulness, he knocked their heads together, took their staffs and used them to break up their squad car. Bit naughty, eh?'

'So he has a criminal record?' The Marshal was fishing for his notebook.

'Ah no!' William wagged his finger and grinned. 'Ah no, no, no. Baby hasn't got a criminal record because if Baby had a criminal record he wouldn't be able to play in the nice football tournament and playing in the football tournament is the thing that Baby likes best. So these things have to be hushed up. Sh! Not a word.'

'I see. The Marchesa.'

'The Marchesa. So if she wants her porter to dress up as a monkey and swing across the roofs he's going to do it to keep his little gorilla out of the nick.'

'And the gorilla himself might . . .'

The Marshal stopped. William's pitted face had turned

pale. The Marshal put a hand out to steady him. 'Here, sit down. I didn't mean to frighten you.'

William did sit down. 'You haven't seen him. He really is frightening and if he had something to do with Corsi's death and I put you on to it, they'll all know by this time!'

'How could they know? They know I'm here, but I've been to see everybody, not just you.'

'Grillo!'

'He saw us come in here, but even so . . .'

'Catherine found out. He always knew everything and she found out—' He jumped from his chair and pulled at a little brass handle on the back wall. 'It's locked.' But a noise as faint as a mouse in a wainscot followed his words.

'I see,' the Marshal said. It was normal in all such great houses to have, in some discreet corner, a servant's door camouflaged with frescoes to blend in with the wall and well away from the room's real entrance. These tiny doors led off a separate staircase so that the servants need not be seen except when absolutely necessary. 'Have all the rooms on the courtyard got service doors?'

'I don't think so. Just on this side, chiefly so that Grillo can get from his lair to the gun room next door to this. You can bet your life he was listening in.'

'Where else can he get to from his passage?'

'Out into the street, of course, through the old tower entrance and up into the tower itself to look after Neri's needs. I think into the Ulderighi apartments as well. There's bound to be a door connecting the new part of the building with the tower at some level.'

'Yes . . . yes, there is.' The Marshal remembered his first visit, going 'up there' and the porter's wife returning with the medicine.

'*All those stairs . . .*'

She had gone by some back route, not by the main staircase. The Marshal's face had taken on a heavy blind look.

'Do you think I'm in danger from that brute?' William wasn't joking any more.

The Marshal only stood there, solid, unseeing and silent. 'Do you?'

But the Marshal still didn't answer. He turned slowly, adjusted his hat and opened the door.

'Of course if I were as big as you and had a uniform . . .'

William's voice followed him softly across the music-filled courtyard. It was only the ballet music now and a woman repeating, angrily, to the rhythmic thumping of a sharp object:

'*Glissade—assemblé—glissade—assemblé—glissade—jeté— temps levé—pas de bourrée! Glissade—assemblé—Glissade— assemblé . . .*'

'Marshal . . .'

Only as he pressed the button to spring the gates did he bethink himself to say, 'No, no . . . I don't think you're in danger . . . because he's not.' And he was gone.

'Marshal . . . ?'

He looked at Lorenzini, frowning in an effort to remember what he'd said. His young brigadier's face showed that he had been waiting some time for an answer. Not knowing what the question had been, the Marshal got up and followed Lorenzini out of the office door to the waiting-room on the assumption that there was someone there he must see to. The small room with its marble-tiled floor and neatly arranged leather armchairs was empty. The magazines on the low table lined up with military precision. The answer wasn't here.

'You'll go, then?' Lorenzini seemed a bit anxious. 'Those two boys on patrol are too young to deal with that sort of thing. You're the only person who . . .'

'I'll go.' He'd got it now. He buttoned his jacket and slid his sunglasses from the pocket. 'Call the boys in.'

'I thought they should stay. The woman insisted—'

'Call them in. And don't go off duty. When I get back I want to talk to you.' He pulled the heavy door to behind him and stumped off down the stairs.

It was practically next door, but if Lorenzini had given him the address he had forgotten it and it was lucky for him that the boys he had called back were coming out of the street door across the piazza as he came down the slope of the car park. One of them was dabbing at his left hand with a handkerchief as the Marshal came up to them.

'What's happened to you?'

'One of them scratched me when I was trying to stop her attacking the old woman. My God, I always thought marital scraps were the worst.'

'Disinfect it as soon as you get in,' the Marshal said.

The two lads went off up the forecourt, giving vent to their astonishment and indignation as they went. The Marshal rang a bell and was admitted to a dark and narrow staircase. He climbed towards the sound of the conflict.

It took him only a few minutes to establish order and insist that all the parties be seated and remain seated. The two women, both dressed in black, were red with fury. One still had tears in her eyes. The one man present was wearing a dark suit that was too tight for him, which was odd, given that he was very small. He was holding his hat close to his chest and pressing himself back against the wall, perhaps hoping to become invisible or at least forgotten. The Marshal would have felt sorry for him, but as a country-bred man he knew well enough that if there had been an acre of land in dispute the harmless-looking chap would have been scratching and spitting with the best of them. God knew there was little enough to fight about in this poor little flat that seemed to the Marshal to smell strongly of drains. He had known the old woman who'd lived there, a neat and busy little soul who suffered badly from bronchitis. Every winter was expected to carry her off, but she had died in the heat of a June day, he didn't know what of, and the funeral had been that morning.

The tearful woman, who turned out to be a sister, blew her nose but let the tears run and trickle down her neck under the collar of her flowered frock.

'It was a promise,' she said, 'practically on her deathbed.'

'Deathbed my foot!' The fat sister-in-law sitting beside her shot a disgusted look at her tearful neighbour. 'You hadn't been near your sister for months.'

'It was last winter. Her bronchitis was so bad I thought then it was the end. I was the one who came and nursed her.'

'Came to be in at the kill, you mean. Vulture!'

'Now, now . . .' A faint protest from the man, who immediately tried to vanish into the wall again.

The Marshal looked at the fat woman who sat now in grim-mouthed silence, clutching a huge black bag of imitation leather between her stout legs. It was the tearful sister, making an attempt on the bag, who had scratched the young carabinieri. The Marshal cleared his throat.

'Now then—'

'Ask her where all the bedlinen is,' commanded the fat woman.

'I don't begrudge her the bedlinen,' the brother said piously.

'Oh, don't you? And what damn business is it of yours? Your sister didn't have a rag to call her own when she married our Ivo and that bedlinen came from my bottom drawer, every piece of it hemmed by my mother—'

'That's as may be, but I gave her the lace tablecloths as a wedding present and they should come to me!'

The lace tablecloths, the Marshal knew, were in that big black bag with the bedlinen. He'd been allowed a glimpse. His mother had had similar cloths, used, if at all, on first

communion days or at wedding feasts. They had to be sent
to the nuns who looked after the altar cloths to be laun-
dered. The ones in the black bag had never been used and
were still in their tissue paper and boxes. The old lady had
no money for entertaining, but she used to spend a few
coins from her pension on feeding the stray cats in the
Boboli Gardens behind the Marshal's station in the Pitti
Palace. She always looked so frail.

It seemed best to let these women have their say. They
would run out of steam at some point and he knew exactly
what to do then. In the meantime, the louder they shouted,
the better he liked it. He could almost wish the scene would
never be over so that he wouldn't be left alone with the
knowledge of what he had done an hour ago. He didn't yet
know why he had done it. Every reasoning force within him
protested, had protested even as he'd driven the car out of
the city instead of going into his office. His very own heart-
beat had made its audible protest as he made his request
with apparent calm and drove away with his parcel to
Borgo Ognissanti headquarters. He had lied again, and
again obtained what he wanted—or he would when the
answer came from Rome. Why had he done it? He knew
what he was risking. He could think of no answer except
that someone else seemed to have made the decision against
his will, and now he was going to have to tell Lorenzini and
swear him to secrecy and he knew just the expression with
which the younger, brighter man would look at him.

He looked at his watch. Lorenzini should have been at
home by now. It wasn't fair to keep him waiting any longer.
The quarrel was petering out. He got to his feet and the
family group fell silent, watching him for signs of sympathy
or at least partiality. His face, expressionless, told them
nothing. His settlement was brief. It began with a warning
against prolonging the matter and letting it get into the
hands of lawyers, which would cost them more than the

value of what they were squabbling over. He then suggested that the silent brother divide the goods fairly but that the sister should have first choice of one of the divisions. Then he left them and went back to face Lorenzini and admit to what he'd done.

6

The tiled corridor with its faint but unpleasant sickly smell stretched out into the distance, apparently without end. The Marshal's feet made no noise as he plodded forward, clutching his parcel under one arm. He had, he knew, been walking for quite a long time. The parcel was getting heavier but that wasn't because he was tired. He knew why. Sweat was breaking on his forehead at the thought but he kept walking forward. Sometimes he passed people who looked at him in silence and he could tell that they knew, or at least suspected, about the parcel. The brown paper wrapping didn't deceive anybody.

The weight dragged at him.

'No . . .'

He whispered the word as if in an attempt to prevent the parcel's becoming what it must become, but there was someone directly behind him, perhaps following, who said clearly, 'That's Corsi's body.'

'It isn't my fault,' the Marshal tried to say, but he wasn't sure that anyone could hear him. His breath was short and his heartbeat very loud. He kept walking since he didn't know what else to do. A man in a long green smock and wellingtons was wiping over and over at a tiny stain on the wall of the corridor which nevertheless did not vanish but got gradually wider. He didn't pause in his work or look round when the Marshal reached him, but he knew what the parcel was and he said, or thought aloud, 'If you take him out of here you're responsible.'

But how could he turn back? He'd signed for the parcel, even told lies to get it. They wouldn't accept it back now.

Outside on the steps he saw traffic streaming by as

though this were a motorway, though there was no noise.

There were people about but nobody stared at the Marshal and Corsi now. It was fortunate that he was dressed, that the parcel had contained clothes, though they weren't the clothes he'd been wearing when he died. The Marshal was sure that they should have been but he couldn't deal with that problem now. He'd thought he had a car with him but now it seemed that he hadn't. How was he to manœuvre the body on to a bus?

No one took any notice. No one helped him, but the shame and fear at what he was doing made him imagine the sort of thing they must be thinking, and besides, where was he going to go with his terrible burden? He couldn't go home. He thought of his commanding officer at Headquarters but was filled with deep embarrassment at the thought of asking for help there. You couldn't just keep a dead body like that. Something had to be done. He must find out what the proper proceedure was and get rid of it . . .

'Try to walk a little . . .' He was so tired of supporting him, but when he looked at the purplish white sheen on Corsi's dead face, stained dark on one cheek, pity overcame his embarrassment. 'Just a few steps, if you can. I can't manage any more by myself.'

They struggled forward together. It had got too dark to see properly and the Marshal kept walking without any idea of where they were going until the thought came to him that he could solve the problem by making for the Palazzo Ulderighi, if that was where the body belonged. Shouldn't the family take responsibility for it?

He began to walk a little faster, but in the darkness beside him the voice of the dead man spoke from the depths of an unbearable sadness.

'Don't take me back to that house.'

'All right, I won't. I promise you I won't.'

But where could he take him? He should surely be buried
. . . wasn't that what usually happened? He couldn't go on
half dragging the poor man around indefinitely. The weight
of the man's grief was getting too much to bear. They had
buried his mother the Marshal remembered now, down at
home in Sicily after her last stroke. She had lain upstairs
in the front bedroom of the old house and then people had
come and buried her. You weren't meant to have to do it
all yourself. He had never had to carry his mother around
like this, he would have remembered.

So he struggled on as far as the old house and when he
had with difficulty found his way in the dark to the front
bedroom he laid his burden down on the big bed.

The dead man's limbs composed themselves but the eyes
remained watchful. The Marshal insisted, 'You have to stay
here.' Couldn't he understand? 'I can't help it. I can't go
on carrying you about with me.'

The eyes were closed. The Marshal covered the
body with a sheet. Then he went downstairs and waited,
sitting in his mother's old place. He was holding his breath,
unable to judge how long he must wait. The important
thing was that Corsi must stay still—had he closed the
door? A first faint noise came from the room above. The
Marshal's fists clenched on the worn arms of the chair
and beads of sweat covered his brow as he stared up at
the ceiling.

'No . . .'

But there was no mistake. He could hear footsteps, slow
and hesitant at first, but then quite normal. He was coming
down the stairs. The Marshal jolted his big body forward
in the chair, seeking its arms for support now but finding
only empty air.

'No!'

'Salva!'

He was blinded as the light went on. He sat hunched

forward in the bed and felt his wife's warm relaxed arm go
around his shoulders.

'You're soaked to the skin. You've never got a fever at
this time of year!'

He was too dazed to answer her, the horror of his dream
was still real.

'I'll get you a pair of clean pyjamas. Have a bit of a wash,
you'll feel better.'

'It was only a nightmare . . .' He got out of bed and went
to the bathroom. His wife's voice followed him.

'Well, what do you expect, eating sausages at ten o'clock
at night?'

'Eight o'clock.' She always exaggerated.

'Don't tell me you couldn't have come in for your lunch
if you'd organized yourself properly. I've told you before:
let those young lads do the running about. That's what
they're there for. I offered to cook you something light for
your supper, those Tuscan sausages are like lead on your
stomach and as for what they do to your liver . . . You
could have had them for lunch tomorrow . . .'

The scolding voice comforted him, pushing the nightmare back into the darkness where it belonged.

'Will you make me some camomile tea?'

He didn't follow her into the kitchen but padded off along
the marble-tiled corridor in felt slippers and went through
to his office. The parcel from the Medico-Legal Institute
was lying where he had left it on his desk.

The expression on young Lorenzini's face was exactly as he
had imagined it would be. Amazement, a touch of pity
perhaps, and that something you could never quite define
that created a cold empty space where before there had
been contact. The something that told you you'd cut yourself off from the others. It would have been better not to
have to tell him, but he had to have help.

'I want him followed. You're the only person I can trust.'

'But the clothes . . . You're not really going to deliver them to the Marchesa?'

There were times when the Marshal, much as he liked and respected Lorenzini, would have preferred a fellow Sicilian to work with him. Someone a little more mellifluous, more tactful, who wouldn't have dreamt of asking direct questions on such a delicate matter. Florentines, now . . . They stared you straight in the eye and just asked. How did he know whether he would really deliver Corsi's clothes to his wife? That had just been the most plausible way of getting hold of them. He was, theoretically, in charge of an HSA inquiry.

Much of the Marshal's discomfort came, he knew, from a sort of hangover left by his nightmare, and it was the nightmare, too, which convinced him that on one would ever ask for the dead man's clothes because nobody cared enough to think of it. But he couldn't explain that to Brigadier Lorenzini. He was hardly likely to start relating his nightmares. In any case, all that mattered was the shoes . . .

Instead of answering Lorenzini's question, he said, 'I asked for priority at the fingerprint lab. I won't get it, but at least they'll get a move on and with any luck I should have something by tomorrow afternoon. After that I'm stuck. This Leo's been picked up more than once and may well have had prints taken but they'll have been destroyed. The Marchesa's seen to it that he has no criminal record. That's why you're following him. We're coming up to the biggest match of the tournament and he's going to get a lot of aggro every time he goes out. If he so much as sets foot in the Santa Croce area they'll try and give him a sufficient going-over to put him out of action for the match. He's a bouncer in some club. Find out which and park yourself nearby. That should be sufficient since he sleeps during the day. He's bound to have trouble with his customers sooner or later that you can mistake for a fight. Don't go after him alone, call for reinforcements. Remember, he plays Florentine football. Built like a tank and behaves like one, I imagine. He knows he can get away with it because of the Marchesa. So watch him, and if he so much as raises his fist in a threatening gesture pull him in, get his prints, then let him go. Fortunately, he's not noted for his brains. Apologize nicely.'

When Lorenzini had left the Marshal got up from his desk and went over to the window, where he stood for a long time staring out at the laurel hedges of the Boboli Gardens without seeing them or anything else. The trouble was that if Leo, the porter's brutish son, wasn't noted for his brains, neither was the Marshal himself. He noticed things, that was what the English lad William had said. He noticed things. That was true enough. But the things he noticed were just ordinary things. It was all very well to remember Corsi's glossy evening shoes which would likely as not carry clear prints if anybody had dragged or carried him. But if he were right, and if the prints turned out to be Leo's, what was he going to do then?

Here is an end of all my woes and a beginning of your own.

They could carve that on Corsi's tomb as far as the Marshal was concerned. It was true enough.

Don't take me back to that house.

How was it that you could invent such a distinctive voice for someone you didn't know, had never spoken to? That was a funny thing. And the truth was that since his dream he no longer thought of Corsi as a man he didn't know but as a man who had no other friend in the world except himself. His wife had only wanted his money to restore and maintain that great house—perhaps that's why the Marshal felt close to him. He was convinced, as his dream showed, that Corsi hated that house as much as he did himself. Not his wife but the house, which exacted tribute of blood and money from every generation. It wasn't that he was beginning to believe in the Cinelli curse. He wasn't the sort to take any notice of that sort of thing, but even so, what an inheritance . . .

His own kids wouldn't have problems like that because he was a nobody, but then what about the little old dear who used to feed the cats? She was a nobody all right and they'd fought like vultures over her few sheets and tablecloths. The house had been rented . . . They ought to buy. His wife brought the subject up periodically and of course she was right. Living in barracks was all very well, but when he retired they had to have somewhere to go and that meant keeping up with the rise in prices. They should have done it long ago but they always got stuck over the question of where. Prices in Florence were astronomical and they had always talked of going back to Sicily some day. Weren't they kidding themselves? The boys wouldn't want to, there was nothing for them down there. They would want to go to university in Florence with their friends. They ought to get on with it and buy something here, but the prices . . . it would cost over three hundred million for a small flat. Three hundred million . . . what would the Ulderighi house be worth? He couldn't even begin to imagine. Billions. But billions meant nothing to the Marshal. A sum of money doesn't have any real meaning unlesss you can say just what it could do or buy. The Marshal knew that a million meant the gas bill and the electricity bill and the phone and so on for two months, but what a billion meant he couldn't have said. Imagine the cost of running a palazzo—and you couldn't sell it, whatever it was worth, because it was a nine-hundred-year-old inheritance.

For some reason, Dr Martelli came into his mind, not because she lived in the Ulderighi house but because of something else she'd perhaps said—no, it was all those ornaments. She'd said what they were but he hadn't caught the name. The point was that she'd said she wasn't fond of the stuff but it had been her father's, that she ought to get it valued. Her whole flat cluttered up with stuff she didn't like but was tied to because it was all bound up with the memory of her father. Well, the Marshal's children might or might not inherit a decent flat and a bit of something in the bank but there was no danger of their being saddled with a roomful of knick-knacks!

He opened the window a little and let in the warm breath of the laurel-scented morning. The sun, by this hour, had moved beyond the far right wing of the Pitti Palace, leaving the Marshal's corner in the left wing bathed in cool shade made deeper and more refreshing by the presence of so many trees. The physical pleasure of looking out on such a morning without the necessity of sheltering from it behind dark glasses for the moment blotted out all the Marshal's current problems. After all, you had to take the bad bits along with the good, and most of the time he liked his job. He had a fatherly affection for the lads who passed through his hands and he got on well enough with the people in his Quarter. It was a decently paid job and, above all, safe and respectable. His father, a peasant farmer, would have given his eye teeth for such a job.

Even as he thought these words he realized that they were not truly his own but his mother's. His father had died before he enrolled, just before, and it had been his mother who, with tears in her eyes, had said, 'It's a good job, safe and respectable. Your father would have given his eye teeth . . .' Had he joined the army because of what his father would have liked to do? Pushed that way with greater force because his father had died? You never know when you do something what the real reason is. You don't think . . .

'*We inherited their dreams . . .*'

The same thing. Those two orphans, William and Catherine Yorke, adrift in a foreign country to fulfil their parents' dreams of freedom and the artistic life. The parents, of course, had stayed firmly in their safe jobs until they died. You could fight against the pressure of your parents when they were there to fight back, but when they were dead? How can you fight against the influence of the dead?

Behind the Marshal the door opened without a preliminary knock, which meant Lorenzini.

'There's a telephone call for you.'

'Well, put it through.' The Marshal continued to gaze out the window.

'Marshal . . .'

He turned then. 'What is it?'

'It's the Public Prosecutor's office.'

Lorenzini's expression, which had every reason to be saying a silent I told you so, showed only sympathy and dismay.

Well, the Marshal, too, was dismayed but, afer all, what else could he have expected? It was true that the case had been played down for the press but everyone in Florence was speculating on the death of someone so important—or should he say the husband of someone so important. Word was bound to get back either from the Medico-Legal Institute or the prints lab at Headquarters.

He sat down before picking up the receiver and waved at Lorenzini to indicate that he should stay. It wasn't a long conversation and the Marshal contributed little to it beyond the occasional grunt of assent. When he hung up, all he said to Lorenzini was that his HSA report was to be delivered to the prosecutor's office by noon the next day, after which the preliminary hearings judge could issue his decree consigning the inquiry to the archives. The body of

Buongianni Corsi was to be released and buried on Saturday. The Marshal communicated all this without a hint of
expression in voice or face.

Lorenzini, uncertain whether to leave the room or risk
trying to satisfy his curiosity, at last ventured to say, 'In
that case . . .'

'In that case what?'

'I just—I mean, this Leo chap. Should I still—'

'Follow him.'

'But there'll be nothing in your report to warrant it,
I imagine. So you might call this, as it were, a separate
inquiry.'

The Marshal stared at him, or rather through him, his
eyes as blank as the windows of an empty house.

'You can call it what you want. And there'll be nothing
in my report. Nothing. What should there be?'

'I don't know. You seemed sure that the patch on his
face—'

'Hypostasis is the business of the doctor who examined
the body.'

'Yes, of course. I only thought . . . I'll start following
him then, tonight.'

'Thank you. The presence of two carabinieri is required
at the funeral in view of the presence of the archbishop, the
chief public prosecutor, etcetera, etcetera.'

Lorenzini waited a moment but his chief made no further
comment, so he left the room and closed the door quietly.

The Marshal returned to his place at the window and
gazed calmly out, his big shoulders rigid as if braced against
an approaching blow.

'Eternal rest give unto him, O Lord, and let perpetual light
shine upon him. May he rest in peace.'

'Amen.'

The priest, circling the coffin behind the officiating archbishop and sprinkling holy water, was the one the Marshal had seen entering the Palazzo Ulderighi the other day. The family confessor. The family chapel. The chapel was a few doors away from the house and, to judge by the stale cold air inside it, had not been opened for years. Indeed, were it not for the presence of the Marshal and one of his boys it wouldn't have been opened to the air yet, since the family entered it from some passage directly connected to the house and passing unseen through the buildings between. This was common enough and, in the case of the Ulderighi, a necessity after the death of the unfortunate Francesco. An Ulderighi didn't pass through the streets in the sixteenth century without risk.

'For Buongianni and for the souls of all the faithful departed . . .'

The Marshal was standing, the small congregation seated on hard chairs which made him remember the concert, the little gold chairs, the young man on a stool near the door whose name he had by now forgotten. On the opposite side stood the lad he had brought with him. A youngster doing his national service who couldn't help forgetting himself so far as to stare down at the important personages seated near him and up at the frescoes on his right. The chapel had no windows and was lit only by a couple of dim electric bulbs and a lot of beeswax candles whose flickering gave life to the figures in their soft glowing colours on the walls. The fresco nearest the Marshal was largely incomprehensible to him but, at a guess, it would seem to have been some sort of Ulderighi family saint seeing visions on her deathbed. Who the saint emerging from a corner of the bedroom wall was he couldn't be sure, but the woman saying the rosary by the bedside of the dying woman was certainly the famous Lucrezia. Was the dying woman her mother, then? No, she was dressed as a nun. An aunt then, or somesuch.

'Let us pray.'

The Marshal ducked his head. He was shivering in his thin summer uniform and it was difficult to imagine the warmth of the June day outside. Every now and then his right arm fell to his side and brushed against the pocket where a sheet of paper was folded out of sight. He didn't want to think about the notes on that piece of paper, only to know it was safely in its place and invisible. He didn't want to think about it because he didn't know what to do about it. He needed time to think in private. He'd do better to think of something else for now. But what, after all, could he think about with Corsi there in his coffin? Against the drone of the requiem mass his thoughts drifted in repetitive circles. The reality of the corpse nailed inside its last resting place, the nightmare of the limbs that wouldn't settle, the eyes that watched him, the parcel of clothes that started it all. The shoes. He had been right, or so he'd thought at first when the phone call came.

Well, you were right. He was carried. Lovely glossy shoes, lovely clear prints. My compliments. Still, you were wrong about the other business.

What other business? There was no other business. I just wanted photos of the prints.

Well, that's what you were wrong about. Oh, I know you said just collect the prints, no point in putting them through the computer. Well, I did, just to be sure. No point in doing half a job. If there was nothing, there was nothing. But there wasn't nothing. Your man's got a criminal record as long as your arm.

But he can't have . . .

Can't he? Theft, grievous bodily harm, robbery with violence, grievous bodily harm again and a nice case of robbery with rape. I ought to explain that our friend is not a thief. He's paid to go along in case any rough stuff's required and he usually sees to it that it is. One of those brutes that enjoys it, know what I mean?

Yes . . . yes, but I don't understand—

Usually known by his nickname, Tiny.

Tiny . . . Somebody told me The Baby.

*The Baby? That's the football player. Everybody knows him!
He's got no record—not that he doesn't merit one but he'd be taken
off the team so he's always protected. Not that he gets up to anything
as lethal as our friend Tiny, just the odd scuffle, bit of admissible
bloodshed on the pitch. No, no, these prints are Tiny's, real name
Gualducci, Rolando Gualducci. I haven't read you his full record,
it'd take all day, but the man's a killer who up to now has been
lucky, you know what I mean? I bet that whoever owns these shoes
is looking the worse for wear after an encounter with him. Or are
they his? Don't look like his style.*

'Eternal rest give unto him, O Lord, and let perpetual
light shine upon him . . .'

The mass was nearing its end.

The Marshal hadn't enlightened his colleague. He was
in need of enlightenment himself. It was a shock. Yet why
should it have been such a shock? He had already thought
that Leo, the porter's son, had been the one to drag Buongianni Corsi by the feet, whatever the reason, whatever else
he might have done to Corsi first. Instead, it had been a
certain Rolando Gualducci. What difference did it make?
He looked around him now and he knew. The family. The
family chaplain, the family chapel, the family retainers. It
would have been natural to call in Leo to help with . . .
with whatever had happened, even so relatively innocent a
deed as covering up a suicide. But Tiny, now. Tiny was
another story altogether . . .

He's paid to go along in case any rough stuff's required . . .

So who paid him? Why did they want him *in case?* Who
even knew him? The Marshal thought he knew the answer
to the last question at least. The only person within the
Palazzo Ulderighi likely to know Tiny was Leo. Two of
them . . . to do what? Just to move a body? Leo could have
done that by himself. How difficult would it be for two big
men to fake the suicide of a third? Close to the Marshal's

face Lucrezia held her rosary between delicate white fingers, her eyes raised to heaven, ignorant of the vision towards which the dying nun stretched out her feeble arms.

'Go, the mass is over.'

'Thanks be to God.'

Thanks be to God was right, thought the Marshal, stretching his cold stiff knees, and he nodded at his boy to go out with him before the coffin. As he reached the door, feeling for his sunglasses ready for the glare outside, his stomach gave what must surely be an audible growl of hunger. Why on earth he should have developed such an urgent appetite in the middle of the morning he couldn't quite understand until he made the connection with the mass. He was very much a weddings, funerals and christenings man himself who left all that sort of thing to his wife, but a lifetime of Sunday mass attendance left its mark. For years the words *Ite missa est* had conjured up his mother's Sunday roast rabbit with rich herb-scented gravy. What an odd business life was. Here was he, suffering nightmares about the burial of Corsi and now, with the coffin being manœuvred rather clumsily into the back of the hearse, he was thinking about roast rabbit.

Grateful though he was for the warmth of the street on coming out of the icy church, his car, which he hadn't been able to park in the shade, was boiling inside and both he and his boy opened their windows as quickly as they could. The journey to the cemetery wasn't long. Corsi was to be buried at San Miniato, surely the most richly endowed church in the city and certainly the most exclusive cemetery. It stood on the side of the hill overlooking the left bank of the Arno and its gilded marble façade glittered so brightly in the morning sunshine that it hardly seemed real.

The Marshal parked in a discreet patch of shade outside the high gates and watched the hearse drive slowly in along the wide gravel avenue followed by the cars of the mourners. He was under no illusions as to the role he was playing. A uniformed presence. The chief public prosecutor rode behind bullet-proof glass with his personal bodyguard and the archbishop's car was followed by four plain clothes policemen. Nevertheless, the Marshal was glad to be there and all but invisible. This was his one chance to get a good close look at the Ulderighi, all of them, and he intended to make the most of it. Until now he had been kept away from them and the fact hadn't displeased him. He had been too afraid of the Marchesa. Not just afraid of the influence she had and the damage she might do him, but afraid of her personally. That day he'd told her of Corsi's death he had stood no more than a foot away from her and yet, afterwards, he couldn't have said exactly what she looked like. He had watched her face, even registered her thoughts and reactions, but her presence had overpowered him to the extent that he didn't know now whether her eyes were light or dark.

'Stay here.' He left the boy in the meagre shade of a cypress tree.

And Neri, the son. He wanted to get a look at him and see for himself whether he looked sick or crazy or both. Yesterday he would have balked at this, too, but today was different. Today there was a slip of paper in his pocket headed 'Gualducci, Rolando aka Tiny', and everything had changed.

A Benedictine monk was stationed near the family tomb awaiting the arrival of the cortège. He wore large black-rimmed glasses that gave him an owlish look and the instant the coffin came into view he began to bustle about officiously. Once or twice his glance caught the Marshal as though he was wondering where to put him, but the Marshal kept just enough distance to be out of earshot of the whispered orders.

The coffin was placed at the entrance to the tomb. Then

the Marshal saw Neri Underighi for the first time. What had he expected? He wasn't sure, but certainly not what he saw. Neri was bigger, bulkier somehow than so much talk of his weakness led one to imagine. In fact, had he not been standing beside his mother with the priest supporting his arm on the other side, the Marshal would never have guessed who he was. There was hardly time for this to register before other people on the Marshal's side of the coffin obscured his view and he was obliged to shift his position as surreptitiously as possible under cover of the Archbishop's prayers which he hoped would hide the noise of his footsteps on the clean gravel. There. He could see them both now . . . and an older woman standing beside the Marchesa, perhaps the aunt. She looked sick, the Marshal thought, her face chalk white with reddish bags under her eyes. She was leaning on a stick.

'Remember, man, that thou art dust and unto dust . . .'

He shifted a little further. As he had imagined, the old aunt's legs were swollen. But Neri, Neri was so unexpected. His stance was that of a middle-aged man. The aunt stood there rigid with the help of her stick. The Marchesa was as upright and immobile as the white marble angel whose wings reared up behind her head against the blackness of a cypress tree. But Neri, even with the priest supporting or restraining him, was restless. His head was never still for an instant. How old had they said he was? In his early twenties at any rate. His hair, blond like his mother's, was already thinning. The head that was never still but bobbing and jerking, this way and that, as if in search of something, was too big even for that large and rather flabby body. He might have been an imbecile, yet the Marshal could just make out his eyes and they were bright and intelligent.

'May his soul and the souls of all the faithful departed, through the mercy of God . . .'

Just a little nearer. He might never get another chance

. . . When he did get nearer he was yet again surprised. The bright eyes, the unquiet stance, the jerking head, all had a very simple explanation. Neri Ulderighi was weeping.

The Marshal's eyes scanned the rest of the mourners. There was a family group, parents and a small girl, who looked as though they didn't quite belong, though they must, from their position, have been close relatives— Corsi's relatives, that must be it. The unfortunate Prince Consort had a family of his own and the Marshal had never given them a thought. There were a number of people in deep mourning who might well have been further branches of the Ulderighi family. Then some obvious city dignitaries, some of whom the Marshal recognized and some he didn't. The family retainers . . . Grillo looking very strange in his tiny suit. He couldn't see the old tata but no doubt she was far too old and frail to go out . . . Leo! That must be Leo, it couldn't be anyone else. Thick-necked and bullet-headed. His hair was shaven, no doubt so that no one could grasp him by it on the field. His parents weren't visible but they would be there somewhere. The retainers hadn't been in the chapel, only the family and the important guests. There was no sign of any of the tenants.

The Marshal wanted a good look at all of them but he couldn't concentrate. His gaze returned again and again to Neri Ulderighi who never ceased to cry during the ceremony.

He was up there screaming . . .

William Yorke had heard him screaming when he thought he'd heard a shot. Screaming in the darkness. The Marshal, too, had heard him in the darkness. At least, he couldn't be sure but he thought he had. Playing the flute in the dark. Not unnaturally, it occurred to the Marshal that the boy might have some problem with his eyes and he looked at him now, from behind his own protective glasses, with even more curiosity. How often it had happened to the Marshal to be stared at by people who thought he was crying when he'd simply forgotten to put his glasses on? But the movements? The way his head kept jerking and falling forward? He was crying, he must be.

The prayers were over and the coffin was being carried inside the tomb, the only noise the feet of the bearers on the gravel, then silence, punctuated by birdsong. The Marshal, looking about him for his boy, was drawn to Neri again and this time, with a little start of surprise, he realized that Neri was looking straight back at him. He seemed to have stopped weeping but he was nevertheless being supported by the priest, who began trying to lead him away. Neri stopped him and spoke urgently in his ear. Then he looked again across at the Marshal. What could he want? The Marshal himself had a strong impression, which he could give no logical reason for, that he wanted help.

Now it was the priest who was talking, his hand gesticulating close to his mouth as though he spoke in a whisper. The Marshal was standing so still watching them that a blackbird hopped right by his big shoes, chinking its love song and hopping away on the grass behind him. The priest's arm went round Neri's shoulder. Neri was much taller and bigger, yet it was plain to see that the priest was controlling the situation. Neri might have been a big child. It was just what a child would have done when thwarted, to turn back as he was led away and insist on staring at the Marshal.

The Marshal could make nothing of it. He glanced at the Ulderighi tomb and then at the tall white angel guarding what he now saw was a small child's grave. Corsi's bones were at rest and tiny invisible birds were singing in the cypresses.

7

'He's a humper at the central market and, by all accounts, every bit as nasty as his mugshot suggests.' Lorenzini had the photo in his hand as he made his bleary-eyed Sunday report. He hadn't worked all night for a long time and his body ached all over. The Marshal hadn't even told him to sit down. He was standing there at the window with his shoulders hunched and his back to the young brigadier and you'd think from his gruffness that he'd been the one to work all night.

'I'm sorry, but there was just nothing,' Lorenzini continued. 'I'll go on trying, of course, but what makes it look so hopeless is that because of the jobs they do one goes to bed practically at the time the other gets up.'

'What about the football? Isn't this Tiny character involved in that?' There must be a point of contact between Tiny and someone inside the Palazzo Ulderighi. Who else could it be but Leo? 'He sounds the type, thug like that.'

'It's the first thing I checked. He couldn't play, naturally, because he's got a criminal record—you may not believe this, but the players are theoretically meant to be the sons of noblemen of the city.'

'Hmph.'

'I suppose centuries ago they were. Anyway, this Tiny did have something to do with it but years ago, well before Leo got involved. He's quite a lot older, you know.'

To Lorenzini's relief the Marshal did at last turn from the window and take a good look at him.

'Why don't you sit down? You look worn out.'

'Thanks.' Lorenzini sank into the first chair he saw but the Marshal stayed on his feet, staring at the map of his

Quarter as if it might reveal to him of its own accord the spot where Leo and Tiny made whatever deal resulted in Tiny's prints on the shoes of Buongianni Corsi.

'What about this club where Leo works?'

'I went there last night. He's a bouncer and on the door most of the night—but not last night because of today's match. It's a private club, a sort of mini disco. Ghastly place, underground and painted grey and black. Suffocating. I looked at the list of members. Tiny's not on it. I showed the mugshot around as well in case the regulars had seen him there as a guest. Nothing. I stayed around till closing time. It seems hopeless. Tiny must start work at dawn when our friend Leo is snoring in bed.'

'Try bars—and restaurants, presumably they're both awake at supper-time. Maybe even that pizzeria opposite the palazzo. No, wait a minute. Go home and get some rest. Give me that.'

The Marshal took the mugshot, got into his jacket and slipped the picture into his top pocket. 'I'm going to the Ulderighi place. I'll make a start—What about his previous convictions? Have you—'

'I spent all this morning on it, but Leo's name never cropped up in any of the reports on Tiny—well, you did say it was unlikely . . .'

'All right, all right. If there was nothing, there was nothing.'

'I haven't even had lunch,' grumbled Lorenzini all but inaudibly. He might as well not have said it. The Marshal wasn't listening, nor was he displeased with Lorenzini's efforts. He was disturbed, and he couldn't have put a name to what was disturbing him if you'd paid him for it.

'Oof!' That was nothing more than an involuntary protest against the fierce blast of the sun as he came out on to the unprotected forecourt of the Pitti Palace. Heat was shimmering above all the parked cars and the Marshal, sheltered by hat and dark glasses, wondered at the temerity of the tourists who seemed to want to expose themselves to burns.

Disturbed. He had been from the start but then he'd put it down to being afraid for his own skin, or at least his job. It wasn't that now because, whatever happened, those prints of Tiny's were a justification for an inquiry. He wasn't harassing the Ulderighi family and he could even be protecting them. He didn't believe that but somebody else might.

'Excuse me . . . Excuse me . . .' Why the devil didn't people move? Standing there blocking the pavement that was anyway only wide enough for one. 'Excuse me . . .' He could do without arriving at the Ulderighi house with smears of ice-cream on the sleeve of his uniform.

It wasn't until he stopped under the scaffolding to ring the porter's bell that he remembered the match. All these people collecting on the pavements were there to get a good view of the procession. What was the matter with him? The kids had been on about the match all morning and all through lunch, still annoyed, of course, that they weren't allowed to go and would have to watch it on television. Teresa had, at some point during the meal, put an infuriated stop to the whole discussion and already he'd forgotten that the match existed. Asleep on his feet. His mother used to say it, his teachers often said it. Teresa, if she hadn't said it in front of the boys, had likely enough thought it, because he hadn't, as far as he could remember, contributed a word to the argument.

'Oh, it's you . . .' The porter's usual greeting, accompanied by the usual piano music.

The Marshal stepped inside without even answering. He was getting pretty sick of being treated like a door-to-door salesman. Once they were through the gates and within

range of the feeble light-bulb the Marshal pressed the
light-switch and thrust the photograph from his pocket at
the porter. 'Have you seen this man?'

'Seen him? How do you mean?'

'I mean what I say. Have you seen him? Has he been in
this building? Is he a friend of your son's?'

'I don't know who he is. All these questions.'

'That's one question I didn't ask you. I already know
who he is. I want to know if you've seen him.'

'Well, I haven't.'

'You might have to swear to that on oath.'

'What's that supposed to mean?'

The Marshal didn't answer but crossed the courtyard to
ring the bell of the music studio. The music didn't stop at
once but continued to the end of a phrase. The Marshal,
glancing behind him, saw that the porter had vanished into
his lair.

'Oh, it's you!'

Ah well, at least he said it pleasantly. He was as spruce
and shining as ever.

'Do come in. Is there any news?'

'Not really. I won't come in but I wanted to show you
this.'

'Heavens! What a monster! I tend to look like a wanted
criminal myself on my passport photographs but this must
be the real thing.'

'Yes. This is the real thing. Have you ever seen him
before?'

'What, in the flesh, you mean?'

'Yes. Hanging around this house, for instance, or with
the porter's son.'

'Absolutely not! Oh, I suppose he doesn't look quite as
bad as that in real life but I think he'd be fairly memorable
just the same, don't you?'

'Yes, I think he would. If you should see him, even hanging about in the street near here, would you get in touch with me?'

The Marshal offered him a card with his telephone number and tucked the photograph out of sight. 'I'll want to show this to the other tenants if they're about.'

'Well, Hugh might well be in but Flavia went away for the weekend, I think.'

'Yes, I think I heard her say she was going away. It's of no importance. I'll need to come back tomorrow, in any case, when the dancing school's open. I'm sorry to have disturbed your playing.'

'That's all right—oh, I knew there was something I wanted to tell you if you came back! It almost slipped my mind but, talking about disturbances, do you know that there was a noise the other night that sounded exactly like a shot? Woke the whole place up and gave yours truly *a fright*! Well, I mean, after what's happened . . . Still, I suppose it could have been anything and we're all present and correct. Wasn't it weird, though?'

'You needn't have worried. It was a firework.' The Marshal had no intention of saying who'd let it off but it did occur to him to say, 'I'm surprised you didn't tell me about this right away, given, as you say, what's happened.'

It wasn't an accusation. He said it very mildly.

'Well, I expect I would have if I'd seen you and you'd asked. I mean, one doesn't go rushing round to the carabinieri to say one's heard a noise, if you see what I mean.'

'Yes, of course.' The Marshal wasn't all that convinced of the logic of this statement but within a day or two he was to be convinced of its truth.

'Marshal . . . a word with you.'

Emilio had returned to his piano. This whispered appeal came from the other side of the courtyard where the lift had just descended. The Marshal peered across through the gloom and saw, standing by the lift doors with the keys in his hand, the family priest. The Marshal walked slowly across to him, the familiar disturbed feeling of foreboding coming to the surface once again.

'Good afternoon, Father.'

'Please . . .' He was being asked to step into the lift. 'It's rather urgent, would you mind . . .' The priest continued his 'rather urgent' whispering as the lift rose.

'I'm sorry,' the Marshal said, 'I didn't hear what you said.' The priest only came up to his shoulder. The hand that he laid on the Marshal's uniformed sleeve was plump and white as a baby's.

'It's all for the best, I do feel that or I wouldn't have dreamt . . . Here we are.'

They emerged on the floor where the concert had taken place.

'This way.' Plump as a waddling pigeon, he bustled along the darkly polished passage in front of the Marshal. The double doors to the two great drawing-rooms were closed on either side. They continued to the end and the priest opened a heavy brass-handled door. 'Just a moment . . .' He turned on a light. There was nothing beyond the door but a staircase, one flight of smooth stone steps leading up to another door like the first.

The Marshal wanted to ask where the devil he was being taken but he was distracted by the thought of somebody saying to him at some point, '*You never see him on the stairs.*' Who . . . He was getting short of breath, but so was the priest. He was slowing down a good bit. Thank goodness for that, anyway. They were steep, these stairs, and slippery and all you could hang on to was a worn and heavy rope looped through iron rings set into the wall. The Marshal's hands were big and he could only just manage a grip on such a rope. The little priest was using both hands. He paused at the top on the brass handle of the second door but didn't turn it.

'I just want to warn you that the minute I've shown you in I shall leave you. I feel it's better that you see him alone.' All this still in a whisper.

'What exactly—' began the Marshal.

'Shh! Now he's very distressed, so I do hope that once he's told you what he wants to tell you you'll leave. You'll find me here. You understand that all this is because there is a serious threat to his health. A very serious threat, otherwise . . . Do go in, do go in.'

And the Marshal found himself hustled through the door, which was shut on him. Behind it he heard the priest's shuffling steps go on upwards. For a moment he stood quite still wanting to be sure that the room was quite empty. It was. He knew by instinct where he was even before crossing the room to look down from the window. The diminished courtyard lay below him. He was in the tower, though not at the top of it. The piano music was still just audible. There was a good view of the entrance. He saw the porter come out and let someone through the gates. A woman. No one he recognized. Not that it was easy to recognize someone from above like that—he'd hardly have known who the porter was if he hadn't seen him come out of the lodge. But this woman had red hair so it wasn't anybody belonging to the house. She started up the staircase and disappeared from view.

'*You never see him on the stairs* . . .' He was pretty sure that Flavia Martelli had said that about somebody, but who and why he couldn't recall. These northerners talked so damn fast you couldn't keep up with all they were telling you. Well, sooner or later it would come to him. Difficult to work out whose flat was whose from here, but if Dr Martelli was away then that one was most likely hers with all the shutters closed. So next door on her . . . left, if he remembered rightly—yes, that was the painter's flat. Easy to see right into it. Surely there shouldn't be that much light in a room on the courtyard where even the midsummer sun didn't penetrate? Must be some special lighting. Probably he was painting. There he was. Waving some sort of coloured sheet about in the middle of the room. The Marshal heard a bell ring quite clearly. Amazing! It must have been the painter's bell because he dropped the sheet at once and went off. Of course, sound always travels upwards and in the enclosed space of the courtyard . . . His thoughts were interrupted by what happened next. He saw the red-haired woman come into the centre of the painter's room. Fido himself followed and encircled her from behind with his arms. Then he stood back. The red-haired woman took off her clothes quickly and lay down in full view of the window.

Once over the initial shock the Marshal began to reason that what the woman was doing was posing. He knew that sort of thing was done—but in full view of the window? With all that artificial lighting he could surely close the shutters. In full view . . . But it wasn't true, not the way he'd thought. The Marshal was looking round the other windows now and it wasn't true. The woman was arranged on some sort of low dais where Fido had thrown the coloured sheet. The flats were on the top floor of the building. The only window high enough to look down on the naked woman was this one.

A faint noise behind him made him jump and he turned away from the window as though he felt guilty. Neri Ulderighi stood facing him, his hands clasped tightly in front of him. He didn't approach the window but the involuntary glance over the Marshal's shoulder and the blush which darkened his face told everything. Almost everything.

'You were very kind to come and see me. Father Benigni said . . . Won't you sit down?' His voice was quiet, or weak, perhaps, as though he were unused to speaking to people. 'Will you sit here? Father Benigni always sits here. You see,

it's comfortable. My chair is close and we can talk.' Neri
had turned a faded round leather chair away from a table
in the corner so that it faced the Marshal. The Marshal,
again, was very conscious of Neri's size and bulk and the
awkwardness of how he held his head. He wasn't crying
now, though the Marshal had an idea that he might have
been not long before because his eyes seemed too bright
and his face was flushed. He had no idea what to say to
him. How could he have? He was a total stranger, an
enigma, and what, anyway, did he want? So the Marshal
said nothing and Neri fixed him with shiny beseeching eyes.

Don't take me back to that house . . .

They were Corsi's eyes, the eyes of the corpse he must
but couldn't abandon, and whatever Neri wanted to tell
him he knew from the sickly feeling of apprehension in the
pit of his stomach that he would be sorry to know it. If he
found words at last it was only to put off the evil moment.
He glanced past Neri to where the table behind him was
covered with tiny leather boxes. 'I heard you were a col-
lector.'

It was as easy as distracting a small child. The anguished
eyes filled with pleasure.

'Oh yes, indeed. It takes up almost all my time. Do you
know much about antique coins and medals?'

'Nothing at all, I'm afraid.'

'Oh dear. But then, why should you . . . You must have
a great deal of work to do and then . . . Father Benigni very
wisely told me that it would be wrong to take up too much
of your time unnecessarily. Father Benigni is always very
thoughtful of the needs and problems of others. He's always
tried to teach me to be like him, but I'm afraid I'm a bad
pupil.'

'You have problems of your own, I imagine. I understand
that your health—'

'Oh yes, yes, certainly, but God never gives us greater

suffering than we can bear. I do believe that's true, don't you?'

'I don't know. Perhaps.'

'Oh, I'm sure of it. Besides which, you know, everyone else has problems, too. I have bad health but I also have a great many expert doctors looking after me. I often think of all the sick people in the world who have no one, no means . . . you understand?'

The Marshal could only gaze at him, perplexed. This strange overgrown child had no guile in him, no hypocrisy, no arrogance. How, in heaven's name had the Marchesa Ulderighi produced such an innocent soul? Was he a throwback to some distant ancestor—the visionary in the fresco?

'I would have liked to show you my collection but Father Benigni . . . it's lonely, you see, sometimes.'

'You never go out?'

'Go out?' The idea seemed to take him aback. 'I—my mother takes me to the country in the summer. The heat here is bad for me, they say. But here I very rarely go out. There's so much noise, the traffic and so on, that for someone with delicate nerves it can be a problem. But people are very kind—for instance, the dealer who sells me most of my coins quite often brings things to show me and I think that's so thoughtful of him since it's out of working hours, don't you?'

The Marshal thought it was very enterprising of him and no doubt very profitable, but he kept his opinion to himself.

'Is it a family collection you're adding to or did you begin it?' The things he would really like to ask Neri! Here he was asking inane questions about a coin collection because he had been summoned to appear before this young man and the shadow of the chief public prosecutor lay over them.

'It was begun by my great-grandfather. The family did have one or two quite important things before then but they were just there, if you understand me. It wasn't in any conscious way a collection.'

'I see.'

'One or two things were sold ... unfortunately ... because ... well, now they're in the Bargello Museum. That's a very fine collection, very fine, so ... Ah, tea.'

'I beg your pardon?'

Neri's more accustomed ear had caught a noise which meant nothing to the Marshal until a concealed service door as in the rooms on the courtyard opened to reveal Grillo struggling with a tray.

'Oh, it's you, is it? Tea for two. Little party.' He banged the tray down on a small marble table and shook his fist at Neri. 'Eat something!'

'I'll try ...'

'You'll do better than that or I'll want to know why. I haven't climbed three hundred stairs with that lot for nothing, or have I?'

He was slapping cups and plates to right and left, hopping from one foot to the other as he did so. It was impossible to know whether he were truly angry or acting. Neri seemed to take him very seriously and to accept his rudeness as normal.

'The steps are hard for you, I know.'

'Ha!' He did a little grotesque dance. 'The Marshal doesn't think so. The Marshal probably thinks I should be in a circus.'

'I ...'

'Now the truth is—' he pawed Neri's big shoulder and wagged his other hand towards his face—'if I had your legs and you had my energy there'd be a normal human being there somewhere.'

'It's true.' Neri seemed delighted. 'But what about brains, Grillo, who's got the brains?'

'You have. But I've got my wits and that's another matter. If you had your wits about you, you wouldn't be entertaining this fellow.'

The smile faded from Neri's face. 'Leave us alone now.'

'I'll leave you alone!' He scuttled back to the hidden door. 'On your own is what you'll be but never left in peace!'

He was gone. The Marshal stared with his big eyes at Neri, longing to ask something, anything, that would elicit an explanation of their relationship which was a mystery to him. He didn't, of course, ask anything, but Neri was quick to understand his look.

'You mustn't mind him. I'm afraid he must have given you a difficult time if you've had to question him.'

'He was a bit strange.'

'But you didn't feel sorry for him?'

'Sorry for him? I—maybe I should have in all conscience but I must confess he got on my nerves so much that—'

'That's why he does it, you see. I have a great deal of time to think about things, and so . . . Grillo has looked after me all my life. Even when I was so small that I had a nanny he was always there, rather like a guard dog. Nanny, who was English and never did manage to follow a thick Tuscan accent, hated him. He tormented the life out of her and she would end up by chasing him, but he could always outrun her and it delighted me. I think now that he did it partly to amuse me because I was so often sick. I think I can honestly say, Marshal, that I have never laughed in my life except at his instigation. I'm grateful to him for it.'

'I can understand that.'

'Can you?' Neri looked at him hard, as though it mattered a great deal to him that the Marshal should understand. 'Yes. Yes, you look like a man who understands things. At the funeral . . . But we were talking of Grillo. The fact is, you see, that someone as small as he is, the

height, say, of a child of eight, is automatically treated
like a child of eight. It's a natural reaction and there's no
unkindness meant, but how would you feel if you were
habitually treated like an eight-year-old?'

'I see what you mean.'

'You wouldn't be wearing that uniform for a start. The
job you did would be entirely conditioned by your height.
You'd be ignored a lot. People would talk over your head,
literally and metaphorically, and if they noticed you at all
it would be to feel sorry for you. Now, you may find Grillo's
behaviour strange, as you say, and unpleasant, disconcerting. Even so, I rather imagine that you haven't treated
him like an eight-year-old and that you haven't tried to
talk over his head. You've felt angry with him, perhaps,
irritated, but you haven't felt sorry for him.'

'That's right. That's very true, I hadn't thought.'

You never see him on the stairs.

That's who it was, of course. Grillo. The tenants were
convinced that he spied on them, that he knew everything
that went on on every floor, though no one ever saw him
on the stairs. They were almost certainly right. He had his
own stairs, and the service doors, to the studios for example,
might be locked but they were flimsy and good for listening
in. At this thought the Marshal's heart began beating faster
and his face felt hot. How much had been said between
himself and William Yorke that time when the dwarf had
been lurking? He couldn't even remember. Whatever he'd
said had been enough to precipitate the release of the body,
the funeral . . . they had certainly talked about the porter's
son, but had he mentioned his intention to pick up Corsi's
clothing? He couldn't remember—of course, that would
have got back in some way whether the dwarf . . .

'Is something wrong? You don't look well? Some tea?'

The Marshal took it and held it without registering what
it was. The dwarf was probably out there now! And where

had that priest gone? How many of the Ulderighi family knew he was here and why? He didn't know himself why but he was being watched, invisibly from all over the building.

Don't take me back to that house!

'You're distressed. You're angry with me perhaps for taking up so much of your time. Father Benigni—'

'No, no. I was thinking . . . I was thinking about your father, to tell you the truth.'

'Of course, yes.' Neri's head began to make tiny agitated movements. 'I am wasting your time and we should be talking about my father. My father . . . I *will* tell you everything. You understand that it's not easy for me. You see, it's so often difficult to confess not the serious things one has done but the petty things, the shameful, squalid little things. It isn't just me, you see. I know very little of the world, but Father Benigni assures me that a man would often find it easier to confess to a murder, say, than to some little socially unacceptable . . . than to . . .'

His breath seemed to fail him and the Marshal, alarmed by not knowing in what his illness or weakness consisted and distressed by his suffering, reached a fatherly hand to touch his shoulder.

'Steady, now. You don't have to confess anything to me. I'm not a priest, remember.'

'But you're something very like a priest in the sense that you are familiar with things that . . . you are used to things and can understand. Besides, Father Benigni agreed that it was right to tell you. He's worried about my health, I know that because my—nevertheless, it's the right thing to do and would be so even were I in perfect health. You've been making an inquiry, they told me that, and you see, you're wasting your time because I know. I know everything, so it's only right. I've been weak and cowardly but there were other reasons, other people—I don't want you to think too badly of me. It matters to me quite a lot and yet I don't

know you. Isn't that strange? I've watched you very often.
You walk very slowly and sometimes you stop and stand
quite still for a moment as though you were saying something to yourself. Then you go on. You've often seemed so
troubled. You may think it strange, but though I can't see
people's faces from up here I can often judge their mood.
For instance, I can tell by the way he opens the gate when
Mori the porter has been quarrelling with his wife . . .'

'I imagine that happens fairly often.' A silly enough
remark, and the Marshal knew he was only trying to delay
what he didn't want to hear without having the remotest
idea of what that was.

'They do quarrel a lot.'

'And when you're not observing the people in the courtyard or arranging your coin collection, you play music.'

'Yes. You knew that? I play the flute. I've studied very
little because it was felt that sustained study would be too
much wear on the nerves. But I do play. I often wish . . .'

What he wished for he didn't say. The Marshal imagined
that there must be a lot to wish for in his life. Why should
he feel for him, though, in just the same way he'd felt for
the dead father—or the dream version of the dead father?
As if he were the only one to care? Surely this young man
was surrounded by care and attention? With a bluntness
that he couldn't help though it sounded so unkind, the
Marshal said, 'Why me? I understand the chief public prosecutor is a good friend of the family. I'd have thought you'd
tell him anything you had to tell.' Was he just being used
again? Was this a trap to make him somehow compromise
himself, the reprimand and the sudden transfer waiting
round the corner.

'Gianpiero . . . Yes, but I couldn't. You're right, of
course, he's a very dear friend of my—of ours, but that's
just why I couldn't tell him—I mean about her, not about
my father—and it would be even worse to have to admit

that I . . . that I . . . It's you I want to tell. It's not easy for me to explain, but I have so much time to watch people, to know them. I've been watching you ever since it happened and at the funeral I became quite sure that you were the one person to whom I could unburden myself.'

The Marshal could well believe it. Story of his life. Other people's problems, other people's guilt, other people's burdens and even their neglected dead. And because he knew that this was what his job was about he didn't protest.

'Tell me whatever you want to tell me if you think it will make you feel better.' And since he had already understood the 'shameful, squalid little thing' that blocked his recounting of the more important one, he helped him.

'You know, I first heard about you and your coin collection from William Yorke. His sister seems to be very fond of you. She told him how you sat for hours together sorting your collection at your desk by this window.' He got up as he said this and went and stood with his back to the window in the space where the desk must once have stood.

'I was looking down myself when I was waiting for you just now. Gave me a bit of a shock. Must have been a trial to you. I mean, after all, we're only human.'

It was a bull's eye all right, but what the relevance of it was to anything remained to be seen.

'I moved my desk.' His face was deep red and lowered towards his tightly clasped hands. His body rocked slightly like an old woman saying her rosary. 'I moved it as soon as I'd confessed to Father Benigni.'

'I see.' But the Marshal also saw from his unshriven face that he had gone on looking after that. 'And what did Father Benigni advise?'

'Oh, he was very kind. He explained that it was only a venial sin, that in a sense I was a special case because, you see, if I'd been well enough my mother would have had me marry before now. You do understand?'

'Yes . . . yes, I do.' *He needs to get married.* Lorenzini's voice but the Grillo's words. 'I understand perfectly.'

'But you realize that it's not just . . . he doesn't just paint them, that he . . .'

Only then did the Marshal think of the portrait of Bianca Ulderighi and remember that where the other tenants called her the Marchesa, or even That Bloody Woman, Hugh Fido . . .

'He was tormenting me, you see. Look for yourself. You can only see from here, only from my window. It was aimed at me all along, although at first I didn't understand that. I only realized it one day when he was arranging a model and he made her lie facing the window, he made her . . . And then he came right to the window himself and looked up. He looked straight up at me. And, God forgive me, God forgive me, even then I went on watching, I couldn't help it! I was shamed to the depths of my soul and I went on looking. I couldn't stop myself. Who else could have helped me except Father Benigni!'

'Calm yourself now. Steady.' The Marshal went back to him and put a hand on his shoulder. 'You trust Father Benigni, don't you?'

'Yes, I do, absolutely.'

'Then remember what he told you. It was only a venial sin.'

'I do trust him . . . But such a terrible chain of events! How could it be that such a small guilt should become so great? I'm sorry. I must keep calm and not waste your time and tell you all the truth that I'm sure of.'

The Marshal could just hear the little priest saying it and he didn't much care for that 'all the truth that I'm sure of' but he made no comment.

Neri's hands were clasped now as though he were praying inside himself as he spoke, which may well have been the case.

'I confessed. I confessed but didn't repent. I moved my desk as I'd promised. Miss Yorke came up that very day, I remember . . . She used to say I should call her Catherine and she was always very kindly, very gentle. She asked me why—why I'd moved my desk to where I wouldn't be able to see properly. That's how kind she was, that she thought of my eyes. They're not very strong. She brought me a box she'd found, a document box which had three coins in it under all the papers. They weren't terribly valuable but she thought of me, and she thought of my eyes, and I didn't know how to answer when she asked me why. She's so far removed from anything like that. I always think she's like an angel from a fresco, don't you agree?'

'I haven't met her yet.'

'Or perhaps from even longer ago . . . "A jar of wine from the Alban hills, more than nine years old . . . *est in horto, Phylli, nectendis apium coronis; est hederæ vis multa, qua crines religata fulges.*" Such long hair, of the same clear gold as the Alban wine . . . "and in my garden there is parsley, Phyllis, to plait a wreath for you; with trails of ivy I will bind your shining hair . . ." Such beautiful hair, like spun gold . . . "with trails of ivy I will bind your shining hair." . . . I wish I could have studied more but my eyes, you see—and she thought of that, so kind—' He broke off abruptly, as though remembering something, a painful memory that flooded his mind and set his hands, which had reposed a moment at the thought of Catherine Yorke, clutching again at each other for comfort.

'Father Benigni said . . .'

The Marshal, for the moment, made no attempt to keep him to the point, if there really was a point to all this. He contented himself with sitting down again and observing Neri Ulderighi, perhaps the most extraordinary person he had ever come across. His body was so decadent, oversized, puffy, the head too heavy for the sloping shoulders, the hair and skin that of an old man. Years of inbreeding had produced his body and its weak but desperate urge to reproduce itself. And out of all this shone a soul purer than a child's—or it would have been had the priests not got at it and burdened it with guilt.

'Father Benigni, you see, is concerned for my health as well as my soul. He's cared for me all my life. I had to tell him that even after my confession I'd gone on . . . gone on—but I was punished, terribly punished—' He was crying as he had at the funeral, his head lolling and then jerking upright.

'Your mother?' asked the Marshal very gently.

The head was stilled. 'You know?'

'I guessed. The portrait and one or two other things suggested . . . an intimacy.'

'You understand that I didn't know what to do?'

'Why should you have done anything? It must have been upsetting for you to think that your own mother—'

'Not to think, Marshal, to see. To see. It was a punishment in itself but I had to confess my own wrongdoing, you must see that. I didn't intend to say more. I swear to you I had no thought of mentioning my—of who was concerned. It's true, you know, what Father Benigni said. It's only our own sins we have to confess. The sacrament doesn't require us to recount the sins of others, and though I hadn't thought of that for myself—I was too upset to think clearly—I nevertheless only intended to confess my own sin. You do believe me?'

'Of course.'

'Of all things you must believe that. But I was very distraught, I think almost hysterical, and somehow it just came out.'

'I see.' The Marshal decided to take over in the hope of avoiding any hysteria now. 'And Father Benigni told your father, is that it?'

'Oh no, not—the secret of the confessional, you see, meant that he—'

'You're not telling me he forced you to do it!' But he had, of course, wasn't that what he'd just done now?

I feel it's better that you see him alone.

'Forced? Oh no, what a shocking thing to think. I know it was the right thing—but he killed himself! He killed himself and I'm to blame with my filthy uncontrollable habit. I killed him!' He started to scream.

8

'And you believe him?' Lorenzini looked almost disappointed.

'Yes.'

How could he not believe him? With a character like his it was impossible not to believe, even without supporting evidence, and there had been plenty of supporting evidence. The Marshal had been doing his job long enough to know that to get the right answers you had to ask the right people the right questions. The right answers were now in his notebook.

It must have been about three in the morning, though I didn't think to look at the clock.

Just one shot—at least I only heard one.

I'll show you. You see? Of course, he'd shot himself by then—I only came out on the balcony when I heard the noise. I'd say that to be hanging over the edge like that he must have intended to fall but he didn't.

We saw it in the paper afterwards. Said it was an accident—of course a family like that wouldn't want it known, it's only natural.

How do you mean, come forward? Nobody asked me. I didn't even know you were making inquiries. Cut and dried, I would have thought.

And even before visiting these people on the top floors of the surrounding buildings the Marshal had followed Grillo up the stone staircase to the top of Neri's tower and looked down. The stones he held as he leaned over had been washed clean, but below him the trail of darkened blood was out of reach. There was no doubt in the Marshal's mind that Corsi had intended to fall, to escape from that house at the last, but he hadn't succeeded.

And all the way down the winding narrow stair the dwarf rattled on and on.

'Heard the one about the chap throws himself off a tower and changes his mind half way down? *Save me! St Anthony, save me!* And a great big hand comes out of the sky and grabs him! Then a voice says, *By the way, which St Anthony were you wanting?* Well, you know how many St Anthony's there are in Italy, so the chap casts about in his mind and comes up with *St Anthony of Paduaaaaaaaaaaagh!*'

The courtyard, for once, had been empty of music. Somewhere outside a fading tattoo of drums marked the retreat of the procession after the tournament. The great doors opened a crack and boomed shut again as the Marshal reached the inner gates. The last thing he saw before escaping was Leo, huge, bull-necked, in purple and white slashed breeches with the tattered remains of a white T-shirt hanging from his scratched and bleeding torso.

'At least, by then, Neri had stopped screaming.'

'Didn't that happen before? I mean, didn't he start screaming like that when that English boy let the firework off?'

'Perhaps it happens all the time.' The Marshal was silent a moment, thinking. Then he said, 'It must happen fairly regularly because they knew just what to do. The Marchesa appeared out of nowhere, as you'd expect, and the dwarf too. Neither of them was surprised and he was given an injection—something intra-muscular, the sort we all do at home but it was the dwarf who had to do it. I've an idea he can't stand his mother being near him. He never mentioned her directly when we were talking, he avoided it, I think.'

'I imagine he blames her for what happened, too.' Lorenzini was still disappointed at its turning out a suicide after the excitement of Tiny's prints.

'You could be right,' the Marshal said, but he didn't sound convinced. Doctors had been sent for then, and the Marchesa had taken the Marshal away to her private drawing-room. There he had sat, discomfited by the comfort of a big velvet armchair, facing the double portraits of Lucrezia and Francesco. He wondered where Fido's portrait of Bianca Ulderighi was but didn't ask. He didn't ask anything, only sat there with his hat on his knees, watching with bulging expressionless eyes. Watching rather than listening. He was a little less frightened of her now but even so, her beauty distressed him. Someone so fine and graceful and with such deeply luminous eyes should have a soul to match. It confused you. The Marshal knew in his heart that this woman was probably ruthless and certainly immoral but the message received by his senses contradicted this just as Neri's ugly decadence had hidden his delicacy of mind and heart. Was it just this generation or had it happened over the centuries that beauty had gone one way and virtue the other?

The faces in the two paintings looked out at him with more life and expression than his own. Francesco, dressed in his wedding clothes, white embroidered with gold flowers, fresh flowers crowning his golden hair. Maybe he was the last of the Ulderighi to have a soul that matched his beauty and he had ended, thrown from his horse against the stone portal of the great doors. Lucrezia gazed out at the Marshal, the same face, he was sure now, that had looked up from her rosary in the fresco. The same face, too, that was inclined towards him now in an imitation of intimacy.

'You can understand, I think, that the natural wish to avoid scandal and disgrace for my unfortunate husband was quite overridden by the danger to my son's health. He is the only heir.'

What did she expect him to say to her? He stared back at her in silence and he didn't care a damn that she must have thought him as dumb as an ox. He'd never made any claim to be bright. She had offered him refreshment which he had refused. She had not been so indelicate as to ask him directly to keep what he had heard to himself.

'But then,' he said to Lorenzini, 'she didn't need to. Who would I tell at this point?'

'But did she offer any explanation?'

'She told me they'd quarrelled, which I knew. Corsi apparently went down and got a rifle.'

And brought it all the way up again instead of shooting himself down in the gun room?

His intention, Marshal, was to shoot me.

'That was when Neri appeared, woken by the noise. He said his father was screaming abuse and was in fact pointing the gun at his mother. Perhaps it was Neri's arrival that changed everything. Corsi pushed past him on to the tower staircase. Neri followed. He saw his father shoot himself.'

'And you're convinced he's telling the truth.'

'He is telling the truth.'

'And everything the Marchesa says corroborates it.'

'Mmph.'

'You don't agree?'

'Oh, you're probably right, only . . .' The Marshal wasn't so good at expressing himself. He hadn't listened to much of what the Marchesa had told him, he'd only watched her. 'I believe him,' he said at last, 'but I don't believe her.'

And no amount of Florentine logic on Lorenzini's part would shake him. In the end the Marshal felt a bit guilty. It was Sunday night and he had dragged Lorenzini away from his wife and baby because he needed someone to tell all this to. And there Lorenzini sat, looking absurdly young in jeans and T-shirt, his face earnest, trying to understand and failing.

'I shouldn't have dragged you out like this. Go home.'

When he'd gone the Marshal sat alone for five minutes or so before getting up from his desk rather stiffly and switching off the lights.

At about one-thirty in the morning he said to his sleeping wife as though they were in the middle of a long conversation—as indeed they were in his own head—'It's true, though, isn't it, that when you go to confession you're only obliged to confess your own sins? Teresa, are you listening?'

'What?' She turned towards him half awake and then opened her eyes wide. 'What's the matter, you're not ill?'

'No, of course not. I was just wondering. I'd never really thought. You only confess your own sins, so even if you know something terrible that ought to be brought to light . . .'

'You'd tell the carabinieri. For God's sake, Salva . . .' She turned her back on him and pulled the sheet round her shoulders with a wrench. 'I wish you'd get to sleep at night, you might be a bit less dozy in the daytime.

'*Grand plié!*' Two heavy thumps on the floor. 'In first two *demi plié*, one grand *plié*, *cambré* forward, in second *cambré* backward, in fourth *cambré* towards the *barre*, in fifth two *grands pliés* and *grand port de bras*, *soussus* and turn.'

The stick thumped again before the music began and the Marshal turned away, intimidated, to listen to another door. The one on his right was closed but the chatter and laughter coming from behind it suggested that there, at least, he wouldn't be interrupting a lesson. He walked straight in and stopped. Twenty or so tiny girls were in various stages of undress, many of them standing on the large table which almost filled the room, hopping and chattering as their mothers pulled pink tights off them, or inexpertly wriggling out of leotards by themselves. To the Marshal they looked hardly big enough to be walking, let alone dancing. He was relieved to see one or two fathers in the fray struggling with all those pink ribbons and frills and it was to one of these that he called over the general racket, 'Where can I find the directress?'

'I think she's—sit down—I said sit down! Here on the edge of the table or you'll rip your tights—sit *still*! I think she's teaching the class in the centre studio, either that or— Come back!' And he was off in pursuit of his little imp, as pink without her satin outfit as she had been in it, scrambling away across the table towards a giggling friend who was trying to do a handstand wearing nothing but pink tights. The Marshal retreated and closed the door on this mini-inferno. Just as well, he thought, that they'd only had boys. He couldn't see himself being able to cope with that.

Intimidated as he was, it was lucky for him that a young woman opened a door further along the passage and looked out, calling 'Are we all here?' She saw the Marshal blocking the passage with his black bulk and looked at him kindly. He hurried towards her and she smiled.

'If your little girl's in the first course they're already out. She'll be in the changing-room. It's Lucilla's father, isn't it?'

'No, I . . . I'm not anybody's father, mine are boys, you see . . . No, I want a word with you about something rather important. I'm sorry if I'm interrupting you.'

'Ah! It's not about . . .' She glanced upward, there was no need to say more.

'Yes.'

'Then of course, but you must come in because I can't leave the children to their own devices, you can imagine.'

After the scene in the changing-room the Marshal could indeed imagine and he followed her inside. Another giggling troupe of fairies, this time in pale turquoise. The young woman, with a dispatch and authority such as he'd rarely come across in the army, had them lined up at the barre, feet turned out, eyes to centre and dead silent within the space of three seconds, and with the simple order 'Warming up exercises!' she switched on a tape of music and was at the Marshal's disposition.

'I saw that they kept it out of the papers, I mean that it was a suicide—not that you could blame anyone for that but I've no time for the woman, myself.'

'The Marchesa?'

'Better keep your voice down. The little Corsi child is in this class—Children! straighten those knees in *relevé*. Fiorenza! hold your head higher and keep it still, that's it, that's better.' She lowered her voice. 'Fiorenza Corsi. Rumour has it that if anything happened to Neri Ulderighi she'd inherit and I think it's probably true. She's named after her aunt, Fiorenza Ulderighi, great-aunt she must be, and goes up to see her after every lesson here. I sometimes think that's the only reason we're still here. We're being evicted, you see. She was glad enough to rent the place when she needed money in a hurry but now some fancy firm wanting a fancy address has offered five times the rent we can afford, so . . .'

'I see. Well, things are different now, of course, as she'll inherit Corsi's fortune.'

'Mm. I don't think that helps us. She's never wanted tenants, so if she can afford to restore without letting we'll all be on the street—I must stop the tape, just a moment.'

She ran swiftly across the room as the exercise came to an end and stopped the music.

'And turn! First position heads high! Let me see you grow! Good. Preparation one two three four *plié* . . .'

The Marshal watched them, less frightened of them now they were under control. Tiny plaits and buns beribboned, delicate hands and feet moving in unison . . . it might be nice, after all, to be Lucilla's father.

The young woman came tripping back to him in her coloured tights and tunic. Her hair was tied back with some sort of scarf of the same colour and the Marshal realized as he looked at her that hers was the first really cheerful face he had come across in that building. She smiled at him.

'I can't leave them more than a minute, you know, so . . .'

'Of course.' He pulled out Tiny's mugshot. 'I'm trying to find out whether this man's been seen in or around the building, and in particular, if he's been seen with the porter's son who lives downstairs.'

She looked hard at the photograph, fascinated. 'I've never seen one of these before. Is he a criminal?'

'A criminal, yes.'

'I've certainly never seen him around here—I mean, my goodness, you wouldn't forget a face like that, it's terrifying—you surely don't want to show it to the children? I really don't think you should. Besides, they're much too young to be reliable, so it's really not worth frightening them—and their parents! If they hear about this they won't send their children! Oh, I really don't think . . .'

'No, no, as you say, they're too young. Don't worry. Perhaps the older students I've seen around?'

'Yes, of course. The best thing would be to go next door. My sister teaches the intermediate class. They're eighteen and nineteen years old so that would be all right. But . . . excuse my asking, but if he committed suicide, then what—'

'It's a bit complicated. Nothing to worry about.'

'Well, if you say so, but I don't like the thought of a character like that hanging around here—No, don't go out again. There's no need. Use the connecting door.'

She pointed the way through and then clapped her hands.

'Children! *Grand plié!*'

The Marshal began to tiptoe across the big room as the tiny creatures dipped and stretched, their faces registering a solemnity matched only by his own. His efforts to get out quietly ended in his putting his large foot into a wooden tray parked near the door and upsetting its contents. A peal of childish laughter rang out over the music. The Marshal grabbed for the door and propelled himself through it, then drew in a frightened gasp of breath as a man's figure came flying through the air in a diagonal leap across the room and landed an inch short of him with an impressive emergency stop.

'Bravo!' A burst of applause and the young dancer grinned at the Marshal, then turned and bowed to his fellow students.

'I beg your pardon. They said I could . . . I beg your pardon.' The Marshal's face was red with embarrassment and he stood where he was, in the corner by the door, afraid to move another step. A tall, white-faced woman in black strode towards him. She was carrying a long white cane and the Marshal was relieved to see that her face, though stern, looked amused. The eyes, large and black, were laughing at him.

'You'd be safer behind the piano.' She pointed her stick and raised her left arm. The Marshal, submitting, was marshalled.

'Two minutes!'

The dancers, dressed in layer upon layer of ragged and complicated bits of clothing, flopped to the floor in alarmingly dislocated attitudes.

'What can I do for you?'

The distracted Marshal came to attention and produced his photograph. Nothing. Not only did no one recognize him but he was quite sure that, as he left the room, he heard one of the youngsters say, 'They beat them up when they arrest them, that's why they look so awful.'

Put out by failure and that last remark, the Marshal was back down in the courtyard before he remembered that he should have gone on up rather than coming down. He didn't know for sure whether that was just a mistake or his reluctance for the next interview. He was reluctant all right, there was no doubt about that. He could have done without seeing anybody by the name of Ulderighi for the rest of his life. Nor was he used to being summoned like a servant. He stood there for a moment in the shadows of the courtyard, trying to settle his nerves.

You walk very slowly and sometimes you stop and stand quite still for a moment as though you were saying something to yourself. Then you go on. You've often seemed so troubled.

Well, he was troubled, right enough, and not least by the idea that within these walls he was always observed. Troubled too by a sense of dread that had never left him since the first time he'd entered this courtyard. He glanced up at Neri's tower. He could make out nothing but that didn't mean he wasn't being watched. He walked to the well and back, trying to reason with himself. An old place like this one—not to mention his having heard such gruesome stories connected with it, would give anyone the creeps. It gave the young Englishman, William, the creeps and he hadn't hesitated to say so. Well, then. That was all there was to that. And as for being summoned by the Ulderighi, wasn't he summoned, and peremptorily at that, by the humblest people of his Quarter? He never minded it. He had endless patience for them, so why not for the Ulderighi, who, Lord knew, had troubles enough to warrant a bit of patience. The father dead by his own hand, the son sickly. No amount of money would make up for that. With an effort at calm and determination he took Fiorenza Ulderighi's letter from his pocket and checked the time of the appointment against his watch. It was early yet. The letter had arrived that morning but not in the post. It had been delivered by hand and unsealed and received by one of the Marshal's men. Delivered by Grillo. Half an hour to kill. He thought of a coffee or something at the pizzeria across the road but he didn't fancy it somehow. Chap there always gave him funny looks for no reason he could think of. On impulse, he crossed the courtyard and rang William Yorke's bell. Having rung it, he realized that the excuse of showing him Tiny's photo wouldn't be very convincing since William had arrived after Corsi's death. Then it occurred to him that the sister should be back by now. That was good enough. He rang again and listened. The door didn't open but he was convinced that someone was in there. The one-roomed flat was so tiny that, despite the thick door, you could practically sense someone breathing. Then he was sure he heard a small movement. He rang again at length. Another movement, and a voice asked, 'Who's there?'

'Guarnaccia. Marshal Guarnaccia.' He listened. It had been William's voice but muffled, blurred.

The door opened a crack. William's face was flushed and sweaty, his hair untidy.

'You were resting. I'm sorry.'

William took an unsteady step backwards and opened up sufficiently for the Marshal to enter. As he did so he passed close enough to William's face to understand that it was flushed not with sleep but with wine, and he remembered the story of the firework. That too had been when he'd had too much to drink. However, it was one thing for someone to say they'd been drunk and another to see it. William was always so spruce, so quick on his feet and sharp with his tongue. This seemed like a different person and the Marshal's only thought was to retreat.

'I won't disturb you. I'm sure you need to rest when you have to work in the evening.'

'I'm not resting and I'm not working—ha . . . good one, that, for an actor, not resting not working . . . If you want a drink I might as well tell you there's none left.'

'No, no. I just called to ask if your sister was back but I see she's not so I'll leave you.'

'Thursday . . .' He mumbled so the Marshal wasn't sure he'd heard right.

'Thursday?'

'Three days to get over it. She didn't come last night so it'll be Thursday. Three days to get over it. If anybody asks for me just say I'm asleep, will you?'

'Yes. Of course.'

'Thanks. Thanks a lot.' He sat down heavily on the narrow divan, took off one of his shoes very carefully and then lay down. Almost at once he began to snore. The Marshal withdrew.

'I suppose you want to know what I'm going to be when I grow up.' The diminutive Fiorenza threw herself into the opposite corner of the long sofa from the Marshal and began stretching out one leg and pointing the foot as though she were still at her ballet lesson.

'And why do you suppose that?' he asked her, sure that, whether he asked or not, he was going to be told. He was right.

'Because it's what all grown-ups ask. Anyway, I'm going to be a ballet dancer and a veterinary surgeon.' The right leg went down and the left shot up to point at the air.

'That's a lot of work,' the Marshal said.

'I don't mind. I shall like it. And I'm going to have a lot of children, eight or nine. How many children have you got?'

'Two.'

'That's not so many. Why do you have your hat on your knees?'

'Because it's not polite to keep it on in someone's house.'

'You could hang it up,' she suggested. Then, after a covert glance at the flame above the peak, she lost interest in his headgear. She glanced over the back of the sofa at an enormous gilded clock with figures supporting it which stood on a long oak table.

'Aunt Fiorenza never comes out of her room until five o'clock exactly. She puts her hair up first and she puts nail varnish on her nails only you can hardly see it because it's not a proper colour. If I were allowed to put nail varnish on I'd choose bright pink or red. That would be much better, wouldn't it?'

'I expect so.'

'But nobody lets me. Aunt Fiorenza won't even let me go in her bedroom and watch. She says "One doesn't" and that's that. She always gives me cake, though.'

'Well, that's nice.'

'First I do my homework and then when she comes out of her room she rings the bell and we have tea and cake.'

'You're not doing your homework today.'

'That's because I'm talking to you. I've got Italian *and* maths to do. You can't do sums, can you?'

'Not very well.' His efforts on behalf of the boys had usually got them into trouble.

'I can't either.' She stretched out both legs now until she was almost lying down. 'Next year when I'm in the third course we'll be doing toe dancing. I want to buy the shoes now but I'm not allowed to because I might hurt myself.'

'Well, I suppose that's sensible. You wouldn't want to hurt yourself.'

'I don't care. I wish I could have them now. You can break your foot or your knee. A girl called Francesca in the intermediate course broke *her* knee. It popped out.'

'Did it?' The Marshal frowned at this painful thought.

'Right out. She was doing a pirouette and she didn't keep her knee straight. You have to keep it straight, and she went over sideways and her knee popped out and she pushed it back herself but she still had to go to hospital. I can do pirouettes. D'you want me to do one for you while you're waiting?'

'No! I—no.' A glance at the slippery marble floor and the thought of knees popping out horrified him. 'I think we should just sit quietly. It's almost five.'

Fiorenza seemed to find this reasonable and went back to contemplating her pointed toes. The Marshal contemplated her. She seemed so tiny and delicate—but then, he wasn't used to little girls. Her fair hair was plaited and wound around the top of her head and a scrap of turquoise ribbon hung from its centre. Her eyes were hazel and there was a faint dusting of freckles across the nose.

'I don't look like anybody, do I?' She suddenly interrupted his thoughts as though he'd spoken them aloud.

'How do you mean?'

'It's what everybody says in this house. Really I look like my mummy, but that doesn't count because she isn't anybody, not like they mean. Aunt Fiorenza would like it if I looked like Cousin Neri. Ugh!'

'You don't like your cousin?'

'No. I don't know him. I was brought to see him once because he was dying, only then he didn't die. He was in bed all the time and he had no toys or books or anything. I told Uncle Buongianni. *I* always get a colouring book and a comic when I have to stay in bed. Now Uncle Buongianni's dead and I saw Cousin Neri at the funeral and his head was all fat and I didn't like him.'

She fell silent for a moment and then, sensitive enough to realize she might have offended him, she gave a sidelong glance at his portly figure and the big hands clutching the hat and said, 'Some people are quite fat but it's nice.'

'Ah.'

'Like Father Christmas.'

'That's right.' He was grateful for the compliment. Coming from such a source, it relieved his feelings of clumsiness for the first time he could remember. 'Do you know a little girl called Lucilla?'

'She's only in the first course—oh, I know why! Her daddy's a carabiniere so you know him.'

'No, no, I don't. I'd just heard . . .'

'Fiorenza!'

The child slithered herself upright and the Marshal got to his feet. Great-Aunt Fiorenza, as formidable an old lady as the Marshal had ever set eyes on, was standing in the doorway leaning heavily on a stick. Her legs and feet were so swollen as to seem boneless and the fine shoes she wore must have been specially made to accommodate this affliction.

'You can have tea in the kitchen with Matthilde.'

The child, released, scampered towards the door. An icy glance from the old woman pulled her up short and she came back to the Marshal and offered him her hand.

'It was a pleasure to meet you.'

'A pleasure to meet you too. Enjoy your cake.' He let go of the tiny hand and, after a tentative glance at her great-aunt, she remembered to walk not run out of the room.

'Please sit down, Marshal.'

Great-Aunt Fiorenza herself sat opposite him on a huge straight-backed chair. It looked extremely uncomfortable to the Marshal but he knew it was probably the only sort of chair she would be able to rise from with relative ease.

'You must forgive me for sending for you like this. I imagine that people who want to see you normally call at your office, which I understand is in the Pitti Palace.'

'Yes, but please . . .'

'I should have rather liked to do that. I haven't been in the Palatine gallery for almost fifteen years. Unfortunately, Marshal, I'm a sick woman and one who has always held to the dignity of independence. I have no intention of leaving this house in a wheelchair.'

'I understand.' There was no doubt but what she was a sick woman. Her face had been carefully made up but the yellowish bags under the eyes couldn't be concealed. Nevertheless, she looked a tough character. She might be sick enough to die tomorrow but she had force in her to carry on for years yet, if she cared to do it. She seemed, now, to be taking his measure with an unblinking stare. In his embarrassment he spoke, clearing his throat first. 'Your great-niece is very pretty.'

'Hm. She has her mother's looks.' The disparaging tone confirmed the child's statement. 'She is not my great-niece, strictly speaking. I should explain this to you since it has a bearing on what I want to tell you. Fiorenza is the daughter of Buongianni Corsi's younger brother who, against his family's advice, married a young woman of American origin. Fiorenza is their only child.

'You see quite a lot of her.' He would have liked to say 'despite your obvious disapproval' but didn't dare.

'I have good reason to, Marshal. Should anything happen to my great-nephew, Neri, Fiorenza would inherit not only from the Corsi but from the Ulderighi. You can perhaps imagine that her upbringing would not prepare her for the Ulderighi inheritance.'

'I see.'

'I do my best, but the influence of a mother of that description and the style of her education such as it's likely to be, are far from easy to combat, as you may easily imagine.'

The Marshal, who couldn't imagine even remotely, was silent.

'I understand you have already met my great-nephew?'

'Yes, I have. A priest, Father Benigni—'

'In that case you'll have realized that he is infirm. I'll be more precise: his heart is weak, congenitally weak. He's unlikely to survive beyond thirty.'

'I see. I'm sorry—but surely, these days—'

'He is hardly in a condition to survive a heart transplant.'

'No, of course not.'

'It is my niece Bianca's wish that he marry and produce an heir.'

'And you're against that?'

'Obviously not.' She interrupted herself to lean forward and press a bell beneath a small table that stood between them. 'I should like, on the contrary, to see him in good enough health for that to be possible. He is weak, very weak. Marshal, I'll come to the point. I understand that you have been conducting some sort of investigation into the death of Buongianni.'

'Well, yes, but it's routine in cases like—'

She raised her stick a little from the floor in front of her swollen legs. The knuckles of her hand tightened around it and the Marshal, staring at the fine, age-spotted skin and the colourless varnished nails, thought for a fleeting second that she was going to hit him. If she had, she couldn't have shocked him more.

'I intend to help you. I want to know what's happening in this house.'

Too stunned to answer, the Marshal was saved by the entrance of a woman with a serving trolley.

'Here, over here! Why isn't there hot water again?—No, no! I'll do that, and don't come back. We'll do without the water. I don't want to be disturbed. Wretched woman! The stupidity of these people who can't learn to do anything properly.'

The woman wasn't out of the room and heard it all, to

the Marshal's dismay. If the old marchesa knew it she didn't care.

'Tea.'

Again! The Marshal almost sighed his dissatisfaction aloud. And if he had, no doubt this woman would have ignored him.

'I had an excellent couple before, but now that my niece has let the top floor apartments we are obliged to rely on these people coming in daily who aren't even capable of learning how to make tea properly. Cream or lemon?'

'I . . . lemon. Thank you.' Well, he would accept it but she could hardly force him to drink it. He placed the cup carefully on the small table.

'Do you believe that Buongianni committed suicide, Marshal?'

He was taken aback. She went too fast for him. What was he supposed to say? He needed to feel his way around before committing himself. What the devil was she after? What had she to gain?

'You don't answer me. Why? Because you don't know or because you know but have no proof?'

Was it the inheritance? He knew nothing about these things. Or a personal vendetta, some old quarrel . . . Did she care for Buongianni Corsi or hate him?

'You're from the South, I gather?'

'Sicily, yes.'

'Hm. Then you won't give me a straight answer to a straight question. If only you knew how tiresome and time-wasting that seems to a Florentine.'

He knew that all right. He'd seen it written on Lorenzini's face every day for years. 'I'm sorry. I'm not sure I understand what you want from me.'

'I thought I'd been perfectly clear. I asked you a simple question.'

'Yes. Perhaps it's the answer that isn't simple.' Did she

want to know whether he knew about Tiny? His one piece of real evidence. Well, he wouldn't tell her, not unless she gave her motive away first.

'It seems,' he went on, his face expressionless as she leaned forward over her stick and watched him intently, 'that Neri Ulderighi saw his father shoot himself at the top of the tower.'

'They found him down in the gun room.'

'Yes.'

'So he was moved. By whom?'

There. It was that she was after!

'According to your niece, by herself.'

'Nonsense!'

'As you say. I said, according to your niece.'

'If you believe her you're a fool. Buongianni was a big man. Heavy.'

'Yes.' The Marshal well remembered the weight of him in the dream. 'You saw and heard nothing that night, then?' It was his first attempt at turning the tables on her, asking her a question instead of the other way round. She seemed to have no objection.

'Nothing. I take sleeping tablets. And if I had heard something, do you imagine I could have gone running up to the top of the tower? My condition is plain, I think. I never leave this apartment unless it is to go down in the lift to the reception rooms on the floor below.'

'I understand. It's fortunate that the dwarf, Grillo, who brought me your letter can act as legs for you.'

She looked at him a moment in silence, adjusting her opinion of him.

'I see you're more astute than one would think, Marshal. Yes, Grillo knows what goes on all over the house. That's what you mean, isn't it? He comes every day to tell me what sort of state Neri is in. As you can imagine, I can't go up there to see him myself.'

'But he could come down.'

'He used to do that. Now he sees no one except the dwarf, Father Benigni—and now you.'

'And his mother?'

'He hasn't spoken to her since that night. They say he won't allow her in the tower. What the dwarf knows or doesn't know I can't say because he won't tell me; what Neri knows is killing him. On that point the doctors have been clear. What I want to hear now is what *you* know. I've watched you walking around down there in the courtyard, day after day. You suspect something. If Neri sent for you, then he knows you suspect something too. The burden of what he knows is killing him. Take it from him.'

'I would have thought the priest . . .'

'You can only confess your own sins, Marshal.'

'Yes. Yes, that's what he said to me himself . . . So you think—his mother or—'

'Yes, Marshal. You see I'm hiding nothing from you. Neri must survive at all costs. I brought my niece up from the age of twelve and I know her. By the time she was sixteen years old I was afraid of her. I want to save Neri, and if I said I intended to help you, the truth of the matter is that I want you to help me.'

'If I can, of course.'

'A Sicilian answer. Also, you know something or you wouldn't be pursuing the matter on your own account. Well, there's no reason why you should tell me. You're the one investigating. Well?'

'I'll do what I can—'

'Do what I can! I'm waiting for your questions. You know nothing about this family, I know everything. Well?'

In silence the Marshal took out his notebook. In silence she looked at it and at him with evident impatience. Nevertheless, he knew that she had straightened her back and was clutching hard at her stick ready for difficult or embar-

rassing questions, perhaps concerning Hugh Fido. He surprised her.

'Tell me something, if you would, about this house.'

'The house? You mean its history?'

'No, no . . . Funnily enough, I've found out a bit about
that in my wanderings about the courtyard.' Observed by
the whole family, as it turned out. Well, he'd felt it from
the start and now he knew it was true. So be it. 'No, the
fact that there's scaffolding outside but no work going on,
though now they say the builders are back. Then this business of the tenants. The house being split up and let. All
happen a bit suddenly, did it? Nobody seems to have been
here more than a year.'

'That's correct. Just over a year. The reason you can
work out for yourself.'

'Shortage of money.'

'Naturally.'

'But a very sudden shortage?'

'There's no mystery about that, Marshal. It was
Buongianni Corsi's money which kept this house going.
The restoration of a building such as this, you may or may
not know, is obligatory. The State makes a contribution
but also determines the extent and quality of the work.
Buongianni, shall we say . . . withdrew his support.'

'And why was that?'

'There was a quarrel. Serious. I don't know any details
but I know that divorce was talked of. Out of the question,
of course, but talked of. That was the end of Corsi money
paying for the Ulderighi estate. According to Bianca, he
felt the house must support itself.'

'The reason for the quarrel couldn't have been Hugh
Fido?' He was watching her face as he asked but it registered neither surprise nor annoyance.

'Of course not. That began when the house was let and
he moved in here.'

'She could have known him before.'

It was obvious that she hadn't thought of that.

'That's true . . . she'd be capable of it, too. Moving him in here once she had nothing more to lose since he knew. But no, Buongianni and he were on perfectly good terms. No, no.'

'Then perhaps the quarrel was about his having someone else.'

She looked at him with a mixture of pity and amusement.

'My dear Marshal, given their situation, I have no doubt whatever that Buongianni had someone, no doubt some person connected with his business and removed from our circle. That would hardly be relevant to the issue. Excuse me if I've offended you. It may be that in the army life is rather more monastic.'

And the priest forever in and out of the place! What people! Only Neri was different, unless . . . Who was to say Neri didn't take after his father? He was a Corsi, wasn't he? Yet the fact that this had only just occurred to the Marshal was an indication of how the unfortunate Buongianni Corsi had been sucked in to feed the Ulderighi clan.

'Buongianni Corsi . . .'

'Yes. What of him?'

'I was wondering if you were fond of him.'

'I was not. Whatever happened to him, he may for all I know have deserved it. I am interested in the health and future of Neri. Please keep that in mind. Visit him. Convince him that the burden he is carrying is rightly yours. Neri's is, in some respects, a brilliant mind but he is in other ways . . . childlike. He sees you as a figure of authority. He trusts you.' She leaned heavily on her stick and got to her feet, staring at the Marshal with her sick eyes. Evidently the interview was at an end and he was dismissed. He got to his feet, ready to offer her his hand, but she had turned from him and was making her way with heavy painful steps towards the door.

Before she reached it, when he was still standing looking after her, she paused and turned to say, 'By the way, Marshal, we received, I should say my niece did, a parcel containing the shoes Buongianni was wearing when he died. They were returned here from the public prosecutor's office along with a form of some description, officially releasing all Buongianni's belongings and a note informing us that you would be the person to apply to for the rest of them. Is that correct?'

'I—yes. Yes. I'll bring them to you.'

'I can see no necessity for it myself but if it's a question of correct procedure, then of course, do bring them. Leave them with the porter.'

9

From that moment until he read Catherine Yorke's letter, the Marshal trod more carefully than he had ever done in his life, and he was by nature a careful man. He trod carefully, but always in the same direction, towards the Marchesa Bianca Maria Corsi Ulderighi Della Loggia. He never saw her, never spoke or attempted to speak to her, but she was his prey. He knew it by instinct though he didn't know why. She frightened him, the house frightened him, the thought of whatever it was she had done frightened him. Only two things encouraged him, and the first of these was the fact that Fiorenza Ulderighi was as frightened of her niece as he was. The second was the removal of the shoes.

'They're your only evidence!' protested Lorenzini.

'I know,' said the Marshal, satisfied. That was something he understood, about the only thing. He'd been baffled by foreigners, Florentine and English, and he'd had enough of it. At last something had happened which made sense to him. A vital piece of evidence had disappeared. He might have been in Palermo! The importance of those fingerprints was confirmed, the vanishing prints demonstrated fear. He was delighted. Lorenzini gave it all up as a bad job.

To the Captain, the Marshal's commanding officer over at Headquarters on Borgo Ognissanti across the river, the Marshal, treading carefully, explained the real problem about the shoes.

'I don't know what she meant, you see. Of course, she may not have known—about the prints, I mean—so that her saying what she did, "If it's a question of correct procedure" . . .'

'Meant exactly that. Guarnaccia, you do have a tendency to read baroque intricacies into a straight line.'

The Marshal only stared, not understanding. Then he said, 'I don't want to be transferred. Teresa . . . The way the shoes were withdrawn from the lab—and, I imagine, nicely polished—the message through the Ulderighi—it's a warning shot.'

'Yes, I see your point there.' The Captain didn't say, 'Of course you won't be transferred, what rubbish.'

The Marshal sat with his hands planted on his knees, looking across the big desk at him hopefully, his stillness and his slightly bulging eyes giving the impression of a bulldog hoping for a titbit. His trust in the Captain in these matters was absolute. He was a Florentine, after all, and an officer too. The Captain, though unable to follow the workings of Guarnaccia's mind, trusted him and always helped him.

They both believed that their mutual reliance was based on the solid facts of their shared work experience. Neither of them knew that it was really based on affection and deep need. The Captain, Guarnaccia always thought to himself, was clever, ambitious and adaptable. Guarnaccia, thought the edgy and over-worked Captain, was fatherly, solid and unchanging. Their thoughts lay buried, unexpressed. They never sought each other out except for reasons of work.

Captain Maestrangelo was a good-looking man, or would have appeared so had he smiled. He never smiled.

'I'll put feelers out,' he said. 'If there's any real threat to you it will be possible to find out. I don't think there is, if that's any comfort to you, because I'd probably have heard already.'

'It might be a comfort to me and it might not,' the Marshal said. 'It depends on the reason.'

'Yes.' The Captain contemplated the bulky, motionless figure before him. 'I doubt . . . with all due respect to your investigative powers, that they consider themselves in any real danger from you. I'm saying "they", having no idea who "they" might be. Perhaps you have?'

'Hmph.'

'Guarnaccia . . . I want to help you but you're not really allowing me to, are you?'

'Yes and no. I don't want to get transferred. I'd have come to you before but I didn't want to involve you.'

'I see. And now?'

'I need two men.'

'And I'm to give them to you without knowing exactly what you're doing.'

'I just thought it might be better, yes.' The Marshal's face remained expressionless.

'All right. Two men.'

'Night duty,' the Marshal said. 'If you should need an official reason, we're coming up to the final of the football tournament. There'll be some trouble. There always is. And Leo and Tiny will be in it.' As far as the Marshal was concerned, that ought to have been the end of their conversation but the Captain was unable to restrain his curiosity and as Guarnaccia got to his feet, he, too, stood up and followed him to the door.

'Wait . . . I just want to understand. You say this boy, the Ulderighi son—'

'Neri.'

'Neri. You say he actually saw his father kill himself.'

'That's right, he did.'

'And you believe him.'

'And I believe him.'

'So you think he wasn't dead, is that it?'

The Marshal stared at him. The Captain had brains, that's what it was. He'd never have thought of that in a million years. Yet it was a solution and a simple one. Neri hadn't touched his father. He'd seen him fire and slump over the edge of the crenellated tower. Then the mother had taken over, sent him down and presumably sent for Tiny and Leo. It was so simple, except . . .

'Surely you can tell me that?' insisted the Captain. 'You must suspect something.'

'Something . . . something that—I hadn't thought of his not being dead. You may well be right about that, only, you see, he was hanging over the edge of the tower, a little push would have finished him.'

'No, no, no. Think of the scandal. The gun room was much better.'

'I'm sure you're right.'

'It all fits.'

'Yes. I'd best be off. I'll expect your men.'

And he was gone.

He trod carefully, he kept his head down, he was dutiful, humble, a little stupid apparently, watching his chance.

By night he watched with Lorenzini, both of them in plain clothes, both of them very uncomfortable, squashed inside the Marshal's own little Fiat. They parked on the pavement of a side street barely wide enough for a car to pass them. From there they could see into the small piazza where Leo guarded the entrance to a disco club which had bulletproof steel doors and a second guard on the inside who, in quieter moments, opened up to poke out his head and chat with Leo.

Ten minutes' walk away, another unmarked car in another side street watched the market square for the arrival of Tiny.

On Monday night nothing happened. When the Marshal and Lorenzini had discreetly followed Leo back to the Palazzo Ulderighi and Tiny was fully occupied humping meat at the market, the four watchers shrugged their shoulders and went wearily home to bed, three of them thinking privately that it was time wasted but not their business to say so.

On the second night, the Marshal was vindicated to the extent that blood was shed over the question of the football tournament.

There had already been a minor scuffle at the door during which Leo had shouldered a group of youngsters away with what looked like more than necessary violence, either because they weren't members—the club was a private one—or because the place was full. They were hardly out of the way when a gang appeared with the clear intention of making a ruckus. They were all men and quite a few of them, even at that distance, were evidently a bit old for disco life. The minute he saw them Leo slapped his hand against the doors behind him. His mate came out and the doors closed.

'Trouble,' Lorenzini said, and got out of the car.

'Don't. He could recognize you!' The Marshal had too much to worry about without Lorenzini's getting involved in a street fight. Besides which, if they didn't recognize him, which was the more likely contingency, he'd probably get himself beaten up or knifed.

The threatening noises were growing louder. There was a plunging in the centre of the group which widened. The fight was on.

'Shouldn't I at least get to a telephone and call a car?'

'Somebody inside the club will have done that by now. They must be used to dealing with this sort of thing. Don't worry.'

It was some time, however, before a squad car did draw up with its light and siren going. By then, Leo and his mate had the situation in hand. Leo had a half-nelson on the most vicious of the gang who had been flashing a knife about earlier and who was obviously the leader. He was smallish and older than the others and was kicking like a mule in Leo's grip. Leo's mate was struggling with a bigger, younger man and getting the better of him by the look of things. The rest of the gang were evidently only there to make up the numbers and contribute threatening noises.

'The two of them seem to be managing all right,' commented Lorenzini as the squad car drew in.

But the two uniformed men who jumped out of it got hold of the wrong end of the stick. Without stopping to ask questions, one of them, seeing the huge figure of Leo fastened on to a smaller, loudly protesting man, drew out his staff and brought it down with a thud on Leo's shaven head.

'You fool!' they heard Leo shout as his hand went up to clutch his streaming head. Then he slumped to the floor. By that time the attacking gang had fled. The half-conscious Leo was booked for assault and the incident was over.

'What do we do now?' asked Lorenzini.

'We wish,' said the Marshal, 'that there'd be somebody there to take his prints at this time of night but there won't be.'

'You never know. They might lock him up for the night.'

'I do know,' the Marshal said, 'and they won't. Follow them.'

So they followed the car to Headquarters and waited an hour or so until Leo was released and taken, still clutching his head, to the emergency department of the hospital of Santa Maria Nuova. There they waited two hours and then they followed him on his journey home in a taxi to the Palazzo Ulderighi. Another night was over.

'Of course, I don't expect you to tell me what's going on,' lied Teresa, shattering his short, tormented sleep the next morning. 'I just think I'm entitled to *some* explanation when you stay out all night, that's all.'

If there was any logic behind that remark, the Marshal, in his much reduced condition, was unable to grasp it. He offered her no explanation. If the worst should happen and his career was blocked, she'd never know he'd asked for it.

The breath of the flute was as sweet and sad as the summer dusk. It had accompanied the Marshal as he puffed up the narrow spiral staircase behind the dwarf, who needed both his hands to pull his short body upwards with the help of a thick rope looped through iron rings in the wall. The Marshal had entered alone by the service door and seen Neri seated near the window but turned a little away from it. He leant forward over the flute, his back stretched, swaying slightly with the current of the music. When it stopped, he laid the flute gently on his knee and leaned back. A sigh that was almost a sob escaped him.

The Marshal, not wanting to embarrass him, crept back a few paces and tapped on the door, shutting it behind him then with a cough. The figure in the chair didn't move or look back.

'You'll tire yourself,' Neri said sadly. 'I don't need anything. You mustn't bring up my supper. Stay here with me and make fun of the idiot child. You have good reason, I can tell you. All these years I've been so afraid of dying and now . . . now, I only feel sad, so sad, for things I'm leaving that I hardly know . . .

'The breath of flutes at eventide,
Mere seaweed on the shore . . .

'Such a weight of sadness. Grillo, stay and make me laugh.'

Then he turned his heavy head. His face was flushed with drugs, his eyes too bright.

'Ah, it's you . . . Forgive me. Tonight I—you're so busy and I should help you . . . tell you things, but tonight I—'

'No, no.' The Marshal laid his big hand on the boy's shoulder. 'No, no . . .'

A sea of expressionless white faces bobbed in and out of the shadows, the gyrating black bodies all but invisible against black walls and against each other. The figures moved as though controlled by an earsplitting drumbeat and their movement was momentarily illuminated and intensified by a flash of silver light that left only a fleeting sense of staring eyes and frozen attitudes as the room blackened again.

Lorenzini was shouting something but the Marshal's attempts at lip-reading were a failure. In any case, there was hardly any need to say it. How could they possibly locate Leo in this crowd? Just their luck that the place he chose to go on his night off—supposedly he was meant to be resting up for tomorrow's final—was the same disco he worked in, a black and airless cellar that was probably meant to accommodate half the number of bodies now crushing each other. If they didn't find Leo quickly the Marshal knew he would have to fight his way out because his eyes were streaming with the smoke and he could barely breathe.

'What?' What was Lorenzini trying to . . . now he was gesticulating and pointing to the far corner behind the Marshal. Had he seen Leo? What an impossible business! The Marshal's idea of meeting up with someone in a crowd was to stand stock still, making a landmark of himself, until they found him. It would hardly do this time, not only because the darkness of his uniform, instead of making him conspicuous, in this place was practically camouflage, but also because Leo, if he did chance to spot his visitors, might well run away. There was only one door, which was something, but the Marshal was intent on keeping his back to it while trying to work out what the devil Lorenzini . . .

At last he caught on. On a raised dais in one corner a

disc jockey dressed in black and wearing large earphones was working at the turntables and a bank of dimly lighted controls. If he was the regular disc jockey he was bound to know Leo and from up there had a better chance of spotting him. The Marshal had signalled to Lorenzini that he should go ahead. The young brigadier was thin and agile, much more suited to wriggling his way through the mass than the Marshal, who felt more suited to his role as blocker of the exit. Lorenzini was swallowed up and reappeared a few moments later on the steps up to the dais. The tall young man with the big earphones, his face lit from below with the pinkish light coming from the control panels, remained heedless of any attempts on his concentration until Lorenzini managed to reach up and tap his arm. Then he looked down, raised a hand to indicate that Lorenzini should wait a moment and bent to do something beneath the control panel.

Ah, thought the Marshal with heartfelt gratitude, he's going to turn the volume down.

No such happy occurrence ensued. The young man straightened up and placed another record on the turntable to his left. Wasn't one enough? Then he held it in position with one finger of his right hand, and with his left raised his earphones. The noise continued unabated but Lorenzini seemed to be making himself understood. The young man in black leaned down from his pulpit to listen and then stood up and looked about him. Further discussion took place and then Lorenzini stepped down and disappeared from view. The disc jockey resumed his earphones and bowed his head in solemn concentration. It was some time before the sweating, suffocating Marshal saw Lorenzini again, but when he did push into view Leo's head was visible behind him, his stitches sprouting from a patch of iodine.

'Thank God,' murmured the Marshal as he puffed up

the last step and came out into the square, his streaming eyes soothed by the sight of the moonlit white marble of the church opposite, his lungs gulping at the night air. Why anybody would pay to be closed into that hell hole was beyond him.

'What's going on?' Leo was blustering, uncertain.

'Just wanted a word with you,' the Marshal said mildly, 'and there was no chance of having it down there with all that noise. Our car's here.'

A squad car tonight, not the Marshal's little Fiat. Lorenzini got into the driver's seat.

'You sit in the back with me.' The Marshal opened the door for him with a gesture so kindly and casual that he might have been showing his wife into a restaurant. The bull-necked, shaven Leo was bristling with tension but he got in as bidden and sat where he was in silence as the Marshal went round and got in beside him.

'Aah . . .' sighed the Marshal, settling into the corner, 'warm, even at this hour of night. Drive round a bit, Lorenzini. Get a bit of a breeze in.' And he rolled down the window.

'Where are we going?' Leo couldn't help breaking his self-imposed silence as Lorenzini drove out of the centre and turned, rather too fast for comfort, on to one of the broad tree-lined avenues skirting the edge of the city.

'Nowhere, nowhere at all . . . That's better. Bit of air.'

Through the car window the night breeze came heavy with petrol fumes mingled with the scent of flowering trees. The Marshal was, nevertheless, acutely aware of Leo's mingled smells of strong aftershave and the sweat of fear.

'I expect you know,' he began, 'that we have informers here and there in the city—well, everybody knows that, don't they?'

'I'm not thinking of turning informer.' Leo sounded

almost relieved. He had expected worse than this. The Marshal knew it and bided his time.

'No, no . . . I wasn't suggesting . . .'

They neared the end of the brightly lit avenue and followed the stream of traffic veering left on to the river bank, then right over the bridge.

Perhaps because their crossing the river appeared purposeful, Leo protested again, 'Where are we going? You've no right—'

'To what?'

Leo had no answer. The Marshal let him wait until they had driven down river and were going back over the last bridge near the park before embarking on his speech.

'Informers . . . these informers I was mentioning, have been saying some strange things about you. Very strange. They're saying there's more to the Palazzo Ulderighi business than meets the eye.'

He paused. Leo made no comment, but the Marshal knew as he looked out the open window at the needles of light shattering the oily blackness of the river that the figure beside him had become rigid with attention.

'More than meets the eye. Now, I'm not usually one to give advice where none's been asked for, but you . . . you've no record. This Tiny, on the other hand, now he's a very nasty character who's spent a lot of time inside. He's experienced, knows what he's doing—mind, I'm not saying you're stupid . . .'

He paused again then to make sure Leo had time to note that he was saying just that.

'Somebody like Tiny, you see, is in a position to haggle where you're not. You've never been inside and want to keep it that way. Everything's at stake for you, whereas he's got nothing to lose. If he thinks the game's up and he's going to have to do a few more years, it's in his interest to tell all and name names in return for our reducing charges.

You can work out for yourself, I imagine, that you'll come out as the chief culprit in his version. He'll have just held your coat, so to speak.'

They travelled another long avenue round the other side of the city with Leo hunched in sweating silence, the Marshal gazing blandly out of the window and Lorenzini wondering where people who weren't working nights found to drive to at that hour. The traffic showed no signs of thinning and it wasn't even Saturday night. The waves of tension he could feel behind his head were such that he didn't venture to ask where he should go next, so he stayed on the ring roads and before long they were back on the tree-lined avenue and heading again for the river.

'Anybody in his position would do the same, I suppose,' the Marshal continued thoughtfully.

Leo's breathing had become audible. The Marshal pulled himself together. If he didn't get on with it they'd be driving round till morning. The truth was that he had this habit, infuriating according to Teresa, of 'going in and out of a coma' and making half-baked remarks each time he came to. If Teresa found it infuriating, it might well be that Leo found it frightening. He was breathing very heavily. If he got too frightened he might be too paralysed to act.

'So what I'm trying to say is that when somebody's got a clean record they deserve a break. Your friend Tiny's done some nasty things in his time. I don't believe the story he's telling and I don't at all care for the way he's telling it. Letting it be known, accidentally as it were, through informers.'

It was a very fortunate thing, the Marshal thought as he talked, that none of this was true. It was a lot more difficult when you had to do a patched-up job on bits of truth and bits of invention. The joins tended to show. But he must keep on or he'd lapse into silence again.

'By tomorrow there'll be a warrant out for his arrest. He'll be taken to Borgo Ognissanti. I want you to come round there—let's say eleven o'clock—you know where I mean, do you?' That was the only moment he couldn't resist a sidelong glance and caught the glitter of Leo's tiny eye.

'What's hearsay can be ignored. When it comes to a written statement . . . you see what I mean. Now, if you're on the spot—and I'm only asking you to come, I'm not accusing you of anything and it's not a trick and then you'll be arrested. If I want to arrest you I know where to find you. If you're on the spot and looking him in the eye, he'll not have such an easy time telling a pack of lies, will he? Turn off here, Lorenzini. We'll take this gentleman back to his club.'

When they got there, Leo was more than a little disconcerted by their getting out of the car and accompanying him right to the door where Leo's substitute bouncer looked a lot more surprised to see him return than he had to see him go.

'Enjoy your night off, then.' The Marshal stood there with Lorenzini beside him and Leo had no option but to go down the stairs towards the throbbing darkness of the disco. He didn't look back at them. When he had gone through the door at the bottom, the Marshal, too, descended the stairs to speak to the two people behind the cash desk.

'One of you the manager?'

A man on his feet behind the cashier spoke up.

'I'm the owner.'

'How many people does this place hold officially?'

'I . . . a hundred and fifty, but . . .'

'How many are down there now?'

'Oh Christ!'

'And how many of them have no membership cards?'

'Listen, I know who's behind all this. We've been closed down at least every two months this year and all because I don't slip an envelope to the right man on the council and the people who do pay up don't want me surviving—'

'I haven't counted them,' the Marshal said, 'and I haven't looked at anybody's membership card.'

The owner was brought up short. 'What's it about, then?'

'Your bouncer, Leo Mori.'

'Leo? He's all right. What's he done? How come he went out with you?'

'It may be that when I've gone,' the Marshal said, staring hard first at the owner and then at the cashier, 'he'll make a telephone call. Is that the only phone behind you?'

'Yes, but—'

'I want to know who he calls, if that's possible, and I certainly need to know what he says. Got that?'

'All right. But Leo—'

'Don't you worry about Leo. He's involved in something a lot more serious than letting too many customers into a club. When he's made the call come outside and tell me. Our car will be out of sight but we'll see you.'

They left, parked the car out of sight and settled down to wait. Every now and then the radio crackled and hummed and the two men outside Tiny's flat reported all quiet.

'I hope I didn't frighten him too much,' the Marshal said.

'You frightened me,' Lorenzini ventured to admit, but the Marshal only gave him a funny look, not understanding.

They sat in darkness and silence for some time, Lorenzini wondering if this were the moment to ask just what was going on. He knew from experience that the Marshal didn't deliberately leave him in the dark. He was just unaware of the fact that his thoughts weren't audible and would often say, 'But you knew that' or 'Surely I told you.' He glanced at him now, a still, expressionless bulk. Perhaps he should just wait and see . . .

A yawn escaped him.

'You're exhausted,' the Marshal said, coming to and noticing. 'Well, it should be over by tonight.'

'What, exactly?' Lorenzini had seen his chance. 'I mean, that letter . . . for you it changed everything.'

'Cleared a lot of things up, that letter. Whys and wherefores. Motives.'

'But not whether it really was a suicide.'

'No.'

Lorenzini waited a bit, but nothing further was forthcoming and the audible sigh he let out as he leaned back in his seat produced no effect.

It had been a very sober and ill-looking William who had met the Marshal at the doors of the Palazzo Ulderighi earlier. The Marshal himself, after his visit to Neri, had been feeling rather low and at first the sight of William cheered him. Then he looked at him more closely in the gloom.

'Are you all right?

'Yes. No, not really, but it doesn't matter. I've been to your office. They said I might find you here.'

The Marshal tried to glance at his watch. He wanted to be out on Leo's tail before long. This being his night off he wouldn't be so easy to watch.

'I won't keep you long. If you have to get back I'll go with you. Only too glad to be away from this place.'

'It would be better.' And a good deal more private without Grillo lurking.

In the Marshal's office William sat clutching his tightly rolled umbrella. His face was pale. An angry red spot was turning septic on his chin.

'I imagine I made a fool of myself. I usually do when I've had too much to drink.'

For a moment, the Marshal couldn't think what he was talking about, then he remembered.

'Ah, well. No harm done. You surely didn't come round here just to apologize for having had a glass of wine too many?'

'No. I do apologize, though, if I . . . I don't know how much I said.'

'Very little. You fell asleep. I gathered you were worried about your sister.'

'I didn't say why?'

'No.'

'I want you to read this.' He gave the Marshal a letter still in its envelope, addressed to William in Venice and postmarked Florence. The Marshal opened it.

'But this—I'm sorry, it's in English.'

'I've translated it for you on the back of the pages. It took me all afternoon. I didn't want to interfere. She was going to be upset enough as it was without her having to be involved with the police. I thought if she came back Sunday I could at least talk to her first. I'm sorry. You're trying to read. I hope you won't think ill of her because she's the most honest, good person I've ever known. I'm sorry . . .'

Dear W,

Tried to phone you this a.m. but you were out or asleep and I think it was just as well—for me, anyway. You could have said 'I told you so'. Of course it was impossible without first finding another flat. I did try—to find another flat, I mean—but it fell through. So: you can't leave somebody who won't be left. You've got to have cooperation. We had it out, or tried to, but he could only see it as an either-or menace on my part. At least you know it wasn't that. I wish I had more experience. Neither of us have—you and me, I mean. Why is that?

Anyway, I couldn't for shame tell any of my girlfriends because of a feeling that they'd laugh at me. I can only tell you the truth, which is that I'm so attached to him in a way I can't explain that to tolerate the wrench of leaving him, which I theoretically did, I needed huge amounts of support and comfort and a shoulder to cry on and the only person I could turn to for all that was him. Every night since I 'left him' he has come down and just held me and let me cry. Nothing else. He won't ask me for anything else but he won't leave me either and I know he's winning. That's the wrong word, I suppose, but that's the way it is. I might as well be a tiny child trying to leave its mother. Father, you'd say. I know you think he's a father substitute but what if that's what I really need? I mean, crutches are a sort of leg substitute but if you've lost your leg you'd better learn to put up with them, or what? I don't know. In my more desperate moments of attempted flight I made a plan for you and me to go back to England, convince whoever's in our old house to sell it to us (for peanuts, of course) so we could start again. Start what? The problems are all mixed up together and nobody knows them all except you, so I can't tell anyone else. I can hear them saying, 'What can you expect if you have an affair with a married man?' and the squalor of it makes me shudder.

It's not squalid. It's not an 'affair'. Does everybody say that? I suppose so, they all think their case is different. I wish I were less ingenuous but I'm afraid it's a question of character rather than experience. I just know I'll always be like that. Tried my usual cure of 'there's always someone worse off than yourself, etc.' this morning when you didn't answer. Went up to see Neri. Each time I see him I'm more touched by his delicacy and amazed by his brain. It flickers like a dying fire. He was translating the ode 'To Phyllis' and gave it to me. Tiny intense

writing—trails of ivy to bind your shining hair—it
reminds him of me, he said. What would he think, feel,
if he knew? If we could get away from this house and
take him with us. Dickensian nonsense. He is part of this
house and dying with it and Buongianni can't bear to see
him. He can't bear it because he *cares*. If he didn't . . .
    If you were here you would make me laugh, no matter
what. Is that the English in us? It's the only thing lacking
with Buongianni. Italians don't laugh at themselves.
Poor Neri. This house and his mother will kill him in the
end and, even though I know that, I have this feeling
that if he were taken away from here he'd die at once.
Ever since I've lived here I've thought about death. I
think you'd better come and make me laugh before it's
too late. In the meantime I'll listen to some Mozart. I've
booked my ticket for the 12th, the first time in my life
I've booked a scheduled flight but I want to be able to
get back at once if I feel I need to, or stay on and go
through with it, in which case I'll stay three days to get
over it and be back Thursday 24th. I don't want to go
through with it. More than anything I hate the assumption by everybody concerned that it's automatic. Not
once has anyone said, What are you going to do? Even
Flavia, who was the one to tell me, only said I could have
it done here but that England might be better as Florence
being so small it would get out. I don't care whether it
gets out or not. It's funny, that, I've tried to think I
should care but I can't. Who is there who'd care—I
mean about me? You, and I've told you. Buongianni and
I've told him. My 'everybody concerned' excludes him,
you know that. He wants a child. I want it. And the only,
the sensible thing to do—according to everybody else,
that is, seems to me *really* squalid. I can't even write the
word, I don't even think it to myself, so how do I go
through with the reality? I don't believe I will. It's so

negative. It would be a sort of death for me too. Could I manage on my own, though? Not financially. And if he can't get away from here can you see me just taking money from him? Can you see me as a kept woman?

New paragraph, new thought. I won't decide about the operation until I'm away from here. Away from this house. When I've decided I'll tell him. I have this feeling that either I'll come back on Sunday and go through with the whole thing—what can La Ulderighi *do* when it comes down to it? Or else I'll give up the child and Buongianni. Either way wait for me. I'll need you (if only to make me laugh).

Love,

Catherine.

'I don't know what to do,' William admitted as the Marshal refolded the letter.

'Have you eaten?'

'What?'

'Have you had any supper?'

'No, no, I haven't but—'

'Go out and have a decent meal, you look like death warmed up. Shouldn't you be back in Venice by this time, anyway?'

'The others have gone but I have to wait for Catherine, if she comes . . .'

'You don't think she will?'

'I'm afraid that if she—if she decided not to have the child, and that's the way it looks now, doesn't it?—then she may have given up on the whole thing like she says . . . And if she told him, then maybe that's why he killed himself. But what if she felt just as badly as he did? You understand that after a thing like that she'd be very depressed and then if she heard . . .'

'Likewise, you'd have heard by now. Surely she'll be

staying with friends—and in any case you expect her back tomorrow.'

'I might ring round a few of her friends in England, anyway.'

'Do,' the Marshal said, 'if it will make you feel better—but have that meal first. All right?'

'All right. I will.' He made an attempt at being his usual witty self. 'If I were as big as you I wouldn't get so easily squashed. It's people tripping over you by accident that gets you down. I've no appetite, to be honest. 'I *won't* have any soup today, Oh *take* the nasty soup away!'

'You have a good big bowl of spaghetti. And get a steak down you. No. If you don't mind, I'll keep the letter just for now.'

Though whether it would be more or less likely to do a vanishing act out of his possession or William's he couldn't have said. At any rate he buttoned it into his pocket and there it still was.

'Did you ever think,' Lorenzini mused aloud in the darkness of the parked car, 'that there must be quite a few telephones in a place as big as the Ulderighi's apartments, so that if she did call him from England whatever she had to say—'

'Yes, I did think of it,' the Marshal said. 'And I imagine that two intelligent people like Corsi and Catherine Yorke would have thought of it, too.'

'I suppose—There he is!'

'Get out and catch him at the corner and watch out for Leo himself showing up.'

Lorenzini jumped out of the car and beckoned to the owner of the disco, who looked furtively over his shoulder before he approached. The Marshal wound down his window.

'Well?'

'He telephoned.'

'Who to?'

'I don't know. That's the truth, he didn't say. He just said "It's me. Listen." Then the other person did all the talking with Leo just protesting here and there. One thing he did say clearly and that was, "Listen, you shit, it's me who's got the protection, you could be out there on your own if I say the word." Something of that sort anyway, it's not word for word. Then a bit more iffing and butting and effing and blinding and they seem to have agreed to meet. At least, Leo insisted on it, but whether the other one was willing or not I don't know.'

'Agreed to meet where? Where?'

'Usual place. That's all he said. "Usual place. Be there." If that's all I'd better get back. If Leo comes out and sees me here . . .'

'You're his employer, aren't you?'

'You've seen the size of him. I don't want him turning on me. I'm off.'

They settled down to wait again.

'Usual place,' muttered Lorenzini. 'I followed Leo for days. What usual place?'

'They'll have been avoiding each other.'

'I know that. But even so, Tiny gets up and starts work when Leo's going home to bed—could just be a street corner, I suppose.'

'No . . .' The radio interrupted them but only to report all quiet. 'No. There has to be a "usual place" for them to know each other at all.'

They fell silent. Except when the disco door opened to release people, letting out a short spurt of light, noise and smoke, the small piazza was hushed and deserted. So hushed that they could hear the trains hooting as they rattled into the central station at Santa Maria Novella.

Lorenzini suppressed a yawn. More to keep himself

awake than anything else, he made another attempt at getting blood out of a stone.

'I suppose this Catherine Yorke is the reason why Corsi
withdrew his support from the Palazzo Ulderighi, as it
were?'

'Mph.'

'Bit of a cheek, though, getting her in there as a tenant
in the circs.'

'Mph.'

'Can hardly blame the woman if she wanted him bumped
off or whatever—that's if she knew.'

'She knew.'

This was progress. Lorenzini sat up straighter and persisted.

'Grillo? The chatty little cricket?'

'Yes. Grillo.'

*He spent a lot of time in here. Many an evening. Playing with
his little pistol.*

Of course he was next door in Catherine's room, and
who would know it better than the dwarf whose web of
service doors and passages gave him access to everybody's
secrets? Then he would scuttle back to his lair and decide
what he should tell to whom so as to maintain the status
quo and his sheltered situation. The Marshal was willing
to bet that he never told Neri anything except what would
amuse him. Neri, no more capable than his servant of surviving outside his tower, was in the same boat. Neri in his
tower watching his mother and Hugh Fido knowing it.
Grillo watching Buongianni Corsi and Catherine. The old
aunt trying to watch them all and find out.

I want to know what's going on in this house.

And after the violence had been precipitated all of them
went on watching. Watching the Marshal now as he circled
the gloomy courtyard filled with music, himself filled with
a sick apprehension that rose and subsided but never left

him. He saw himself pacing heavily round and round and from each window eyes were watching him as the dwarf dodged in and out between the columns, grinning and beckoning.

'Come on! Come on!'

He hadn't played the game for years and had never been any good at it anyway. He was too slow. The old tata sitting among the red lights of her icons and who, as it turned out, was his mother, was watching him from behind her closed door.

'Come on, Salva! You're so slow. You never win.'

'He's off!' cried the dwarf. 'Warmer and warmer . . . No! Cold! Cold!'

The Marshal didn't care. There was a heap of clothing near the well and he wasn't going near that no matter how the dwarf taunted him. It was probably Corsi's clothing and the thought of touching it made him shudder. He stayed under the colonnade and kept walking, ignoring the dwarf's shouts of 'warmer' and 'cooler'. All that mattered was that he should keep walking until the piano music stopped and then . . . Or was that musical chairs? No wonder they all laughed at him as they watched him trailing round and round without even knowing what he was trying to do. Asleep on his feet, that's what they were saying. Asleep. Was he asleep? He was, he must be . . .

'Marshal?'

'Eh?'

'I said, if we find them together what do you intend to do?'

'I don't know . . . I think I must have nodded off. What time is it?'

'Closing time. Look.' The last clients were pouring noisily out of the disco. Leo wasn't visible among them.

'As late as that?' The Marshal sat up, wide awake now. 'But Tiny? We haven't heard anything.'

'But they called in ages ago.' Lorenzini couldn't hide a note of irritation. 'They said " He's off". They're following him to the market—there's Leo.'

He came out with the owner and stood talking to him for a moment until a taxi drew up. The owner got in and Leo went off in the wake of the last bunch of clients. Lorenzini started his motor. 'What do you want me to do?'

'Wait.'

They waited only six or seven minutes before the radio message came.

'He's stopped work and he's standing looking about him—Damn! There's a meat truck pulled up, we can't see . . . wait, it's backing up . . . He's still there. He's talking to somebody—'

'Describe him,' the Marshal interrupted. 'Is he big, shaved head, dressed in black?'

'Nothing like. Not your man—he's too old. I reckon Tiny's asking him to take over. He is. Slapped him on the back and now he's crossing the road . . .'

'Don't lose him!'

'No fear of that. He's going across to the café where they all have breakfast. Nowhere else he can be going at this hour. This could be what you're looking for.'

'We're on our way.'

Much as Lorenzini would have loved to take off at full speed with lights and siren on, they had to go slowly and discreetly for fear of overtaking Leo. When they got near to the market square they parked and continued on foot. As they walked the vegetable-littered streets dawn was breaking, the sky as clean as a pink pearl, but the lights were still on under the glass roof of the big market hall. The lorries that had converged on the square during the night were mostly emptied and gone but there was still a lot of noisy activity among smaller traders with their tiny three-wheel trucks. It was easy enough to spot the café. Everything else along the street was closed and shuttered and a lot of traders were heading across for their breakfast.

'There it is,' said Lorenzini. 'What now?'

There was no occasion to decide. A sudden commotion inside the café caused those approaching it to rush forward for a look and, almost at once, one of the plain clothes men pushed his way out to look about him desperately. Lorenzini and the Marshal began to run.

By the time they got inside, a number of Tiny's equally large mates had got Leo off him but they were having trouble keeping him off.

Four men were holding on to Tiny. One of them screamed, 'Get him out of here! Get him out or he'll kill him!'

It was true. Leo himself, infuriated, had been brandishing a knife which was now lying at his feet but it was Tiny, his eyes glittering and a low, uncontrollable whine issuing from between clenched teeth, who would have killed, and killed with his bare hands. He didn't even notice the presence of two uniformed men. Leo noticed and lunged impotently forward in an effort to free himself.

The Marshal nodded towards Tiny indicating that he should be immobilized first. Lorenzini, like a hunting dog let loose, bounded forward with handcuffs. It took all the strength of the men already holding him plus the two plain clothes men and Lorenzini to get Tiny down on the floor on his stomach with his wrists handcuffed behind him. Even then one of the plain clothes men took a hard kick in the stomach, which put him out of action.

Then they made for Leo. He flung himself backwards, crushing a man against the bar counter. A lot of the customers were getting out for fear of being hurt.

'Not me!' Leo bellowed, 'you're not taking me! I never

touched her except to hold her down! You can't do me for it, I was never meant to touch her at all. He made me because she was fighting like a cat—but he was the one raped her! He was the one killed her! Not me!'

10

TO THE PUBLIC PROSECUTOR'S OFFICE
FLORENCE

At approximately 21.45 yesterday, June 24th, in the course of duty, namely the examination of the cellars of the Palazzo Ulderighi . . .

The Marshal typed fast with two thick fingers. He had been right to leave it until after lunch and Teresa had been right to insist on his having a sleep. He had thought he would be unable to drop off but he was away in seconds and she'd had to wake him at a quarter to five.

'Not that I want to know your business, if you don't want to tell me, you don't, but I hope whatever it is will soon be over because if you don't get a night's sleep—'

'It's over.'

Over except for the one decision and now he had made it. He only had to type it.

In the presence of the undersigned . . .

Lorenzini knocked and came in.

'This is ready. Will you sign it? I'd rather you checked through it first . . .'

'Give it to me. Has the doctor signed?'

'Everyone except you.'

The printed form was filled in by hand and contained the description and recognition of the cadaver. The section marked 'Describe position and clothing of the cadaver' had been filled in by Lorenzini. The lower part of the body, unclothed and curled up tightly on itself, showed damage from the masonry. The Marshal forced himself to read on, determined that his decision must encompass all that Catherine Yorke's terror and suffering and death might evoke in him, all that he had walked away from that evening in the cellars when the stone of Cinelli's wall tomb had been removed and he had seen her hair flash golden in the strong spotlights.

'*With trails of ivy I will bind your shining hair* . . .'

The men around the body were wearing masks, the Marshal wasn't. When one of them noticed him retreating he probably thought that was the reason.

'Will you stay?' he had murmured to Lorenzini. 'The brother . . .'

'Of course.'

A click of the technician's camera. He had photographed the stone, too, before they removed it.

> Here is an end of all my woes
> And a beginning of your own.

The courtyard, for once, was silent. Emilio had deserted his piano and stood under the colonnade with Flavia Martelli and Hugh Fido. They spoke in whispers and in their glance at the Marshal, even in that dim light, he thought he detected a twinge of guilt. It was almost certain that the other two had known about Hugh, but then didn't they, too, have an interest in maintaining the status quo? However much they might grumble, flats were hard to come by. 'Better a corpse in the house than a Pisan . . .' He knocked on Catherine Yorke's door.

'Come in.'

William was perched on the edge of the single bed, his knees pushed tightly together as though to prevent him from falling, his eyes glittering. The Marshal's glance took in the room and found the glass and bottle on Catherine's desk.

'It's all right. I'm perfectly sober. You've come to tell me something's happened to Catherine, haven't you?'

'Yes.'

'I knew when I saw them going down to the cellars . . . I feel as if I'd known all along. She's dead, isn't she?'

'Yes.'

William sat as still as ever but his face seemed to dissolve as the tension was released and his tears flowed in silence. The Marshal held his shoulder for a moment and then sat down, turning the chair at the desk to face him. There was no need to tell him everything. Not all at once.

'I shan't know what to do . . . you'll help me? I mean . . .'

'I'll help you. Don't worry. Most of the formalities will be dealt with by us. Afterwards, when you feel calmer, you can tell me where you'd like her to be buried.'

'I don't know. She had no real home, did she? If she's buried here she'll be alone. There's nobody else, only the two of us . . .'

'Perhaps where your parents are buried?'

'My parents . . . If I'd been in that day she called—'

'No, no. Don't do that. Don't start thinking like that. You'll only upset yourself more and it can do no good now.'

A rumbling of drums in the distance announced the arrival of the cortège on its way to the final match of the football tournament.

'Leo. Leo and that other one, the one in the photo.'

'Yes.'

'You have to tell me what happened. I don't want to find out from anybody else, I want you to tell me.'

The Marshal understood his need, but even so he would have tried to hide some of it had the boy not been too intelligent for him.

'And it was La Ulderighi paid them to do it.'

It wasn't a question.

'Nothing's come out yet.'

'It won't, will it?'

'Perhaps not.'

William's body remained more or less upright at the edge of the divan but it was like the body of a puppet whose strings have dropped in a tangle. His arms and hands seemed too long. His face, still and expressionless, was bathed in tears. His nose was running. The Marshal gave him a big white handkerchief, but though William accepted it he didn't make use of it.

The drumming outside grew louder and trumpets played a fanfare, but it was all muffled by the thick walls of the palazzo and seemed to come from a great distance.

William shuddered. 'Is she in the house?'

'The Marchesa? No. I believe not, but she's expected soon. Don't you think you'd be better off away from here? I can arrange a *pensione* for you, if you like?'

'You're afraid I might get drunk and go for her, is that it?'

'No.' The Marshal remembered his remorse about having let off a firework and frightened the sick Neri. He wouldn't hurt a fly. 'No, I don't think that. I only think this house distresses you and that you'll pass a bad night here alone.'

'Yes,' William admitted, 'you're right and I'm grateful to you for thinking of it, but I'll stay. I let her down, you know, by not being there when she needed me. You don't know—it's no use trying to comfort me, you don't know. In her letter she said I was either out or asleep . . . Well, I'd been drinking the night before and I didn't get up to answer the phone—'

'You couldn't have known.'

'That's not the point. That's not the point. It shouldn't have happened. I drink, you see, because I don't know quite where I am—sexually. I like women but men like me. I suppose I shouldn't complain, as long as somebody's taking an interest there's hope for me, wouldn't you say? I don't want you to think better of me than I deserve just because I've lost my—'

He was unable to get the word 'sister' out. His head dropped forward as the word choked him. Then he took a deep breath and tried to pull himself together.

'I feel exhausted, as if I'd made a long journey and been beaten up at the end of it. Perhaps I could sleep if I covered myself up a bit. I feel cold.'

The airless room was unbearably hot. The Marshal helped him to get himself under the counterpane. William lay still, his eyes half closed.

'Lift your head.' He gave him the pillow which had fallen to the floor. He looked to be in shock and should have someone with him. The Marshal decided to get Flavia Martelli to come in. William's eyes were closed now but as the Marshal began to tiptoe away he murmured, 'Wait . . .'

'What is it?'

'You didn't come to the theatre.'

'What?' With a start the Marshal remembered. The complimentary tickets were still in the pocket of his uniform.

William's eyes had opened but he didn't look up at the Marshal, only stared ahead. 'I wish you'd come. I'm not so good at life but I'm good on stage. I wanted you to see me, I don't know why.'

'I'm sorry.'

'It's all right. I'm glad you were here today. They did it . . . They did it in the cellar, didn't they, not in here?'

'Yes. She must have been working.'

'Will you arrest them?'

'I already have.'

'It was written on that document she was restoring . . . funny . . . "Whoso foregathers with great people is the last at table and the first at the gallows."'

William said nothing else and after a while his eyes closed and he slept.

Also present were two Radiomobile units and an ambulance of the Misericordia. Dr MARTELLI Flavia, being present as a resident of the Palazzo Ulderighi, was asked to proceed to an external examination . . .

The Marshal himself had suggested it because the doctor who had done the preliminary examination of Catherine Yorke's body had left. It had been easy enough to tell William not to think like that, not to go over and over the story, telling it the way it should have been if only . . . Who was there who could tell the Marshal not to do it, not to retrace his steps and do in his head what he ought to have done? If, for instance, it had occurred to him to put Lorenzini in the dwarf's place?

The S on his typewriter was dirty. His mind went blank as he stared at the page with each letter S almost a solid block.

The phone rang.

'Guarnaccia?' It was Captain Maestrangelo.

'Captain.'

'I hope you got some rest.'

'Yes, thank you, I did.'

'Well, I thought you'd want to know. Charges have been brought and, as we expected, two very expensive lawyers are now with us.'

'And their story?'

'The girl was Tiny's girlfriend and he found out she was two-timing him with Leo. He came to the Palazzo Ulderighi to have it out with her on June 11th. She was in the cellars sorting documents. Tiny claims he had intercourse with her there with her consent. Leo came down and caught them *in flagrante* and a fight ensued. Leo says the girl took his part and Tiny turned on her and strangled her. Breaking open Cinelli's tomb was Leo's idea but it turned out to be a lot smaller than they expected. In Tiny's words: "We had to double her up. She might have got scratched a bit when we

pushed her in." Incidentally, your fears that she might have
been walled in before she was quite dead were groundless.
Her neck was broken. As for their being paid assassins—
well, if it's any comfort to you I know you're right, but I
think that's about all the comfort you can expect. These
lawyers are good. Neither Tiny nor Leo can afford to talk.
With a story like theirs they could get away with man-
slaughter and when they come out they'll be rich men.'

It was true. If they involved the Marchesa Ulderighi
it would be murder, and murder for financial gain. They
wouldn't see the outside world again.

'I'm sorry,' the Captain said. 'You did an admirable job,
anyway.'

An admirable job. There had been two deaths and his
'admirable job' had caused a third.

'Are you still there?'

'Yes . . . yes, I'm still here.'

'You sound depressed. You shouldn't be. You realize
we'd never have got them at all if you hadn't found out
how they knew each other.'

'That's true.' For what it was worth. Funny how it hadn't
registered there and then—though not that funny, considering the panic in the café. So simple. Half, or rather more
than half, of the people having breakfast were market
people, their early morning faces shiny and pink, their
clothes old and dusty. The women wore aprons with their
money in a wide pocket in the front. And the others were
exotic in leather and black lace, the girls' faces white and
slashed with purple lipstick. Some of them strung out and
weary, others still high from the disco. All of them stopping
there for breakfast before sleeping the day away.

'I'm probably interrupting you,' the Captain said coldly,
annoyed at the lack of reaction.

'I . . . No, no. I was writing my HSA report for the public
prosecutor's office.'

'I see.' The coldness left his voice. 'He's putting you under a lot of pressure.'

'Yes. But it doesn't matter.'

'Well, if you need any help . . .'

'Thank you.' But he repeated, 'It doesn't matter.'

'As you wish. By the way, we need to call in this character they refer to as Grillo. Can you give me his correct name?'

'Yes. Just a moment.' He was obliged to look it up in his notebook. 'Filippo Brunetti.'

He kept the notebook before him after he'd rung off. According to the Captain, they intended to call Grillo as a witness to the relationship between Catherine Yorke and Leo Mori. Once that would have been a safe bet but now . . .

At approximately 21.45 yesterday, June 24th, in the course of duty . . .

Filippo Brunetti . . . There must have been a time when someone had called him Filippo. His mother, if he'd known her. Before he became just Grillo, just a dwarf.

The Marshal had found him that evening on the spiral staircase after he'd left William. He knew he must go up and see Neri, but Grillo was blocking his way and the Marshal had stood there, amazed at what he was seeing. Three stairs above, the dwarf laid a tray of food, mostly covered by a cloth. Clutching the thick rope to help himself, Grillo hauled himself laboriously up two of the high stone steps, stopped to breathe deeply for a moment and then moved the tray up three more steps. Another pause for breath and he grasped the rope again.

'Can I help you?'

The dwarf had been too absorbed in his task or his heavy breathing had been such that he hadn't heard the Marshal's approach. He whipped his head round now, still clinging to the rope, but he didn't acknowledge the offer, only flattened himself against the wall to let the Marshal pass him. This the Marshal did as best he could, trying not to push against the dwarf but it was impossible to avoid it. He expected some wisecrack about his size but it didn't come.

The dwarf only said, 'Be careful,' as the Marshal, with the help of the rope, took two stairs at once to avoid the tray. But it wasn't the Marshal he was worrying about.

'He hasn't eaten for two days. I've made him soup. Maybe he can get that down . . .' And he resumed his laborious climb.

The tower that night was as silent as the courtyard. No flute. No sound at all. When he entered the room the Marshal found Neri's habitual chair empty. He came back out on to the staircase. Far below him, still struggling, the dwarf jerked a finger, pointing upwards. The Marshal climbed to the next floor. There he found only a bathroom and what appeared to be a dressing-room though it was difficult to make out in the fading light. The next floor was a bedroom.

Neri was not in bed but lying on the coverlet, clothed and with a thin dressing-gown over him. The shutters were open and there was a little more light up here beyond the roof of the palazzo. A suffused pink light of a midsummer sunset. He was sleeping. Not, the Marshal thought, a natural sleep, but drug-induced. His face was flushed and a small trickle of saliva escaped the corner of his open mouth where it pressed on the pillow. He had seen dying people sleep like that when they had been given morphine to ease their pain. Their limbs collapsed in abandoned attitudes. Only babies slept like that naturally. The Marshal sat himself down quietly by the bed and waited. In the silence he listened to Neri's breathing. The intake of breath seemed to require an effort. A pause, then, as though too much energy had been expended, the lungs collapsed with a low bubbling snore.

The only other noise was the dwarf's slow progress on

the stairway. One two, one two, pause. The scraping of the tray. One two, one two, pause . . .

Neri caught his breath. Nothing outside had disturbed him. He was dreaming. His head began to move slowly from side to side on the pillow, then more quickly, each movement accompanied by a brief moan. The movement became more violent, the protest articulate.

'No. No. No. No. I won't do it. I won't do it. No. No. No. I won't do it.'

'Wake him!' The dwarf was in the room. Dumping his tray, he ran to the bed on his short wobbling legs and clutched at Neri's arm. 'Wake up! Can you hear me? Wake up!'

Neri's eyes opened. They focused on the dwarf's face hanging over his own and at once tears poured down his flushed cheeks.

'You promised to keep me awake. Grillo, you promised. Don't let me fall asleep again, for God's sake don't let me . . .'

'Hush. I had to get you something to eat.'

He could hardly have seen him up to then because Grillo had been blocking his vision, but now he stood out of the way.

At the sight of the Marshal's large, still figure a ray of hope lit Neri's feverish eyes. His head had left a patch of sweat on the depressed pillow.

'You've come to talk to me. You'll help me to stay awake. The doctors don't understand. They say I must sleep, but I must keep awake at all costs . . .' He tried to hoist himself into a sitting position but he was too weak. The Marshal moved to help him but the dwarf was there first.

'Thank you.'

'Thank me by eating your soup.'

'I'll try. Leave me with the Marshal now—but don't go far.'

'I'll be on the floor below so I can hear you.' He shot an angry look at the Marshal as he left, clearly thinking that his presence would interfere with the soup.

Whether or not that were the reason, Neri ate nothing, though he tried, and in the end he asked the Marshal to put the tray outside the door.

'Just the smell of food makes me feel ill.'

When the Marshal came back he said, 'Sit here as you were before. I'm glad you're here.'

William had said that, too, but what comfort could he offer? What could he offer to soothe the nightmares of this ageing twenty-four-year-old who, anyway, knew he was dying?

'As long as you're here, you see, I can talk to you and stay awake. You can't imagine the nightmares . . . and yet nothing ever happens, nothing frightening at all, so that when I tell Grillo he laughs. Of course he laughs to make me laugh . . . And sometimes I do laugh. But the minute I close my eyes they're there waiting for me. The very minute I close my eyes . . .'

'Who's waiting?'

'I don't exactly know. I can't see their faces but they're people I know or people who know me and they give me the box, a small oblong box, and expect me . . . they expect me . . .'

Sweat rolled down his temples and he clutched the Marshal's arm. 'Don't let me fall asleep, please God don't let me!'

'I won't. Steady, now.'

'I'll get up!'

'Are you sure you're fit to—'

'It's wearing off now. They give me tranquillizers, do you understand? They make me helpless and the nightmares overwhelm me. It's wearing off now. Help me to get up.'

With or without help he was determined to get out of

bed, and so the Marshal helped him. There was a sickly
bluish tinge around Neri's lips that frightened him.

'Here. Have my chair and I'll bring another one.'

'Thank you. How kind you are to me. Bring it close. It's
strange. Everyone is kind to me and yet the people in the
nightmares are so cruel and relentless.'

'What do they want of you?'

'They give me the box . . . They give me the box and I
have to stick something sharp into it. That's all. They don't
say anything but I know that's what I have to do and I
won't do it! I know it sounds stupid. What makes me so
afraid is that if it goes on, every time I close my eyes, I'll
give in and then—I'll give in and—'

'Don't distress yourself. It's all over now. That's what
I've come to tell you.'

It wasn't true. It was all over, but what could he tell
Neri?

Everything in the room was suffused with the fading pink
of the dying sun. Soon it would be dark. The Marshal felt
a great weight of sadness dragging him down. He had felt it
for Corsi's disembodied presence and now it had transferred
itself to Neri, whose eyes, the same eyes, were looking at
him, waiting for help.

'Is it over?' Then he turned away to ask, as though he
didn't quite want to hear the answer, 'Catherine?'

'We found her body an hour ago. The two men who
killed her have already been arrested. It's over.'

Neri dropped his still averted head and was silent a
moment.

Then he began to murmur in a very low voice, '*Est in
horto, Phylli, nectendis apium coronis; est hederæ vis multa, qua
crinis religata fulges . . . Qua crines religata fulges . . .*'

The voice faltered and a tear fell on to one of his big limp
hands.

The Marshal, thinking he had been praying said 'Amen'.

Describe the position and clothing of the cadaver.

The body lay prone with the head turned to the left in the direction of the well in the centre of the courtyard and was correctly dressed.

The Marshal's two big fingers paused over the keyboard. It had occurred to him, after Neri had received the news of Catherine's death, to leave him to assimilate it and make his own decision about what he wanted to know, what he wanted to tell. The idea had been to go down a moment to William and check up on him and then to have a word with the men down in the cellars. He wanted the ambulance to draw right up to the cellar door—there was space enough and to spare—so that the girl's body could be removed discreetly. It had just crossed his mind that if he didn't interfere they would naturally ask William to identify the body there and then and in its present condition . . . He had gone so far as to get to his feet but he was unsure, even then.

'Excuse me . . .' He had gone over to the window and looked down. There were a lot more people there by now and, though it was impossible to be sure from such a height, the Marshal reckoned that a few journalists had got in. The big double gates had been opened, which meant that the ambulance was expected. He had decided then to go down. But suddenly Neri was behind him.

'Marshal. I beg your pardon. It was only for a moment— I was particularly fond of her, you see. Her kindness and . . .'

'Of course, I do understand.'

'Father Benigni . . . He was right, you see, that if there'd been no truth in it I would have caused dreadful pain and upset for no reason—and Catherine did tell me she was going away and so I waited. I waited . . . but now, I must do what is right in God's eyes but I want to ask your indulgence—please sit down.'

Perhaps Neri was right about the drugs wearing off. His

face, though the lips were still tinged with blue, had a more normal colour. Or was that because the rosy light had drained away from the high room?

'Father Benigni was right about two things: we can't confess the sins of others and people do say wild things in anger which have no basis in truth. They are said to wound. In this case, Marshal, they wounded my father to death and I . . . I began it all—'

'No,' the Marshal said firmly. 'You began nothing, you harmed nobody. You loved Catherine Yorke, didn't you?'

He was taken aback. No doubt he had never given his feelings a name and perhaps, anyway, the subdued and childlike turmoil that lived inside his head feeding upon itself could not rightly be called love. But whatever its true nature, it existed and was yet another source of guilt for this overloaded soul.

'My father loved her—perhaps you know that by now.'

'Yes.'

'He said that night that she was—that she was expecting his child. I understood him then. There was never any time to tell him, to talk to him, and now he's dead. I understand that though he loved Catherine, what had made him so determined was the thought of the child. A healthy normal child, Marshal. Look at me. What sort of son was I for him? He has a brother, you know, though you may not have seen him. I always thought he envied his brother. There's a little girl, Fiorenza. They brought her to see me once, I don't know why because I was too sick to talk to her but I remember her, even so. Very tiny and full of energy. I saw her again at my father's funeral and I understood. That's what he wanted, children like that. I know there were times when he couldn't bear to look at me. I used to dine down there with them but I could see how I disgusted him, so now poor Grillo drags my tray up here.

I'm a burden to everyone and I have nothing to offer in return.'

The Marshal felt the truth of this and felt no inclination to offer banal denials. But he remembered Catherine Yorke's letter.

'There was a letter,' he told Neri, 'from Catherine Yorke to her brother. She talked about you. She said that she and your father talked of you often, that your father suffered, as you saw, but that it was because he cared. She said, "If only we could take him with us."'

Neri's eyes were alight. 'She said that?'

'And she meant it. She said coming up to see you helped her when she felt sad.' It occurred to him that he was offering the poor creature affection coming now from beyond the grave and so he added, 'Your Aunt Fiorenza has spoken to me about you. She is afraid for your health and wants to see you well. She asked me to help you. I can do that only if you feel you can help me.'

Neri was silent. Again there was a moment when he could have got up and left and gone down to William, done something useful instead of insisting on this truth which he could never use except for his own satisfaction. And was his personal satisfaction worth a life?

Then Neri said, 'I'll try.'

After that nothing would have dragged him away.

'Try, then, and tell me what happened on the night your father died.'

'There was a quarrel . . .'

'Where were you?'

'I was . . . in my bathroom—I'd got up, you see. Well, from there you can hear. Then I went down to my sitting-room where there's a connecting door. I was frightened.'

'Why were you frightened?—Do you mind if I switch a light on? Would it bother you?'

'Afterwards. Let me tell you this first . . .'

For him it was still the confessional. The Marshal felt
uncomfortable at being forced to play the priest but there
was little he could do if he wanted to hear the truth. He
must accept this great burden of guilt from the innocent.

'I went down because their quarrels were sometimes so
violent. Because my—I was afraid for my father. Even so,
I shouldn't have listened behind the door like that. It was
cowardly. In my heart I want to do what's right but my
actions always come out as cowardly, vile.'

'It wasn't so unreasonable,' the Marshal pointed out, 'to
want to be on hand if violence broke out but to be reluctant
to interfere otherwise. Surely anybody would have done the
same.'

'Do you think so? Do you really think so?'

'Well, I'm only giving you my opinion.' There was no
getting away from it. He really wasn't quite right in the
head and this childlike trust in his burning eyes, evident
even in the half light, irritated the Marshal. It wasn't normal and it upset him. That, too, may have contributed to
the way things went afterwards.

'Well—' Neri clasped his large hands together and began
squeezing them rhythmically—'I'm glad you see it like that
and yet, if I'd opened the door at once, my—she wouldn't
have said those things, not in front of me. I'm sure she
wouldn't, and then my father would have lived.'

'What did she say to him?'

'They were quarrelling about divorce. They had before,
more than once, but this time my father had made up his
mind and how he did it was up to her. If she wouldn't agree
he would use Hugh Fido's name—you see! That was my
fault, too, because he would never have known but for—'

'What answer did she give him?'

'She laughed in his face. Sometimes, when she's really
angry she laughs. It can be very frightening.'

'Were you frightened that night?'

'Yes, I was. There was something—I don't know—something unreal about the quarrel. Of course, now I know . . . It was unreal because she—'

'Are you all right?'

The Marshal leaned forward to peer at him closely. The glazed look caused by the drugs had gone but he looked ill now, perhaps the strain of telling this was too much for him. But then, how else was he to unburden himself?

'It's my heart . . . there are some pills I should take but it doesn't matter—He told her then. He told her that Catherine was expecting a child and I understood. I wish I could have talked to him. I wish I'd had the chance to tell him that I understood.' He was still squeezing his hands in anguish.

'It's always the way,' the Marshal said, 'when someone dies. We think of the things we never said. I felt that way when my mother died.'

'Did you?' Neri's voice was soft, wondering. 'But she didn't die the way my father . . .'

'No, no, she was sick. But you feel it just the same when they're gone.'

'I've talked to him in my prayers but I can't reach him. I haven't even a memory of him, of us together. I was always sick and he was so busy. But once . . .' He stood up shakily, looking about him, his hands still gripped together. 'Once when I'd been very sick he came to see me and brought me something . . .' He went to his bedside cupboard and took from it his father's present. It was a news magazine. The date was the November of four years ago. The Cellophane wrapping was unbroken. 'He thought of me, you see, and brought me this and said, "It might cheer you up to read what's going on in the outside world." It was a kind thought, don't you think?'

'Very.' The Marshal recognized the kind thought as being Fiorenza's but it was touching that Buongianni had tried to follow her advice. 'You never did read it, though?'

'Oh no. I much preferred to keep it intact and now I'm very glad I did. It's something to remember instead of remembering the sight of him up there, the sight of him—'

'Try and keep calm. You'll feel better when you get it off your chest. How did the quarrel end?'

'He said that Catherine had gone to England to think things over but that he intended to go after her the following day, because on no account did he want her to—to not have the child, and then—that was when she started screaming with laughter and she told him that he could save himself the journey because his—his tart was right here . . .' Neri's voice was reduced to a hoarse whisper, as if the words hurt him physically. Then it became harsh and it might have been Bianca Ulderighi herself speaking, watching what had been her husband crumple before her eyes.

'Just what she deserved. As she was offering her services I found her two suitable clients, people on her own level, and if they accidentally broke her neck there was no harm done. Where are you running to? There's no need for you to interfere. I've seen to everything. They put her body into Cinelli's tomb—I thought of that. And what's so amusing is that instead of Cinelli's bones in there we found those of a dog that dissolved into dust at a touch! So much for the curse. So you see it's all settled. There will be no divorce.'

Neri paused, breathing deeply, searching for his own voice.

The Marshal shuddered as though Bianca Ulderighi were in the room with them. He spoke loudly himself to dispel the sinister atmosphere. 'Is that where he went when he went down in the lift? To the cellars?'

'Yes, I think so. I didn't watch him. I'd been behind the door all that time and then when everything was silent I opened it. She was standing just as he'd left her, very erect, her head high. She looked very serene, almost smiling, and I thought that none of it could be true, that now she would tell me that it had all been a cruel joke to frighten my father. We've—we were always very close. She never left my side when I was sick, and she used to tell me everything. So I waited.

'Then I realized that she wasn't even seeing me. I was right there at the door facing her and she went on standing there, smiling and smiling . . .'

Neri lifted his grief-stricken face to the Marshal's.

'I've thought about it so much and I've prayed. I've prayed for him and for what he didn't do.'

'I understand,' the Marshal said. 'He intended to kill your mother and didn't. She told us that.'

'He came up my staircase, Marshal, not in the lift. He came up my staircase and only when he didn't find me in my bed did he run back down and go through the door where he found us together. I don't know why he didn't shoot both of us then. Now that you've told me about Catherine's letter I wonder if that—*She* cared about me.'

'What she said was that he cared about you.'

'In any case I've forgiven him for what he wanted to do because I can understand. He must have suffered terrible anguish, I know that. Father Benigni insists that suicide is as much a sin as murder and I know he must be right, but God will forgive him because he suffered so much, I believe that.'

'Did he go up to the roof then?'

'Yes. I think . . . I think it was just to get away from us. I ran after him but it was too late. He was stronger and faster and I couldn't keep up.'

'But your mother could surely—'

'Oh no. No. She didn't move. When I came down to tell her she was standing exactly as I'd first found her. She was still smiling. I told her he was dead and all she said to me was, "Go back to bed." I said I can't carry him, not by myself. We can't leave him up there. I've got him off the parapet but I can't carry him. What can I do?'

'Go back to your room. Wash yourself.

'She was still smiling. It was still as though she couldn't see me. As I went away I heard her telephoning someone. I suppose she had my father taken down to the gun room. I heard them a long time afterwards, I heard them on my stairs dragging . . .'

The Marshal's ear caught the sound of a siren. He went to the window. The ambulance was coming in. There was a lot of noise, voices, instructions, but it was spent and distorted when it reached this height.

'I must go down.'

'I've never spoken to her since.' Neri's face was composed, his eyes focused on some faraway point visible only to himself.

'I must go down,' the Marshal repeated. 'I'll send Grillo up to you.'

When he reached the door he heard Neri remark quietly, 'I was right, wasn't I? I said they'd make me do it in the end and they have.'

The Marshal looked back over his shoulder, hesitating. Neri had his back to the door. He might have been addressing the Marshal or only an idea of the Marshal. In any case he didn't turn. 'She was in that little box. And now I've done it. I've destroyed her.'

'I'll send Grillo up,' the Marshal said again because he didn't know what else to say.

The left hand and arm were folded beneath the trunk and the right arm outstretched. (See enc. 1 Photographic file.)

Though the square of sky above was still pale turquoise, no light by then penetrated the courtyard and the atmosphere was tense and subdued now the fuss of the ambulance's arrival had died down. The Marshal had been right about the journalists. The magistrates were still down in the cellars and once they came up the press would surely be evicted, but in the meantime they were huddled together under the colonnade near the old tata's door, smoking to keep their spirits up in the gloom. They'd get a fright all right if she opened up and attacked them, but no doubt she heard nothing, locked in to her own icon-lit world by her deafness.

He found Lorenzini talking to one of the ambulance men and gave him instructions as to the discreet removal of the body because of William.

'Then you don't want him to identify?'

'I think I'll ask Dr Martelli. She was her patient.'

'Right, I'll tell them—' Lorenzini interrupted himself and caught the Marshal's arm. 'Look who's arriving.'

Someone behind them, probably one of the journalists, whispered, 'The Marchesa.'

She was dressed, very elegantly, in deep mourning. She was followed at an almost imperceptible distance, by the chief public prosecutor. Inside the gate she rang the bell for the porter, then walked towards the central well and paused. She looked at the ambulance and said something in an undertone to the chief public prosecutor. The porter came hurrying up to her, buttoning his jacket. Without looking at him, she said, 'When these people have finished, go down and see how much damage they've done.'

She saw the Marshal. She looked him straight in the eyes. She didn't see the shrouded stretcher appear behind the ambulance. Then the dwarf began to scream, brief staccato screams not of fear but of rage. The Marshal ran to the entrance of the tower, knowing what the dwarf's rage meant. The Marchesa and all the extraneous people in the courtyard gazed after him. He pounded up the stone stairs, round and up, up and round, never pausing for breath, his heart fit to burst and yet he knew that he would be too late and the hand that reached and grasped at the rope was sweating and sliding.

He overtook the dwarf quite near the top. He was still hauling himself up by the force of his arms and chest. His tiny legs had almost given out completely and he no longer had the breath to scream rage at his impotence. Tears were mixed with sweat on his streaked face and breathless incomprehensible curses issued from him. When the Marshal had got past him he slumped down on to the stairs, still clinging to the rope.

The turret was empty. The Marshal stopped, holding his chest and closing his eyes at the searing pain in his lungs. Above him the turquoise sky was deepening to midnight blue and the first star shone peacefully. It never occurred to the Marshal that Neri would have made an attempt at last to leave the Palazzo Ulderighi as his father had seemed to do. He knew before his slow steps reached the wall, before his big hands touched the warm stones of the parapet, that Neri would be a huddled heap by the well at his mother's feet. Slowly, he leaned over to look down on the death he had failed to prevent. Slowly, the first firework drew its soft glittering design across the sky in honour of San Giovanni, the patron saint of Florence. On the night of June 24th.

The cadaver presented injuries to the head and the right hand. (See enc. 2)

The right hand had been broken. Probably from hitting the well, but the Marchesa ignored this as she had ignored the crushed head. She had been distressed by the superficial grazes on the hand and had called repeatedly above the noise of the fireworks for water and bandages. When the ambulance men tried to get near with a stretcher she became angry.

'Can't you see he's sleeping? He always did sleep face down . . . I used to worry so much but the doctors . . . Why isn't there water? Bring me a bandage. For God's sake, can't anyone see that he's hurt his hand!'

In the end they had been forced to bandage the dead hand. Then she allowed herself to be led away by the chief public prosecutor. 'I told you,' she said, 'that in time he'd come back to me.' She was smiling, her face intermittently lit by the blue, red and green explosions above her.

The Marshal never saw her again. She was to die many years later in a clinic in Switzerland. She never regained her reason and nothing ever again disturbed her absolute serenity.

The cadaver was removed on the authorization of the substitute prosecutor Dr Mauro Maurri at 22.25 and transported by an ambulance of the Misericordia to the Medico-Legal Institute to be detained at the disposition of the competent authorities.

This morning's interview with the chief public prosecutor and substitute prosecutor Maurri had been brief. They had come full circle and arrived at yet another HSA report.

Nevertheless, their attitude to the Marshal this time was very different. All of them knew that, even should she regain her reason, which was unlikely, Bianca Maria Corsi Uldcrighi Della Loggia would never be prosecuted. The Marshal knew everything and could do nothing. The expert lawyers of Tiny and Leo would have their way with the case. The difference was that the Marshal was treated with respect instead of disdain; he was being implored, not threatened. In the circumstances it was perhaps unnecessarily wicked of him to go away without offering any comment, to let them sweat it out until his written report arrived. It would arrive soon enough. It was all but finished. And it was, after all, the only satisfaction he would have out of the whole business, this letting them wait for his decision. They would never know he had reached it without any reference to them and that annoyed him. Perhaps to Captain Maestrangelo he could explain, but then, he wasn't so good at explaining things so it was probably better not to try. Only he would ever know what was in his head at this moment. A twilit image of a young man dying in an old man's body, mourning the loss of what he had never known. Another, happier image of a small freckled girl who didn't look like anybody and on whose frail shoulders the entire Ulderighi inheritance would fall. The Marshal had great hopes of Fiorenza Corsi. If she didn't sell the place, which was likely, she would fill it, with animals or ballerinas or her numerous children, or at any rate with life. And he would lighten her burden to the extent in his power. The Palazzo Ulderighi had claimed yet another victim but the Marshal had the last word. His two plump fingers typed doggedly on to the end of the page.

. . . *that in the presence of the undersigned, Neri Corsi Ulderighi Della Loggia, in attempting to observe the events taking place in the courtyard below, either through an attack of the chronic malady from which he suffered or through loss of balance, accidentally fell to his death.*

His tongue protruded slightly from the corner of his mouth as he concluded with the standard phrase.

Referred in accordance with the obligations incumbent on my office—

MARSHAL IN CHIEF
STATION COMMANDANT
(Salvatore Guarnaccia)